DOWN IN THE BASEMENT

The basement seemed foggy today, but Lydia wasn't sure if the haze was in her eyes or the room. Sleep had not been a friend to her in a while.

The sensation of something being here was present, as always, and she hoped that by acknowledging it, she would feel less spooked.

"Hello?" Lydia called. A sense of despair washed through her in a wave, and the hairs stood up on her arms. Her vision swam, more blurred, as if she were caught in a dense fog. She could almost make out forms swirling around her, gaps in the haze that let in the room light.

She saw images on the floor. As she squinted her eyes, she thought she saw shackles bolted to the floor. She leaned over to touch them and they evaporated as if an illusion.

Over on the wall, she saw more shackles, and long chains hanging down from them. She walked over, pushing aside the swimming forms with her hands like seaweed. When she got to the wall, again the image disappeared.

Her hair was standing on end and she tried to push it down but she couldn't. It was as if someone was hanging on to it.

"Are you here today?" she asked. "I want to help you."

The room seemed to sigh, another wash of anguish flooded her and then she felt a sudden stab of pain, as if she were being gutted from her neck to her belly.

Sèphera Girón

House of Pain

LEISURE BOOKS NEW YORK CITY

A LEISURE BOOK®

August 2001

Published by

Dorchester Publishing Co., Inc.
276 Fifth Avenue
New York, NY 10001

ISBN 0-8439-4907-4

Printed in the United States of America.

ACKNOWLEDGMENTS

Although *House of Pain* was inspired by a horrendous real-life serial killer case, it is in no way meant to glamorize it. In light of the theme of the book, be warned to never let your guard down especially when you fall in love, for you never know who you are really dealing with!

No book is ever written in a vacuum, although it sure as hell can feel like it while you're writing it! In this age of technology, it is much easier to connect with other writers all over the world and share our agonies and ecstasies as we work, trying to create stories that will thrill and delight our audiences. I would like to thank my friends both online and off, who got to hear me moan and groan and who inspired me or supported me in some way as I wrote *House of Pain:* Yvonne, Nancy K., Cecile, Julie, Sandra and Brett, Sara and Jill, Cathy and Shirley, Caro, Jimi, Tina, David N., Julian, Heather and Dave E., and Tom P.

I also would like to thank various English teachers who encouraged me throughout the years. W. Schell, R. Bondy, S. Cassan, b. p. nichol, and J. Schaefer are a few names that come to mind.

Thanks to my agent, Lori Perkins, for her endless enthusiasm and for keeping me working my butt off!

Thanks to my children, Adrian and Dorian, for putting up with my wacky hours and mood swings, and thanks to my parents for putting up with me for three decades.

A big thank you to Don D'Auria, my editor, for all his wonderful encouragement and support over the years.

House of Pain

Chapter One

The sky hung heavy with clouds, darkness tumbling into light, pregnant with seasons changing, a swirling vortex of shade and shadow, a collage of turbulence biding time.

The woods glowed with orange crimson slashes, leaves blanketing the paths, a playground of crunching, crackling death. Just beyond the woods to one side, a river glistened in the sporadic sunlight, darkly hoarding secrets beneath its glimmering veneer.

Ten-year-old Tony crouched behind a bush that had lost most of its leaves, making the game a little less challenging on this crisp October day. He was slight, a wiry child whose baggy jeans bagged lower than most, even with a belt tightly cinched around his waist, his monster movie T-shirt flapping when he walked. His dark blue eyes were doubly vibrant today under a shock of dark brown hair, as he scanned the trees thoughtfully. Jeff, Tony's blond-haired buddy, peeked out from a nearby tree. Tony grinned.

"Come on," Tony whispered, waving his hand frantically. Jeff stared around to be certain the coast was clear and then hightailed it over to the bush where Tony waited. Jeff slid into position beside Tony.

"Shhh . . ." Tony put his finger to his lips, laughter bubbling up through his body. The boys giggled breathlessly at their game, clamping muddy fingers over their mouths so they wouldn't give themselves away.

This forest had been their playpen for the past few months of their ten-year-old lives. It was a small woods, not far from their homes, a place of adventure and spying, of forts and caves.

A place to hide away from the rest of the world.

Today, however, it appeared the rest of the world had descended onto their secret place.

Tony and Jeff watched as people gathered around the small wood-and-brick house that stood on the edge of the woods. In fact, the woods were part of the property belonging to the owners of the house. The boys had never paid much attention to the house or the young couple that lived there. They had seen the couple from time to time, coming and going in their shiny red sports car. A blond couple with nice clothes and few visitors. The boys weren't interested in how the couple conducted their existence, except in trying to stay out of sight of the house so that they wouldn't be caught trespassing. They weren't sure how tolerant the couple would be of three little boys playing spy games and going for the occasional swim. The boys' main interest was in the woods, the river, the caves where they could thumb through comic books and gorge on candy, make weird little weapons and play with lighters and jackknives. And listen for the sounds in the shadows, especially when the sun was beginning to set. The time when their imagination would really run wild.

Sometimes they imagined they were stalking a fantastical creature, and their imaginations would steer into overdrive. Shadows stretched long and frightening, morphing into monsters they hunted with giggling trepidation. More than once, the shadows would seem almost too real, and on those evenings, they would give up the game and run home.

Today, they hadn't come to play in the woods. They were aware that this house had been in the news a lot lately, aware that something horrific had happened here and aware that things would be changing dramatically today.

One by one, cars rolled up the driveway, crunching on the gravel, spitting rocks from beneath their tires. People stood huddled around the house, whispering and crying, arguing and *tsk*ing their tongues in disbelief. A small procession dressed in black coats and hats walked slowly up the driveway, clutching Bibles to their chests, chanting the Lord's prayer.

"Check them out." Jeff nudged Tony. They watched as the black-garbed people formed a ring around the front door of the house. One of the men produced a flask from his pocket and poured the contents across the front step, over the piles of flowers left in the past few weeks. He then put his fingers to the flask and drenched them. He slowly and carefully traced the image of the cross along the wooden front door, wetting his fingers frequently with the contents of the flask.

Tony noticed that steam wafted from the door where the man's fingers touched it. Perhaps it was from the heat of the morning sun, as sporadic as it was, for though the air was chilly, the sun still glowed with white-hot heat through the clouds.

Another man stood by the door, waving a large golden cross complete with golden-fleshed Jesus nailed to it. Even from the distance, Tony could make out Christ's rolling eyes and anguished open mouth. The men were chanting as they performed their rituals.

"What are they saying?" Jeff asked.

"I can't hear them . . . let's get closer."

The boys peered around, looking for the next safe barrier. There was a short hedge that bordered the side path, where they could still see the activity at the front door. Tony sucked in his breath, and assumed racing position. He stretched his toes anxiously, waiting for people to look away. Would the flow of people ever stop?

More people wandered along, joining their friends, placing flowers along the stairs so as not to disturb the religious group.

Tony waited until the black-clothed people were huddled in a semicircle staring at the doorway as the curious onlookers watched and gossiped. Tony counted to three and then sprinted over to the hedge.

He arrived safely unseen, then turned and signaled to Jeff, who followed. They crouched down again, this time the need for giggling dissipating as they witnessed the hollow-eyed grief of so many mourners.

The boys could now hear snatches of conversation.

"They will burn in hell."

"Goddamn them."

"My poor child . . ."

One of the black-clothed people, a man, started to sing softly. "We shall overcome . . ."

One by one the others followed, their voices growing stronger over the chaos slowly unraveling around them.

"What are they doing?" Jeff asked.

"Praying, I guess." Tony shrugged. He was starting to piece together a vague notion of what was going on. Snatches of his parents' whispers, bits of info gleaned from the news, glaring headlines splashed across the papers over the past few months, all leading back to here.

This house.

A place of unspeakable evil.

"But it's not Sunday," Jeff said. Tony nodded slowly, trying to pull together all the pieces, his eyes dreamily watching the glitter of crucified Jesus catching in the sunlight.

"Oh . . . look!" Jeff said.

The boys' attention was drawn toward the loud roaring and clanging of a bulldozer creeping up the long gravel driveway. Smoke belched from its exhaust, a stinking black cloud that hung suspended in midair.

The black-clothed people held hands, while policemen tied yellow tape around trees, creating a barrier away from the house. More policemen corralled the onlookers back behind the tape. The hand-holding procession was led by the man with the cross back behind the line.

A woman ducked under the tape and fled to the front of the house, carrying a large assortment of flowers. Tears streamed down her face as she fell onto the steps sobbing, the flowers scattering and mingling with the others.

"My Belinda . . ." She ran her hands along the stairs, caressing the worn wood. Her body shook with grief. One of the policewomen knelt beside her, touching her arm.

"Sorry, ma'am, but you're going to have to step back." The policewoman tightened her grip as if to lead the sobbing woman away.

The woman jerked her arm away from the policewoman's grasp. "No . . . Belinda's blood is here. . . ."

"Please . . . I know you're hurting . . . it will soon be over. . . ."

"You don't understand, they took her from me. My baby . . ."

"There, there, Mrs. . . . Mrs. Greenstone . . ."

A male police officer approached the women. He knelt down beside Mrs. Greenstone. "Come along, Mrs. Greenstone. You know nothing more can be done. The sooner we get rid of this house of horrors, the better everyone will sleep at night."

Mrs. Greenstone looked at the young officers before her. She touched their faces.

"Oh, William, Sandra . . . I still can't believe she's gone," Mrs. Greenstone cried. "She was so young. Barely into her teens."

"We know, Mrs. Greenstone." William firmly held Mrs. Greenstone's arm and helped her to stand.

"There are so many of you . . . that's why we have to do this," Sandra said.

"But her blood is still there . . . her last words, her last thoughts . . ."

"Shhh . . . don't torture yourself. You know she is at peace now."

Mrs. Greenstone started to walk with the police officers, then stopped and stared back. "But is she? Is she really at peace?"

Tears began to fall again as she took her place with the others behind the tape.

The bulldozer belched forward, this time picking up speed as it approached the house.

Without stopping it rammed right into the front stairs. The crowd of people cheered as wood splintered. The bulldozer backed up and barreled forward again, making further headway into the porch.

Connie Bellows, the local news reporter, dragged

her cameraman, Bob, over to where the bulldozer was backing up, readying itself for another go at the house.

"Ready, Bob?" she asked, positioning herself where Bob could get the bulldozer wreaking havoc. Connie tugged at her miniskirt.

"Rolling," Bob said.

"This was the scene of so much horror, so much death and torture. Look at all the lives that have been touched by this destruction. With Donald and Debbie Johnson safely behind bars, awaiting execution, there is hope that peace can once again be restored to this little town with the demolition of this house of pain."

Connie leered and Bob put down the camera.

"Was that all right?" she asked, touching her short red hair. Bob nodded as he checked the bite through the viewfinder.

"Looks good," he said.

"All right, let's get some more shots of those religious wackos."

Connie and Bob walked near to the hedge where Tony and Jeff hid.

"She's so pretty," Tony said, staring at Connie's shapely calves.

Jeff shook his head. "She's a bitch."

"Maybe, but she's still pretty."

"Get over it."

The cheers and crying were nearly drowned by the grinding of the bulldozer. The house shook with every ramming slam. The sound of screeching and groaning echoed through the woods. The house leaned, back and forth, as if trying to dodge the next battering, moaning as foundation posts were weakening.

There was a rustling behind Tony and Jeff. They turned to see what was making the noise and found themselves face-to-face with their best friend, Buddy.

"Hey, you guys got a great seat for this show." Buddy grinned with teeth too large and gaped for his mouth. He had red hair that fell in an unwashed tangle to his shoulders and more freckles than stars in the universe. His eyes were a weird color of reddish brown; they almost seemed to match his hair on some days.

"Where you been?" Jeff asked. "You missed most of it."

"Nah, I was over on the other side. Hey, caught me a frog, wanna see?" As Buddy reached into his jeans, Tony looked back over to the house.

The roof was sagging.

Buddy pulled a tiny toad from his pocket. He patted its head, giving it a little kiss. "Hey, little dude, you wanna watch the show too?"

Buddy held the toad up between two fingers,

lightly enough so as not to kill it, but firmly enough so that the toad squirmed, kicking its hind legs.

"Cool," Jeff said, glancing at the toad and then back at the house. Tony looked at the toad but his attention also was drawn back to the wrecking of the house.

"Holy shit," Tony breathed.

The bulldozer was backing up again as the house teetered. The walls fell in on themselves, dirt and dust, wood and stone flinging into the air as if a bomb had been detonated. The house shrieked and groaned as it sank into itself. A thick gray cloud puffed into the air. The onlookers coughed and choked and clapped. The cloud hung over the house, enveloping it from sight for a moment, like a heavy blanket. Tony stared at it, his eyes burning from all the dust and dirt.

The cloud seemed to swell and pulse, rippling in thick, heavy, undulating waves. Tony's body trembled, as though a shard of electricity had wormed its way into his body and was dancing through his veins. His blood was on fire, surging through him with a boiling roar, his mind flooding with blackness ringed with a sense of *bad things*. Images flashed through his mind. He could see a basement, a dark dingy stone dungeon where thick silver chains attached to heavy metal rings were cemented into the floor, where unknown bodies lay broken and bleeding. He saw shiny instruments, sharp and pointed. He saw leather straps and canes. He saw knives and ropes and candles and burning jars of something, smelled a sweet smoke, felt angst and confusion fleeting through him, thoughts that weren't his own yet he felt them just the same.

The walls seemed to breathe, stone walls that pulsed like a heartbeat. He watched as they thumped, each pulse pressing the stone forward like rubber, then sinking back into itself again. Pushing farther, stretching, splitting until tiny cracks snaked along and burst open, leaking streams of a dark, thick, garnet-colored liquid. All the while there was a hideous shrieking, squawking noise, like a giant machine clanging and grinding rusty gears.

Tony put his hands over his face, pressing on his eyeballs, willing the vision to be gone. He prayed for blackness, for darkness.

When he opened his eyes again, he was looking at the ruined house. The cloud had dissipated, smoke into the air, as fine and distant as any other cloud of dust.

Tony gasped and looked at his friends. He couldn't tell if they had experienced the same feelings, the same vision. Then he saw the toad in Buddy's hand as Buddy watched the cloud float away. The toad hung limply, its little eyes bulging, blood bubbles leaking from its tiny mouth.

Tony sucked in a couple of breaths of air and turned his attention back to the demolition.

Within minutes, the house was nothing but junk.

Several people started to move forward, but the policemen held them at bay.

"Everyone, stay back. It isn't safe."

A tall lanky teenager crept around the human barricade and snatched a brick from the rubble. William spotted him. "Hey, you. No souvenirs. If you take one, then everyone will want one. This is still private property."

With two officers flanking him, the teenager reluctantly dropped the brick. "Shit, man, that would have been so cool." He returned to his buddies, who slapped him on the back.

"Nice try," they said, scowling over at the cops.

The boys watched as the choir launched into another hymn. Connie was still wandering around, prattling on about her insights to the camera, shoving her microphone into the face of whomever she passed by. Mrs. Greenstone sat on the grass, clutching a red carnation, twirling it in her fingers, back and forth, back and forth, her eyes glassy as she watched the smoke cloud rise above the trees.

"She's still there," she muttered to no one in particular. "They are all still there."

"All right, everyone, the show's over. Let's clear out now."

The police waved their hands and tried to shepherd the audience back down the driveway.

"I want one of those bricks," Jeff said, his dark brown eyes glinting.

"Yeah, that would be so cool," Tony agreed.

"How are we going to get past the cops?" Buddy asked, making his toad fly with little airplane noises. He stopped and looked at the toad.

"Oh, man, he's dead."

"Shit, you killed another one, Buddy. Jeez, when are you going to be more careful?" Jeff scolded.

"God . . ." Tony sighed, pretending to notice for the first time. "You squeezed him to death."

"Man, I just wanted to play with him." Buddy's eyes filled with tears as he laid the toad gently in his palm. He dabbed at the bubbles of blood around its mouth. "I was trying to be so careful this time."

"Well, you did it again," Jeff scoffed. "Just get rid of it."

"Maybe I should bury him." Buddy started to dig at the loose leaves where they crouched.

"Shhh . . . don't make so much noise," Jeff warned as Buddy scooped out the damp bug-ridden dirt.

"I didn't mean to kill him . . . I didn't," he

sobbed, tears streaming down his face.

"Stop it. Who cares, it's just a fucking frog," Jeff snapped.

"Just a frog." Buddy stopped digging and stared at Jeff. His red-brown eyes, normally small and narrow, were now wide open. "Just a frog!"

"Yeah, it's just a fucking frog."

"I suppose *you* are just a person. Just one fucking person out of a million, but, boy, would you be pissed if someone came along and squeezed *you* to death," Buddy snarled.

"Shhh," Tony hissed. "Come on, guys, cut it out."

Jeff shook his head and crept back over to where Tony was watching the activity. Buddy continued his burial.

They watched as the cops hurried people down the driveway, and cars roared into life and began crunching back down the gravel.

"Look, they're so busy getting everyone out, they won't notice if we plan a sneak attack. Over behind that way!" Tony said, pointing a pathway from bush to bush to where a pile of bricks had fallen.

Two officers stood guard by the ruins, pacing back and forth while the rest helped the crowds out. The black-clothed people were walking slowly down the driveway, their singing barely audible over the noise of cars and chattering.

"So, who's going to go?" Jeff smiled. "Who's the fastest?"

Buddy patted the earth where the toad lay buried, and scooped a few leaves over the spot. He grinned, his drying tears leaving dirt-smeared trails along his face. "We all know Tony's the fastest!"

Tony shook his head. "No, I'm not."

"Sometimes I can beat you," Jeff agreed.

"So who's gonna go?" Buddy asked.

"What if we get caught?" Tony said.

"Maybe we should sweeten the pot!" Jeff smirked. "Whoever goes gets five bucks from each of us! That's ten bucks for the person who steals three bricks."

Tony thought about all the things he could buy with ten bucks. He studied the cops and how relaxed they were becoming now that almost everyone was gone.

Everyone except that Connie Bellows still dragging around her cameraman. She was trying to get closer to the house, seemed to be trying to see down one of the holes exposing the basement. The police officers noticed at the same time Tony did, and walked over to her.

Tony didn't need to think twice. He raised himself into squatting mode and counted to three. While the cops were talking to Connie, he broke into a run, then dived behind a small pile of rubble.

He crawled on his belly, dragging himself with his hands toward a small clump of bricks.

He grabbed three bricks that appeared intact. He shoved two of them into the side pockets of his baggy pants. The third one, he held in his hands. He was just getting ready to go back to the hedge when he heard the cops shouting at him. His heart sank. Busted. He saw Jeff and Buddy creep away. Jeff gave him their secret hand signal before he slinked into the woods. Tony nodded slightly, giving his secret hand signal replay, by tapping the brick.

"Hey, hey, you, get back here," one of the cops called out. Tony scrambled to his feet. He saw the cops on the other side of the gaping hole to the basement.

"Put down those bricks."

Tony watched them stumble across the debris. He was torn. He knew he should obey the law, but he also really, really wanted to keep these bricks. He wanted the brick and he wanted ten bucks.

He broke into a run.

The cops finally made their way across the rubble and picked up speed as they followed the boy into the woods. Tony had the advantage in that he knew the woods by heart, but he was severely handicapped by the lack of leaves on the trees and the noisy crunching of the dead ones under his feet.

He zigzagged his way along the bigger trees,

stopping now and again to catch his breath, still hearing one of the cops panting in pursuit.

"Hey, kid. Put it back. Don't make me come after you."

Tony laughed. He already was coming after him, wasn't he?

He ran down by the river's edge, where the marsh grass was still high. His sneakers sloshed and slipped in the mud, sinking up to his ankles, the suction so great that he thought he'd lose his shoes, but it was still quieter than the leaves crunching in the woods. He heard the cop sliding down to the edge.

"Jesus Christ, I'm not going into that shit," the cop muttered. "Hey, kid. You got your bloody souvenir. And mark my words, nothing but bad luck will come your way if you keep it."

The cop half smiled to himself as he picked his way back out of the swamp grass and made his way back into the woods.

Tony stared at the brick in his hand. He was home free!

The three boys sat in their cave fort, examining the bricks by the light of several flickering candles.

"Wow, these are so cool," Buddy said, turning one over in his hands.

"Bricks from the house of horrors! We're the only ones!" Tony grinned.

"Oh, I'm sure others will steal things too. They can't guard that place forever," Jeff said.

"Well, we have the first ones." Tony smiled. "So pay up, guys. I want my ten bucks."

Jeff and Buddy stood up and felt in their pockets. Jeff pulled out two crumpled-up one-dollar bills. He held them out to Tony. "Here . . . I only have two for now, but I'll have more later."

Tony snatched them. "You better or I'm taking it back."

He unrolled the money and looked at it, holding it up to the candlelight to make sure he wasn't getting ripped off. "And you? Buddy . . ."

Buddy pulled some change out of his pocket. A mixture of pennies, some nickles and a couple of quarters. He dropped them into Tony's outstretched hand. "I'll get you the rest as soon as I can. . . ."

Tony sighed and counted it, shaking his head. "It's even less than Jeff. Jeez . . ."

"You know I don't get much allowance." Tony looked at Buddy and nodded. Even though they were just kids, they already understood about Buddy and his hard life with an alcoholic mom on welfare and a succession of new daddies.

"I know, Buddy. It'll be months before you pay

me back. Maybe I should hang on to that brick just to make sure you do."

Buddy's eyes grew wide. "Aw, you don't hafta do that. I'm good for it. I really am."

"Well, we're gonna thump you if you don't come through," Jeff said, raising his fist.

"Well, what about you? I don't see you paying up in full either."

"Well, I could have if I'd known. Besides, Tony knows I'll never steer him wrong."

"Hey, he knows I'll never steer him wrong either," Buddy pouted. "I just don't have rich folks like you two."

Tony winced. Buddy's words hit home. Sure, they weren't rich, but middle class seemed rich to a kid like Buddy.

Tony stood up, holding the three bricks. "Hey, guys, we're best friends to the end." He held a brick out to each of them.

"Cool," Buddy said, turning his over in his hand. "Thanks, man."

"A toast," Jeff said, imitating his parents at the dinner table with their wineglasses, and held his brick up. The boys held their bricks up over their heads and touched them together.

"Best friends forever!" Jeff shouted.

"Best friends!" said Tony.

"Best friends!" said Buddy, smiling.

The bricks sparked, sending surges of electricity down their arms. The boys jumped back, the bricks falling from their hands. The bricks landed with three successive thumps onto the dirt floor of the cave, smoke wafting from them in the candlelight.

"Holy shit," Jeff said, staring in disbelief as he rubbed his palm against his leg.

"What was that?" Tony asked, also rubbing his hands to get rid of the tingling surge.

"It felt like when I stuck my knife in the electric socket once," Buddy replied, inspecting his hand. "Like a big jolt of electricity."

"That was weird," Tony said. He crouched by his brick and poked at it with a stick. There was nothing.

Cautiously, he picked up his brick. He turned it over in his hand. There was no feeling in it now, nothing unusual at all.

"Hey, guys, it's okay now," he said. The other two watched warily as Tony touched all three bricks.

"I—uh, I'm gonna go home now," Jeff said, carefully picking up his brick. He inspected it and found it to be just a plain old brick again. He shoved it in the waist of his jeans. "I'll see ya guys later."

"Yeah, I'm gonna get going too." Tony nodded, rubbing his eyes. The musky cave of candle smoke was getting to him.

Jeff stumbled out of the cave. Tony and Buddy stared at each other wordlessly. Tony turned his brick over and over in his hand.

"It was real, wasn't it?" Tony asked. "We couldn't have all had the same dream."

"Vision." Buddy smiled, his face suddenly looking old and wise in the shadows of the cave. "We had a vision."

Tony was filled again with a sense of dread and wanted to put the brick down. But he also knew this was a very valuable souvenir. It might even be worth money to someone somewhere. Besides, he didn't want Buddy to think he was a wus.

"See ya later, Buddy," Tony said.

Buddy nodded. "Yeah. . . ."

"And don't forget the money. A quarter a week, man. I mean it."

"Thanks. I won't let you down. Promise."

Tony shrugged, wondering if he'd ever see money from either one of the boys. He walked out of the cave and into the late afternoon sun.

The days were so short now. The long languorous days of summer had flown by and now darkness came so early and stayed so late.

A wind had picked up, blowing in a chill from the lake.

Tony held the brick in his hand as he wandered along the edge of the lake. His lips were pursed in a whistle as he strolled along, trying to focus on the song he was creating instead of the weird and wild thoughts running through his mind. It had been a full and strange day. A day he didn't think he would ever forget.

As he walked along, he grew more aware that his hand was throbbing—actually, he realized, it was burning. He looked down and saw that the brick was pulsing. The sides pushed out and then collapsed in again as easily as a rubber balloon.

The brick was breathing.

Tony stopped and stared down at it. The brick expanded and collapsed, each expansion pushing out farther. He saw little cracks tearing along the sides, saw droplets of moisture leaking out. He held the brick closer to his face, trying to see what was making it do that.

It must be trick of some sort. Maybe Buddy or Jeff playing some kind of practical joke and had switched the brick on him. Maybe the whole business with the sparks had been some sort of setup too. He wouldn't put it past them.

The brick breathed again, stretching so far that it was almost translucent. The sides heaved so far that he thought it was going to burst.

One of the cracks split open farther and a wash of thick red liquid leaked out. Tony gawked at it as the wash turned into a river gushing over his hand.

As he stared speechlessly at the bleeding brick, it burst into a fountain, spraying him from head to toe with thick syrupy liquid.

Tony screamed.

Chapter Two

His screaming woke her fully.

With her heart pounding, Lydia watched the man beside her flail and hit at dream demons, the glow of the moonlight giving just enough substance to shadow that she wasn't sure if maybe there wasn't something there. Of course there wasn't. Whatever he was fighting was locked in a battle with his subconscious. She watched him crying out, his hands reaching, grabbing at something. Lydia rolled over to the far side of the bed, protecting herself from getting hit.

Tony jolted upright, and his eyes popped open, glittering in the moonlight. She saw him staring beyond the wall, his mouth opening and shutting like a fish as he breathed his panic. His dark hair was tousled and she could see droplets of sweat running in gleaming streaks down his face.

For the three years she had known Tony, he had suffered from nightmares. Sometimes weeks would go by and she would think they were safe from them, that they had finally left him alone, only to find him screaming and thrashing or cowering and crying once again in the dead of night.

Now that Tony was settled, Lydia pulled herself up to sitting position, and slowly ran her hand along his arm.

"Tony," she cooed. "It's Lydia . . . You okay?"

Tony shivered and shook his head, more to clear it than as a response. His earring glittered in the half-light.

"I'm . . . I'm okay," he gasped.

Lydia ran her hand through his hair, comforting him. "You're soaked again, honey," she said. "Let me get you a cloth."

"No. no. I just want to go back to sleep," Tony muttered.

Lydia squeezed his arm. "What was it that scared you so?"

"I can't talk about it." Tony sighed.

"You have to talk about it one day," Lydia said. "And I bet the minute you get it out in the open, the nightmares will stop once and for all."

"If I talk about the nightmares, then I will be pulling them into *this* world," Tony muttered, lying back. He nestled his head back into his pillow like a little boy. Lydia pulled the blankets over him, but he was already asleep again.

She watched his dark lashes flutter in the darkness, his lips slightly parted as deep relaxing breaths passed in and out of his mouth.

She wondered what haunted him so. What was this trauma that he dared not speak about?

Maybe once they were married, he would open up more. As well as she thought she knew him, there was so much darkness locked inside. It both intrigued and frightened her.

"Wow!" Lydia said as Tony stopped the red sports car, avoiding a puddle left from the melting snow. Tony grinned, the little boy he once had been revealed for a glancing moment. Tony had grown into a tall, slender man of thirty. His dark hair was trimmed very short, emphasizing the pronounced widow's peak of his hair line and the expressiveness of his blue eyes. He had a small hoop earring on one ear, and today, a pair of sunglasses protected his sensitive eyes from the glare of the sun.

Lydia too wore sunglasses over her dark brown eyes. She was twenty-nine, with long brown hair, and had a lovely figure, the classic hourglass shape with ample bosom and rounded bottom. They both wore sweaters and jeans, befitting the long ride from their home in New York City out here to the countryside just under two hours away.

Lydia climbed out of the car and looked at the lot at the end of a long gravel driveway. Tony got out and held the door open for Lydia's dog, Pilar. Pilar was a mahogany Belgian Tervuren, with a black muzzle, a purebred derived from a long-ago encounter between German shepherds and collies. She looked like a longhaired German shepherd with a regal mane like a collie. Pilar bounded up beside Lydia as she walked toward the vacant lot. Tony watched his fiancée, enjoying the view of her jean-clad butt before he caught up to her.

"So this is where we're going to build," Tony explained. "Do you like this area?"

Lydia looked over at the trees, tall and towering, new buds sprouting as winter broke into spring. There were small clumps of icy snow looking out of place among the new green grass.

Lydia wandered over to the tiny piles of rubble surrounding a large boarded-up area flush with the ground. There was a bit of old chicken wire haphazardly surrounding the covered-up pit.

"I thought we would build right here, over the original basement." Tony pointed, leading her over to the plugged-up area. "We can always add on, wings even!" He laughed. "When we make it big!"

"Wings, my, but you dream big." Lydia smiled. She looked along the boarded-up basement pit and saw a few rocks and bricks stained with black charcoal smudges.

"Did this house burn down?" she asked.

"No, there was a fire years after the original house was destroyed."

"What happened?" Lydia asked.

Tony reached into his pocket and pulled out his cigarettes. He offered one to Lydia, who took it. He lit them both. After he took a deep puff, and watched the smoke release into the cool air, he turned to her.

"You know, I don't really remember the reason. Maybe there were faulty gas lines? Or maybe the people didn't pay the mortgage. I just remember being ten years old when a great big bulldozer came chugging up this driveway and smashed that little old house to bits."

"Ten years old . . . that must have been something to see," Lydia said, examining Tony's face. She couldn't read his expression behind his glasses. She couldn't tell if he was telling her the truth, or trying to "protect" her as he was wont to do in that stupid macho way that men often had. She decided to let it drop for now.

"Are you sure you really want to move back here? To your hometown?" she asked.

"I've given it a lot of thought, Lydia. It is perfect. It's only a train ride into the city when we need to go, and we both have the sort of job that we don't have to go in every day anymore. Gotta love technology!" He grinned. "And my parents are still around, so when we start our family . . ."

Tony reached his arm around Lydia and pulled her close.

"I know how much you want to start a family," he whispered into her ear. "As soon as we move in, we'll start making plans."

"That sounds like a great idea," Lydia said. "I hope I make a good mom. I've been out in the business world so long, I don't know if I'll be able to deal with staying home full-time."

"We'll cross that bridge when we get to it," Tony said. "First, we have to build this house."

He took her hand and led her around the basement. "I hope you like it."

"I'm sure whatever you decide will be fine," Lydia said.

"Do you want me to show you the design?"

Lydia thought for a moment. "You know what, if you think it's a good one, then surprise me!"

"Then surprise you I will."

Tony took her hand and led her into the woods.

"You know, we own a great deal of this forest too," he said.

"Really? How far?"

"I'll show you the surveyor's map when we get home. But first, you have to see it."

They picked their way along the mud and left-over icy bits, fallen branches and little mountains of unmelted snow. They slipped and slid, giggling as they leaned on each other until they reached the river's edge. Tony led her to a spot that was naturally curved in more than the rest of the bank.

"Our own swimming hole!" he said. "I know how much you love to swim, and now, here, you can swim all summer long! We'll build you a dock and everything."

"Oh, my God, Tony. This is amazing. . . ." She threw her arms around him and kissed him on the lips. Then she hesitated. She removed his sunglasses from his face and looked into his eyes.

"Can you afford it?" she asked very seriously.

The side of Tony's mouth twitched, giving him a lopsided boyish grin. It was a look she adored, a look that she was seeing less and less of as he climbed his way up the ladder of success. She hoped that one day it wouldn't just disappear.

"I can afford a dream house for my beautiful bride."

"Are you sure? It's a hell of a lot of property, and then building a house on it . . ."

"I've been saving for this place forever," Tony said, putting his glasses back on. "I always knew it would be mine, no matter what the cost."

Lydia turned her attention back to the shining water of the river. The sun's rays danced along the surface, creating a glass illusion that hinted at darkness lurking below. She wondered how deep the water was out in the center. The sound of splashing caught her attention.

Pilar nosed along the weeds and pond grass, half of it dead from the previous year, with lush green new growth woven through.

"Pilar," Lydia shouted, following the dog down. Pilar was up to her chest in the water. "Oh, God, now we have a wet dog to take back with us."

Pilar splashed and played, attacking beetles skipping along the water's surface. Lydia forgot about trying to keep the dog dry as she laughed at Pilar's antics. Lydia looked around on the ground and found a big stick. She threw it out into the water, where it landed with a splash. The current caught it and it twirled and swirled lazily downstream. Pilar swam after it, snatching at it with her teeth, gulping and coughing until at last she had it in her grasp. Once it was in her mouth, she paddled back to shore, heaving and puffing like a steam engine.

She dragged herself up the muddy shore, now even more slippery due to her soaking paws, and dropped the stick at Lydia's feet.

"Not bad for a city dog!" Lydia laughed. Pilar shook, spraying muddy water all over Lydia. Lydia covered her face.

"Hey, you're going to have to learn to shake somewhere else if we're living here."

Pilar bounded back down to the river again while Lydia looked over at Tony, who still stood staring out across the river. His mouth was set in a grim expression, his dark eyebrows furrowed above the sunglasses.

Lydia wandered back over to him. "Hey, handsome, what's wrong with you?"

"Huh?" Tony snapped back to reality.

"You are so far away . . . what are you thinking about?"

Lydia wrapped her arms around his waist and leaned her head against his chest.

"I was just remembering . . . how much fun we used to have here," he said. "Me and the guys."

"You and the guys . . . sounds like a pretty tight group you had."

"We were. . . ." Tony nodded. "Yeah, we were. . . ."

There was a rustling beside them and Lydia turned, expecting to be rained on again by Pilar. Instead, she was startled to see a man lurching from the bushes. He was dressed in filthy clothes, his face covered by matted copper and gray hair that sprouted from his head to his chin. He wore an old baseball cap, and in his hands he carried a dirty burlap sack. He stopped, clearly as startled as the couple was.

"Holy shit . . . y'all scared me," the man wheezed, banging his chest. He started to cough, a deep rattling noise that racked him to bending over. He stood up and hawked onto the ground. Lydia winced.

"This here's private property now," Tony said. "You can't be hanging around."

"No shit . . . someone's finally bought this sorry-ass place." The man chuckled. "After all this time. . . ."

The man stopped laughing and stepped closer to Tony. Lydia instinctively stepped back.

"Hey, man. Take off those shades for a moment," the man said.

"Why?"

"Jess wanna see something . . . come on . . . lessee your face."

Tony shrugged and pulled his glasses off. The man leaned forward, peering. Tony leaned back, a waft of the man's body odor hitting him.

The man widened his eyes, cocked his head and then started to laugh.

"Why, shit . . . I'd know those baby blues anywhere! Tony, my man . . . how's it hanging?" He slapped Tony on the back so hard that Tony nearly fell over. Tony stared at the man, trying to see the face beneath the hair. Then he saw it, the gap-toothed grin of a boy he once knew.

"Buddy?" Tony asked as if speaking to a ghost. "Is that you, Buddy?"

"The one and the same."

"No shit. Man, I was just talking about you. Lydia." Tony waved Lydia over. Lydia took a tiny timid step forward, wrinkling her nose as the foul breath of the man washed over her.

"Lydia, this is Buddy. One of the three guys I used to hang out with . . . in these very woods."

"Apparently still hanging out in these very woods," Lydia said, staring around at the budding trees.

"So what's the deal? You buying this place . . . even after everything?" Buddy asked, his eyes wide.

Tony furrowed his eyebrows. "I'm the new owner. I'll have the final papers drawn up this week."

"Wow, you're brave, man."

Lydia looked from man to man.

"No, I'm just buying a piece of property, to build a home on where we will live after we are married." Tony put an arm protectively around Lydia. As he did so, he flashed a finger signal at Buddy. Buddy caught it and nodded with a sly grin.

"Lovely woods, these." Buddy sighed, staring around. "I like to come fishing here. You won't mind if I come fishing here?"

"It's up to Lydia. She's the boss." Tony winked teasingly at Lydia.

She pushed him playfully. "That's right, I'm the boss, you heard it here! Fishing . . . I don't see it being a problem . . . I don't think," Lydia mused.

There was a moment of awkward silence.

"So, what do you do? Are you like some hotshot executive or something?"

Tony laughed.

"Close. An up-and-coming hotshot executive . . . I'm the financial advisor for an entertainment firm in New York City."

"Making the big bucks then!" Buddy winked at Lydia.

"No, not yet. It's a new company, but we have high hopes. Big dreams," Tony said seriously.

Buddy nodded and turned his attention to Lydia. "And you, pretty lady. What is it that you do?"

"I'm in advertising."

"Hmmm . . . entertainment and advertising." Buddy nodded with approval. "Sounds like a good match."

"And you, Buddy . . . what do you do?" Lydia

asked, staring at the mismatched mud-caked rubber boots on his feet.

"As you can see, life hasn't been near so kind to me . . . I . . ."

Out of the corner of her eye, Lydia saw Pilar barreling toward them.

"Oh, no . . . cross your arms over yourself, quick, my dog . . . *Pilar!*" Lydia screamed. Pilar lunged for Buddy with a growl. She tackled him and they fell to the ground. Buddy reached up to her fur as Pilar's growls filled the air.

"Come on, girl," Buddy said as they rolled over. Lydia realized that Pilar was playing. Instead of biting Buddy, she pinned him on his back and licked his face. Buddy laughed and grabbed Pilar by her mane.

"Don't know what it is, but dogs always take a shining to me," he joked as he wrestled with the dog. Buddy pulled himself back to standing position with a grunt and tugged at her fur. They played back and forth, Pilar barking and springing. Buddy found a stick and threw it for her. She scrambled off through the debris to fetch it.

Lydia stood with her mouth agape. "Nice guard dog. . . ." She sighed.

"You didn't tell her to attack," Buddy pointed out.

"Buddy always was the Dr. Dolittle of the group," Tony said. "He . . ."

"Shh . . . listen. . . ." Buddy put his hand up, cocking his head. "Do you hear that?"

"What?" Lydia listened.

"I don't hear anything," Tony said.

The wind rustled, a little stronger. The leaves fluttered along the ground, a bird whistled somewhere. Pilar had gone back down to the river's edge with her new stick and they could hear her splashing in the water.

"You don't hear it?"

"I hear Pilar," Lydia said.

"Oh, no, I don't mean Pilar." Buddy sighed. "Listen."

Again the three stood as still as deer frozen in the middle of an open meadow.

"What are we listening for?" Lydia asked, frustrated. "I don't hear anything I haven't heard before."

"Well, maybe not today, maybe not tomorrow, but you will hear it. Sometimes, when it's real quiet like, you can still hear them screamin'," Buddy said, his reddish brown eyes narrowing to a glassy slant.

"Uh, Buddy." Tony tapped Buddy's shoulder. "Like, don't scare my fiancée, man."

"Hmmm?" Buddy was startled from his trance.

"It's all right. I'm a big girl," Lydia said. "Tony, look at the time, we have to get back to your mom's place."

Tony looked at his watch. "You're right. Well, Buddy, it was nice to see you again. We'll have you over for a barbecue once we get settled in."

Tony took Lydia's hand and they walked away. Buddy waved, still stuck halfway in his dream-world.

"I hope you aren't serious that we're having that smelly bum over for dinner," Lydia scolded once they were safely out of earshot. "Really. . . ."

"Hey, I bet if we cleaned him up . . ."

"*We* cleaned him up! What are we, his parents? Hell, he's the same age as you and he looks like he's sixty-five."

"Life isn't so kind to some people. His life sucked from when he was just a little kid," Tony said, remembering the times he shared his lunch with the starving child.

"Well, yours wasn't so hot, and neither was mine."

"Hey, mine was all right. I was a middle-class kid without too much baggage."

"Oh? Then why the nightmares? How come at least twice a week you burst awake in the grip of some god-awful nightmare?"

"Everyone has bad dreams, Lydia . . . even you."

Lydia stopped and stared at him. "But not like yours."

Chapter Three

"Oh, my God!" Lydia cried as Tony slipped the blindfold from her eyes. She stood at the foot of freshly painted stairs leading up to a wide porch and stared up at their newly completed home.

It was a modest two-story dwelling, an A-frame style with lots of windows. The porch already had a rocking chair on it and a couple of long cement planters filled with yellow flowers. Smaller pots of flowers perched on the railings. The deck circled the house like a moat.

Beyond the house, the woods were green and lush, full of growth and life. A long, tall, overgrown hedge framed the far side of the driveway, providing a barrier from the woods. Beside the house, a small rosebush was already clinging to the new wall with tiny tendrils, as well as some wild ivy.

It was late June, so the heat of the summer hadn't kicked in yet, but the damp smell of rain and woods and flowers tickled Lydia's nose. She breathed in dreamily.

It smelled like home.

Her home.

Their home.

She ran up the stairs to the porch and crouched by the planters, touching the petals and lowering her face into the flowers, breathing in their sweet perfume.

"Oh, they smell so pretty. Like summertime." She touched the tiny petals. "New beginnings . . ."

Lydia jumped back up and tried to peer into the house through one of the windows, but the curtains were closed and very thick. She rattled the front door handle but it was locked.

"Patience, my dear," Tony said.

"I have to see it," she said, turning to Tony. "I feel like a little kid!"

"It's locked, honey. Here, just wait for a second," Tony said, digging in his pocket for the key.

"Oh, yes, this is perfect, so absolutely perfect," Lydia cried, running her hand up the banister as she tried the front steps again.

Tony slipped the key into the door. "Now remember, I haven't gone furniture shopping. That's your department," he said as he pushed open the door.

Lydia stared inside, the smell of fresh lumber and recent painting flooding her nose. The walls were all white and the floors were a shiny dark mahogany. Over along the far wall was an old-fashioned brick fireplace with a large mantelpiece.

"This is the living room. A bit cozy for now, but once the money starts rolling in . . ." Tony nodded.

"It's lovely the way it is. You and your money," Lydia said, running her hands along the brick of the fireplace.

"Those are some of the original bricks," Tony said. "From the original house."

"Wow, historic as well as beautiful," Lydia said.

"Come, you must see the kitchen." Tony took her hand and led her into a bright open kitchen. There was a glassed-in breakfast nook that faced the narrow backyard that led to the woods. There was a built-in table with cushioned benches, diner style.

"Coffee is going to taste ten times as good in here." Lydia plunked herself into one of the couches and stared into the woods. She watched light and shadow play as the trees rustled in the breeze.

"Hey, have you seen that creepy guy around lately?" she asked.

"Creepy guy?"

"Yeah, your old school friend. Buddy."

"Oh, Buddy . . ." Tony gazed into the woods. "Not in a long while."

"I really hope that he isn't going to be hanging around here much."

"Don't worry, Lydia, we're going to be far too busy to be hanging around with the likes of Buddy. Hey, did you check out the indoor grill on this oven stove thing?" Tony pointed to the stove island.

Lydia hurried over and inspected all the conveniences. "I've always wanted one of those. How did you know?"

"You're my wife, aren't you?" Tony pulled her close and kissed her.

"Only for a couple of weeks!" Lydia blushed. "If you keep making me as happy as I am now, this marriage will last forever."

Lydia slipped from his grip and wandered back into the living room, listening to her footsteps echoing in the hollow empty room.

"Once you pick out your furniture, we'll paint the walls to match." Tony grinned.

Lydia turned to him. "I love you. No one is more perfect than you." She kissed him on the cheek.

He laughed. "Go on, go look around some more. Tell me what you think. I'll go let Pilar out of the car."

"Make sure you wipe her feet, it's pretty muddy out there."

Lydia climbed the stairs to the second floor and walked down the hallway. There were two small bedrooms and a fair-sized bathroom that was accessible from either bedroom and the hallway. She continued to the end of the hall and pushed open the door to the master bedroom.

It was bright with high ceilings, and large long windows. Two walk-in closets had racks and built-in shelves and there was a bathroom. When Lydia walked into the bathroom she was thrilled to find two sinks, a toilet, an oval Jacuzzi and a shower stall. She looked at herself in the mirror over the sinks. Her dark eyes were shining with joy.

"You are blessed, Lydia. Whatever shit you've been through so far, consider yourself blessed from this moment on." Lydia studied her face, searching the faint lines around her eyes and in her forehead for answers, for revelations that she truly was finished with the crap that had dragged her down before she met Tony.

She wondered if moving back to his hometown would make Tony's nightmares worse or better. How she hoped he would finally be able to exorcise some of his own inner demons.

Lydia twisted one of the faucets. The pipes

groaned and a few drops of rusty-colored liquid leaked out.

"Euw." Lydia grimaced.

Lydia opened the faucet a little more and an explosive burst of rusty water flew out, spraying her blouse.

"Oh, shit." She sighed, staring at the stain. She was loathe to touch it with her hands. Looking around the bathroom, she saw nothing to wipe it with, not even toilet paper, and her purse was still in the car.

"I guess I should just consider myself baptized into this new house," she muttered, rubbing at the stain with her fingers. The water ran clear now, and she put her hands under the spray. It smelled musky but she knew it was from lack of use. She turned the spigot off again and left the bathroom, wiping her damp hands along the sweater, trying to soften the rust splotches. She was careful not to get drips on the plush white carpet of the bedroom.

She was distracted from her task by the large wide bay window and, built in below the window, a window seat.

"I've always wanted a window seat," she said to the empty room. She could imagine exactly what kind of curtains to get for this room. Sheers and pretty valances, wrought-iron rods. She smiled as she imagined a canopy bed.

The outside view was similar to the breakfast nook, but higher. The backyard, the woods and then just beyond, a glimmer of the river. Lydia sat down on the soft, checkered cushion, leaning against the wooden frame. She thought about how nice a swim would be, once the summer came. The sun climbed higher in the sky, already above the edge of the woods. Pockets of shadows twisted, forming odd patterns along the trees. She watched as bushes swayed and branches trembled with life running through them.

One tree in particular was active, swaying with the weight of several birds. Leaves and branches rustled and shifted. The movement grew more frantic, a flurry of activity, and leaves fell to the earth. Suddenly, about a dozen blackbirds burst forth from the tree, screaming and cawing as they took flight. They soared high into the sky, circling and swooping. One of the crows had something in its talons. The other crows followed it, dive-bombing it, trying to snatch the object away. The fleeing crow outmaneuvered the others as long as it could, but eventually tired of the game. It circled and swooped, landing in the backyard.

One by one the other crows descended, cockily walking over to the crow with the prize, cawing bossily. They picked at whatever it was they had been fighting about, with flapping wings and stabbing beaks.

They chattered and squawked among themselves. Lydia cranked open the window to hear them better. She could see a flash of a dirty white something that the birds pulled and tugged at, dropping it, snatching it from each other, feathers flying.

Pilar bounded across the backyard, right into the thick of the birds. They screamed and shot back up into the air as Pilar barked and circled them from below. The flock sought refuge once more in the woods. Satisfied they were gone with one last "stay away" bark, Pilar sniffed around where they had been and found the mystery object. She chewed on it.

"Drop it, Pilar," Lydia shouted from the window. The dog looked up and, seeing her mistress so far away, continued to gnash, the crunching audible even to Lydia's ears, until it was gone.

"I hope you aren't going to get sick later." Lydia sighed. Pilar set to work sniffing and searching and found the trail of something else. With the plume of her tail wagging, the dog disappeared into the woods. Lydia spotted her mahogany mane darting through the trees as she headed down to the river.

"Are you happy, Mrs. Blackstone?"

Lydia jumped.

"Wha—?" Lydia put her hand to her heart. "You scared me."

"Sorry. Boy, there sure was a lot of noise for a while there. You going to be able to handle the country life?"

"It's great. Sure beats watching the bums squabble over a half-dead whiskey bottle," Lydia joked.

"Yep." Tony nodded.

"I've never been so happy, my handsome husband," Lydia purred, reaching up to Tony. She cupped his face in her hands and stared into his eyes. Her lips pressed against his gently.

"You are perfect. Absolutely perfect." She sighed. "How did I ever get so lucky?"

"I ask myself all the time, how did I ever get so lucky?" Tony said, putting his hands on her shoulders, stroking the soft fabric of her blouse.

They kissed again, this time more hungrily, hands roaming, exploring. Shirts were pulled from each other and fell to the floor as they kissed and touched each other in the window seat.

"Mmm, I want to eat you up." Tony sighed, and led her to the floor. Lydia lay back sinking into the soft carpet. She reached her hands up to Tony and pulled him down on top of her. They kissed, stroking each other's face, touching each other's hair.

Lydia heard a noise, a distant cry, almost like a wailing.

"What is that?" She lifted her head. Tony nuzzled her, his tongue licking her ear.

"I don't hear anything," Tony said, nibbling her as one of his hands cupped her breasts.

"I thought I heard . . ."

"Pretty jumpy for a city girl," Tony teased.

Tony's mouth covered hers again. Lydia responded, pushing thoughts of noise from her mind as her hands ran along his back, feeling his warm flesh beneath her fingers.

She pulled him closer to her, reveling in his strength, imagining herself trapped as she slipped her hands beneath his jeans, sliding them down the round mounds of his butt. She wrapped her legs around his, searching out his mouth again and again.

The sound was back. Soft, yet persistent. Almost angry, like a hive of bees, or a cat, but she knew the sound. It was the sound of a newborn baby.

It whined persistently in the background until she could stand it no longer. She pushed Tony off of her.

"Don't you hear that?" she asked, sitting up.

"Again with the noise. Come on, Lydia. Get a grip . . . relax." Tony ran his hand along her arm. He kneeled so that he could see out the window. "It's probably a motorboat or something. You just aren't used to the noise of the country yet, that's all."

"Oh, a motorboat. . . ." Lydia nodded thoughtfully. "Sure . . . I thought it was a baby crying."

"A baby crying."

"Like a newborn baby. You know how they always sound like a hive of angry bees, or an angry cat."

"Well, no, but if you insist . . ."

"You'll know."

Tony hugged Lydia thoughtfully. "Mmmm . . . a baby . . ." He breathed in the essence of her hair. "Yes, let's make a baby today," he murmured in her ear.

Buddy shuffled into the backyard, his burlap sack in one hand, a long wooden walking stick in the other. Every now and again, he'd have to use the walking stick, especially on days like today, when his right knee just did not want to behave as well as it should. It was an old injury from when he was a teenager. Now he suspected some sort of arthritis had taken hold. Well, he knew it was going to rain later on, if nothing else.

He hobbled over to the spot where the crows had been fighting over their prize. Buddy kicked at the grass, but there was nothing there. He poked around the soft earth with his staff. Nothing. Not even a crumb.

Buddy knelt down heavily with a groan, and then crawled on his hands and knees, examining the ground, blade by blade, dirt mound by dirt mound. Whatever evidence there had been was long gone now. He shrugged and stood back up again, slapping loose grass and dirt from his filthy, baggy pants.

His attention was caught by movement in the upstairs window. He knew they were here, he had watched them drive in. He had even played a bit with Pilar before she took off to the river.

Up in the bay window of the master bedroom, he could see Tony and Lydia staring out at the woods, in between kisses. Through the open window he could hear their soft murmuring. He wondered what loving words they whispered to each other. He wondered what loving words anyone whispered to each other. What sorts of secrets did lovers share?

His heart pounded as he saw them gently touch each other's hair, faces closer, hands rhythmically stroking, more kissing and whispering. Soon their heads disappeared once more as they sank back to the floor.

Buddy nodded and stared into the woods. A wind was picking up. The leaves rustled, *shssh*ing against the branches. The open window of the master bedroom swayed back and forth, creaking on its hinges. Buddy raised his eyes to the sky, watching as gray clouds rolled and tumbled into sight, mixing and melding with the white ones. The wind grew stronger as the sky grew darker. An eerie howl wove through the forest. A low moan, the groaning of trees bending, of branches snapping, of seasons blending and melting.

Thunder boomed as the sky rippled and spun.

Buddy closed his eyes and imagined Lydia and Tony, clothes scattered across the room, their flesh joining and parting as their sweat glistened between flashes of lightning.

Tears filled his eyes as a hollow ache flooded him. To be caressed by another, to feel soft touches dancing along his skin, to be gazed at with eyes filled with love and passion, pupils large, possibilities endless. His hand clutched the staff, fingers gripping. His arms were so empty, his heart hadn't been filled with love for another human being in years. But now, thinking about the newlyweds, he realized how achingly lonely for human companionship he truly was. How his life consisted of day-to-day existence, wandering around, gathering food, occasionally making his way into town for the odd grocery run when his check came, sometimes making small talk with those who weren't too afraid to talk back, and those who remembered him as that poor child of Tildy's.

Of course, he had his animals.

There were always the animals.

Never judging, always loyal . . . it was amazing how loyal so many of them had been over the years. Humans would never be so loyal to one another. So unconditionally loving.

The wind was so strong now that his burlap bag started to tumble along the ground. Buddy caught it just as the first few drops of rain began to fall.

He stared up at the window, seeking shelter under one of the nearby willow trees. He sat down heavily against the trunk, wondering how it felt to have the press of lips against his. He raised his hand to his mouth, absentmindedly. It had been so long he could barely remember. A kiss. A simple, gentle kiss.

Again the ache trembled through him. This time it wasn't a tremor but a full-blown avalanche.

The ache of all love lost, the ache of all love never found, the endless ache of unrequited love flooded him. He remembered snatches of moments when perhaps he had once been happy, once thought he was loving and being loved. And how fleeting that time had been. What a disillusionment that had been.

How cruel life and love could be to so many.

How many misunderstandings had there been?

Love hoped for when in fact it was mere illusion, a carrot held for the donkey to move . . . *move on, horsie, lead on, Buddy, he don't know no better.*

Let's laugh at Buddy, he's too crazy to git a girl. What girl would spread her legs fer the likes of Buddy?

Or maybe Buddy likes boooyyysss. . . .

Buddy rested his head on his knees and hitched a sobbing breath. Sadness and loneliness washed through him as the rain beat down. And with the cleansing, he was able to think again. For pain brought clarity, and with his heartache mourned, he now remembered exactly what it was that had brought him here, what had lured Tony here after all this time.

He started to giggle. The summer storm accelerated with fury. The willow tree slapped him with flailing branches and he laughed at the sting. Pilar came skulking by, drenched from the rain, hungry for human companionship in this strange stormy land.

"You will be part of it too." Buddy laughed, tears streaking his face as the rain soaked his hair. He leaned over to pick up his walking stick. He ran his hands along the half-finished carvings whittled into it. Carvings of wolves, jaws open, teeth snatching, tongues lolling.

"My beautiful wolves . . ." Buddy stroked their faces. He searched his pockets, patting himself until he found his old jackknife.

"My lovely wolves . . ." Buddy started to dig at one of the half-finished wolf faces, ignoring the rain dumping down on him. The point of the knife hitched into the wood, falling away to reveal more of the face, the cunning eyes, a beautiful scruff around the neck.

"Oh, yes . . . it begins again," Buddy sang. He looked over at Pilar, who lay against the trunk of the tree, watching him apprehensively with large brown eyes.

"Oh, yes, indeedy, Pilar, it begins again. . . ."

Chapter Four

Lydia stared at the piles of boxes around her. Wedding presents, mementos, clothes, books . . . it was endless.

She sighed and leaned back against a box of books. Where to even begin?

Lydia reached into her pocket, digging out her cigarettes and a lighter. Staring at the sun gleaming across the shiny wooden floors, she inhaled deeply and thought about how she had even gotten to this point.

She had been so lost for so long . . . tied to her work, each day passing by in a haze of successive days until the months flipped into years and the years threatened to roll even further. It had been best, to bury herself in her work. She had always been a loner. Didn't make friends easily. In high school, she was the geek eating lunch in the library, devouring mystery novels and scribbling in her diary. She was L'etranger.

Never finding a clique to hang with, never feeling the urge to tumble on the mats or don freakish clothes to prance around on stage. She didn't belong to the chess club or the film club or work on the paper or do cheerleading. She just existed, every day as though she were invisible, wafting through the hallways, pressing to the sides so that no one would see her, no one would know she was there.

Her sense of invisibility carried through to the university. At least here, she was more assimilated, a large portion of her advertising and computer classes were shadows of herself. But like shadows, the people in her classes wrinkled back and forth in time, maybe borrowing notes on a coffee break, perhaps meeting in the pub for a Christmas binge, but on the whole, more at home with the phosphors and keyboards than with each other.

She had a couple of love affairs. Guys that she enjoyed but inspired no great spark, no sweeping urge to abandon herself, to lose herself in a great emotional wave. At least, not in the way that she knew she could be. When it came, there would be an all-consuming yearning to be entwined in another person's life. The heartbeat racing, the aching of loins in moments apart, looking for e-mail, waiting for the phone to ring.

She knew *it* existed. At least for others.

There were books about this, movies about this. People died for this, yet for her, men were a bland nothingness. Friends to pass the time with, but there was no heat, no electric connection. She began to wonder if the songs were all lies or maybe she was just wired wrong.

Then she met Tony.

Just the thought of him, even after three years, made her heart beat faster.

The songs were not lies.

With her little knife, Lydia sliced through the tape sealing one of the boxes. As she ripped open the top, her mystery hardcovers gleamed in the sunshine. She scooped up a few books into her arms. As she slipped the books onto the shelves, she thought about that very first day Tony appeared in her life.

She remembered when he had first walked into the offices. Tall, thin, self-assured yet an aura of gentleness shimmering beneath the surface. Even before she sensed his charisma, it was his eyes that drew her in. He smiled, holding out his hand in the expected business ritual, yet as she took it, she fell into those bottomless blue eyes and never returned. In that instant, she finally understood what it was to be swept away.

When he called a few days later to presumably go over some information relating to the account, he asked her out for coffee. They met at a nearby café, and found they shared a passion for cappuccino with cinnamon.

"How is it someone as lovely as you has not been whisked away and married?" he asked, studying her face.

"The same reason as you, I'm sure. Just haven't found my mate yet."

Their eyes locked in that instant, his intensity sweeping over her in waves. Her body was electric as she drank in his face, his dark eyebrows, his thick short hair with that high forehead and widow's peak. He had reached over and taken her hand. He held it a moment, studying it. She remember wishing that she had painted her nails that day, how they were chipped and cracked. He didn't see that. He didn't see her fingers that were neither lovely nor graceful, he didn't notice how she trembled at his touch, or maybe he did. He had taken her hand and pressed it against his cheek for a moment, almost as if he were in a dream. His eyes were far away, and in the years that followed, she would get to know that dreamy look, a place where she couldn't reach him, that place where she couldn't follow.

He had looked at her hand once more and pressed his lips against it. The tremor that had been fluttering through her now flowed forth. Their chemistry had blended a perfect cocktail and they were together ever since.

She stared at the boxes. Already so many memories accumulated in such a short amount of time. Memories of dreams planned, of lives unfolding together. The future seemed so bright and so ready to be filled with limitless possibilities.

Her heart pounded as she thought about Tony. Never had she felt such passion for another human being. She was his shadow, basking in his glow, hungrily reveling in his success, craving to please and to be consumed by him. She still could not believe how it was that after so many years of grinding loneliness, she had found her soul mate.

She could not imagine a day when he would disappoint her. She didn't believe that he ever could.

The only problem, the only block that didn't quite fit into the wall of perfection, was his desire for a baby.

Lydia sighed. This was the only part of the dream

that wasn't clicking properly for her. Baby. Where there was a baby, there was a mom. And a dad. And then there was usually another baby after that.

Tony wanted a baby.

Lydia wasn't sure if she did.

Well, she knew that she *did.*

Someday . . . an elusive someday in a soft fluffy-cloud future. A someday with white rocking chairs and pink pillows, rays of sun and pretty white nighties. A someday she could dream about.

But someday was suddenly very, very near.

Someday was pressing urgently closer.

Since their marriage, he was more persistent. What had once been a vague sort of dream was now being pulled into reality. An anchor, that final grounding that would forever link them.

Marriage in itself had been a terrifying proposition. Despite the joy of finding her soul mate, marriage was a whole different deal. Endings and beginnings. A life shared instead of the independence she had grown accustomed to, a life that was once hers alone to fill as she pleased, now resonated as two. Even living together didn't have that clank of finality. Yet she didn't think she could imagine a life without Tony now that she had found him. So she swallowed her reservations of being his mate till death parted them and took the plunge.

Now, that far-off wedding day was suddenly in her past.

How quick yet endless that day had been. Forever smiling, grinning, laughing, shaking hands, patting beads of sweat from her glowing forehead, dusting her aching cheeks, carrying herself proudly in the heavy, corseted silk contraption that bound her up in the steaming summer sun. Meeting endless streams of relatives, how would she ever remember all of their names? Feeling the silent disapproval of that most important person, Tony's mother.

Lydia wasn't sure what the problem was that Sybil had with her, but it was there all right. From the first moment they had laid eyes on each other, the coldness of her future mother-in-law was like the unblinking stare of a snake.

Lydia thought for sure the woman would warm up after a few social dinners, but there was no thawing out this ice queen. Sybil would warily watch her, like a cat ready to pounce on the prize canary when no one was looking. When others were out of earshot, she would whisper cryptic things to Lydia. Snatches of "when he was dating so and so" or "too bad you don't understand how he really thinks" and veiled insinuations that she, Lydia, the woman who had been by his side for over three years, would never be good enough. Even when they announced their engagement, it seemed to take every fiber of her being for Sybil to attempt to hug the object of her son's adulation.

The only good thing Lydia could say about the woman was that the wedding ceremony went rather smoothly, her sharp tongue was held in respectful check.

Lydia didn't kid herself. It was all for appearances' sake. Mustn't upset her son. Mustn't have anything but perfection for the wedding ceremony, even if the bride herself was not. Every flower, every cheese cube, had been organized by Sybil. Lydia's parents barely had a hand in the preparations at all, and all Lydia could do was thank God it had been a relatively small affair.

How could someone as warm and loving as Tony have such a shrew for a mother? Lydia wondered.

His father, Walter, on the other hand, was a little less uptight. He still wasn't the warmest person on earth but at least tried to hide it, especially when the required dinners were held in a public setting or around extended family. Walter let the mask of formality slip now and again, even as he held court, twinkling blue eyes glancing at his wife, who'd sniff aloofly as he'd relay an amusing anecdote or two. With a few drinks in him, Walter could actually loosen up and be a bit fun. Lydia thought he'd be a decent grandfather, if Sybil would let him.

The past three years had been lived with many, many miles between them. No need to cross paths except on holidays and the rare special occasion.

Now, she lived in the same tiny town as these people. And it was tiny.

Lydia hoped that she would be able to survive.

At last, most of the books were on the shelves. She ran her fingers along the spines. Some were old favorites from high school, *Clockwork Orange, Lord of the Flies, Gone with the Wind,* and then there was her growing collection of mystery novels.

She loved a good mystery.

Mysteries were the genre that saved her from all those jerks that she had to deal with day in and day out at the high school. Sometimes she wondered if she hadn't missed her calling and maybe should have been a private eye of some sort.

Well, it was fun to read about mystery and murder, but dealing with the reality of it on a daily basis was dangerous and just plain depressing.

She could never understand why husbands plotted against wives, why wives embezzled from husbands, why there was so much blood and hatred when divorce was legal. . . .

Hell, murder and espionage were practically the norm in these little fantasies.

But that's what they were, fantasies.

And that is why people like her read them. To escape and be entertained. And to be grateful for what normalcy there was in her life even if her mother-in-law was Queen Bitch.

Several empty boxes lay around her. She knew she should cut and fold them like a good little re-cycling girl, but she just couldn't be bothered right now. The best thing to do would be to get them out of the way, so that she could feel that at least a small amount of progress had been made.

Well, hell, that's what basements were for!

She gathered up a couple of boxes and headed through the kitchen and down the stairs.

The smell hit her like a wall. Damp, muggy . . . decay . . .

She breathed through her mouth, putting the boxes down as quickly as she could before going back up to get more. She couldn't understand why it stank so bad down here. Was this not a brand-new house, with a brand-new basement? Should not the scent be fresh paint and sawdust, wood and glue and turpentine? But it wasn't. It was the stench of death.

She wondered if an animal was rotting away in a corner somewhere, trapped between the walls during construction.

As she stacked the boxes against the wall, a chill wafted across her, an ebbing undulating across her arms, leaving goose bumps in its wake. She shuddered and wondered where this draft was coming from. Her hair tickled as if it had caught on something. She ran her hand along the back of her head but her hair was fine.

The naked lightbulb swung lazily. Certainly when they had more money, they would fix up this basement, put in proper lighting, walls, a floor.

She kicked at the concrete floor, cracking already in places. The basement had always seemed rather odd to her. The brick wall had been erected about halfway down the room. She knew the basement was much larger, had seen it with her own eyes when Tony first showed her the hole in the ground. Yet for some reason, this wall had been placed in this strange spot. She looked up at the ceiling, at the boards and beams supporting the upper level. Maybe it had to do with the ground level and the foundation.

It also seemed strange to her that the wall was brick. Not drywall or plaster or cinder block, but brick, old bricks . . .

She ran her hand along the bricks. They were icy cold. The prickling sensation ran along her hair again, the lightbulb now swinging in a circle.

Out of the corner of her eye, she thought she saw something, but in turning her focus to it, there was nothing there but the dancing shadows from the light.

"There is nothing here," she hummed softly to herself, her eyes darting around the room, double-checking the corners.

She hurried back up the stairs to get more boxes.

Wasn't she being a baby, getting all creeped out in her own basement? A basement in a brand-new house.

It's not as though there would be any monsters in a new house, even if it was built on an old foundation. This was real life, not some B movie. Of course, she'd seen all those creepy films, from *Poltergeist* to *The Sixth Sense* to *The Exorcist,* and their echoes stirred faintly in her subconscious.

Besides, there were no such things as monsters. Except for those assholes that had tormented her as a teenager.

Perhaps all those stupid memories about high school had triggered something. Those crazy bitches that just couldn't leave someone alone. Why did they feel her business was their business anyway?

She remembered being in the locker room and being taunted in the shower for her round body, having a bottle of baby powder poured over her head by some anonymous asshole that to this day she had no idea who it was . . . all those crazy memories, those crazy hurts. It was as if it had happened to someone else in some high school high-jinks movie. Yet, she had been one of the so-called losers. Just because she wasn't cool. Couldn't figure out what cool was . . . couldn't even pretend . . .

She could hardly wait until a few more years had gone by, a few more years to even the score, to give her strength and to ride hard on those skags whose youth and beauty would be betrayed by booze and rough nights waitressing in bars, waiting for balding, fat, ex-football-captain hubby to come home and fuck her and smack her. Lydia smiled, knowing that she had been watching way too many TV movies, too many episodes of *Jerry Springer* and *Jenny Jones*, but she liked to pretend, even for a moment, that there was karmic balance somewhere, somehow, and that one day, she would get hers.

The stairs creaked under her feet. For new steps, they were noisy. Perhaps, though, it didn't matter if steps were new or old, perhaps some steps just creaked no matter what you did. She shifted the box and carefully stepped back down. The light flickered and she stood still, staring at the glowing bulb. She wondered what kind of lighting fixture she should put up down here. This naked bulb just wasn't necessary in such a new home. In fact, the whole setup of this basement area was a contrast to how everything should be.

Lydia reached the bottom of the stairs and slid the box on top of the other one. This room was so tiny. Perhaps there were other things that she could not see. Like furnaces and wiring and plumbing bits that an apartment dweller like herself knew nothing about.

Her eye was drawn back to the lightbulb, gently swinging now on its long stringy cord. Dust motes clung and swirled around the glass, forming a second ring. It glowed like a planet hovering in a miniature galaxy.

The planet began to sway, round and round, each epileptic swing spreading into a wider and wider arc. Lydia gasped as she watched the shadows bobbing and bouncing on the far wall. The gloam around the bulb didn't move at all. It hovered, a weird little cloud chunk, suspended as the bulb swung farther and farther. Another rush of cold air welled up from nowhere and shimmered down her bare arms. Lydia ran her hands across them, her fingers dancing along the millions of goose bumps as she headed for the stairs. She felt her hair lifting, the tugging again.

"Who's there?" she called out, turning around,

her hand grabbing the ends of her hair, feeling as though she had reached through a fog patch that shifted and floated back up to the lightbulb.

Shadows shifted.

The lightbulb sizzled, then popped.

Darkness.

Lydia ran back up the stairs.

He held the brick in his hand. It was bigger than his palm, his ten-year-old fingers could barely wrap around it. Tony hefted it up and down a couple of times.

This brick . . .

This brick was witness to so much. . . .

The tales this brick could tell.

He ran his other finger along the rough surface, could feel the stone rising beneath his fingers like baby beads of braille. He closed his eyes, willing his fingertips to dance along the brick, garnering whatever message he could receive.

The brick pulsed and swelled beneath his fingers like a sigh. He kept his eyes closed, knowing that this was how the vision usually began. This was the gateway to the dreams.

Colors flowed in and out of his mind, ribbons rippling like streamers on the ends of the batons the cheerleaders used at the local high school football games. They always started off like traces of echoes; then the colors would grow brighter and brighter until he was mesmerized by their vibrancy. When the shimmering started he could feel the color, he could taste the color, it was illusion, it was sound . . . it was the string of molecules that huddled until he was ready to jump through the flow and break the gap.

The brick pulsed hot, throbbing in his hand as the colors throbbed in his head. The heat of yellow, of orange, of white-hot white seared into his mind.

Then suddenly, there they were, waiting for him, enticing him into the gap.

He leaned forward, his child mind knowing without knowing all that he desired and that merging with these colors would take him there.

The thumping of his heart was terribly loud in his little room. The thump of orange, of yellow, of white-hot white pulsed into his temples. The once hazy fog now crystallized into a form. Shadows shifted and stretched into long limbs, into gaping mouths and ripping flesh.

The boy stood beneath a ridge of shadows. His feet were cold on the cement floor, but above him he could feel heat. The heat of soul, of flesh emitting one last spark before the sullen cold damp of despair sank in.

He glanced up and saw them. This time he didn't

scream. This time he made himself look.

Really look.

He was underneath several bodies that swung as if on invisible beds. He could see backs and buttocks torn, hair hanging in matted clumps, blood dried and caking, fresh and dripping, falling like rain around him.

He only made himself look at the flesh, hanging like giant dolls. He held his hand out for the droplets, the rain of pain, and stared mesmerized at the precious jewels glimmering in his palm.

The blood stung, a heat that seeped into his skin and burned into his body. With the burn came a sense of exhilaration. His heart beat faster, and again he looked up at the hanging bodies. He stood underneath what once had been a girl, a teenager on the verge of graduation, until she was led here by whatever temptation. She hung on hooks like a slab of meat. Three hooks down her back, one jammed through her butt. Where once had been breasts were now gaping holes, dried-up coagulating blood forming a seal to keep more of her insides from spilling forth.

Her body was crisscrossed with scars and slashes, gouges as if she had been horsewhipped, then lanced with a machete in places. Her face was frozen in dread, mouth opened, bound with wire, darkness where her eyes should have been. There was nothing in the crusting sockets full of pus, and little Tony swallowed back his bile.

The colors, concentrate on the colors, he told himself.

Tony tore his gaze away from the revolting sight above him and ignored the other bodies. The colors danced and swirled before him and he saw a figure walking toward him.

His heart pounded and he wanted to run, tried to run, but his feet were firmly anchored to the floor. There was no escape, he would be forced to face whatever it was that wanted him.

The figure came into focus. Reddish brown shaggy hair, reddish brown wild eyes. A tiny nervous laugh escaped from Tony's throat.

"Buddy . . ."

Buddy stared at him wide-eyed. "Oh, man . . . it's you . . . Tony."

The boys stood close together, willing their hearts to settle.

"So, how did you get here?" Tony asked.

"I was playing with the brick . . . and now I'm here." Buddy looked wide-eyed above him. "Shit. . . ."

"It's pretty horrible here."

"Well, thank God this is just some crappy nightmare and I'll be waking up soon." Buddy sighed, wiping his hands on his pants.

"A nightmare, huh?" Tony asked. "You think we're in a nightmare?"

"Of course we're dreaming. As if this could be real. As if we would be in each other's dreams. . . ." Buddy giggled, just a bit too loud and giddy for Tony.

"This is no dream . . . I don't think this is a dream. I've been here before."

"Well, shit, I've been to lots of places in my dreams over and over again. My momma done tole me when you dream the same dream over and over it means you have a problem you need sortin' through."

"That's a dream. *This* . . . is no dream," Tony said.

"You're pretty funny, Tony. I can hardly wait till I wake up and tell you all about this tomorrow at school."

"Yeah . . . well, all . . ." A darkness swept over them coupled with a wretched screeching noise. The boys dropped to the floor, covering their ears. With the darkness came a rancid smell. The floor rumbled as the horrible noise pierced their ears through their hands. The boys' stomachs rumbled. Their heads spun as they gasped for air, trying not to make any noise, trying to will the blackness and excruciating noise away. Tony's stomach spasmed and a surge of bile gushed up his throat and out onto the floor. Once the vomit was let loose, he puked again and again, not caring who heard or saw, only knowing that the vile sour liquid flowing from his mouth gave him a sense of cleansing, a focus away from the evil that hovered above. If he was going to die he was going to die and there was nothing he could do about it.

He heard Buddy retch and, looking over, saw that he too was braced up on his hands, emptying his stomach out onto the floor. Their waste, their panic, their fear, pooled along the floor, mixing with the puddles of blood. Tony's head spun, watching the blackness swirl into colors. The scintillating colors grew and shifted, then became white-hot white. . . .

Tony was back in his room, staring at the brick. A string of puke still hung from his lip. He threw the brick down and ran into the bathroom. Without even taking off his clothes, he turned on the shower full blast and cried.

Chapter Five

Lydia popped an old Faith No More CD into the deck and floored the gas as she sang along. The road between her house and the little town was usually devoid of traffic this time of morning. Rush hour was over, school was out and there was little reason for anyone to go anywhere. She watched the trees, the wide sprawling fields of farmland. It felt so weird to be in wide-open space like this after living in the confines of New York City for so long. The sky was so amazingly blue with small puffs of clouds dotting the horizon. There was a dot alongside the shoulder of the road. As she roared closer, she saw that it was an old man wearing a huge hat riding a bicycle. It sure would be hot peddling along on a day like today. As she got closer, she realized that what she thought was a hat was actually the man's head. She whipped on by, glancing at the biker in her rearview mirror. Her heart skipped a beat as she saw the misshapen face of a teenager with obvious Down's syndrome.

She wondered about the boy. Did he know where he was? She slowed a bit as she glanced in the rearview mirror again and saw him peddling purposefully, a vacant smile on his face. He didn't seem upset or panicked. What little she knew about people like that was they were very capable of getting to where they were going, as long as you didn't distract them. She hoped that he knew where he was going, and revved the car back up again.

Lydia pulled into the parking lot of the grocery store. It was not the huge store of the suburbs but not a tiny fruit market either. She double-checked the locks on her car and flicked the alarm system. As she wandered through the parking lot, she was amazed to see so many cars with the windows half down. There was something to be said for small towns. At least *those* people wouldn't be returning to a scorching sweatbox.

Still humming a snatch from a song, she grabbed a cart and went inside. A large woman in a flowered shift and long gray hair stood perusing the vegetables and was blocking the aisle. Lydia took a moment to examine the strawberries and put a couple of quarts into her cart. The woman still hadn't moved. Lydia stared at her, mesmerized by her face. She could see years of pain lining the woman's face. Years of smoking and drinking and crying. The forehead, the sagging cheeks, the many layers of flesh hanging from her chin. Faded blue eyes peered from behind the glasses as her short stubby fingers trembled, delicately holding a cucumber. The woman was in her sixties and incredibly large, probably close to four hundred pounds. Lydia's gaze traveled down to the woman's elephantine ankles. Bulging with veins, the flesh was a weird sickly yellow color, almost doubling over her flip-flops.

The woman belched.

Lydia jumped.

Lydia's movement startled the older lady and she fixed her with a glassy stare.

"Oh, I was just waiting . . . you know . . . to get by," Lydia sheepishly explained. The woman continued to stare at Lydia, examining her from head to toe. Lydia crossed her arms over her thin cotton T-shirt.

"Uhm . . . can I get by . . . please?" Lydia said.

The woman grunted and narrowed her eyes. She moved her shopping cart over and stood sideways. Lydia tried to push her cart by but there wasn't enough room past the woman's fleshy girth.

"I'm afraid . . . oh, never mind, I'll just go back. . . ." Lydia turned around and went back down the aisle and around. Suddenly the fruits and vegetables didn't seem so appealing. She'd grab something at one of the roadside stands.

Lydia went over to the household section and picked up more cleaning supplies and several cans of air freshener. Somehow, she'd get the smell out of the basement. She wasn't sure how, but it had to be possible. It was a new house, after all. . . .

She turned around and was startled to see a young mother standing and staring at her. Lydia squinted her eyebrows and looked at the toddler in the child seat. A little girl of about two smiled and waved her lollipop at Lydia. Lydia smiled and waved back. The mother turned and pushed her cart away. Lydia frowned and looked at herself. She was dressed normally, she thought. T-shirt, wasn't too tight or too loose, and no slogans or bands on it. She wore tight jeans but so did the young mother. She touched her hair, still in the back braid. Maybe she should have put makeup on, or maybe she had a smudge of some sort. She peered into one of the sponge mops, trying to see her reflection. Through the distortion she couldn't tell what she looked like but she was pretty certain that if she had a smudge or something on her face, she'd be able to tell.

If she had B.O., she would surely smell it.

Lydia wandered down the pet food aisle and bought some treats for Pilar. She would hit the pet store for the good-quality food later. As she re-emerged from the aisle, she peered back over to the produce department. The lady was gone now. She pushed her way back over, deciding she wasn't in the mood to stop at some fruit stand that may or may not have what she wanted. She threw lettuce and cucumbers, tomatoes and onions into her cart, all the while aware that the various patrons in the store were watching her and whispering to each other.

Christ, I'm paranoid, she thought. *Really, as if they are all staring at ME. That's utterly ridiculous.*

Well, I am the new kid in town, so I guess it's inevitable they would want to check me out. After all, everyone probably knows everyone, and they all probably knew Tony at some point or another.

Lydia looked over to a cluster of young women giggling together and smiled. They froze, as if they were deer caught in the headlights, and then continued their whispering.

Lydia decided to forgo the frozen food section and headed to the checkout. The cashier, a young woman with streaked blond hair pulled high into a ponytail and a pierced nose, stared lazily at her, chomping on a wad of gum. Lydia slowly pulled her purchases out of the cart and stared at the girl's name tag. Bev.

"Do I have something on my face?" Lydia whispered. Bev inspected her.

"Nope. You look fine to me." She started to scan the items.

"I was just wondering . . . because it seems like everyone is staring at me."

Bev laughed.

"Don't mind them. I swear this is one of the most closed-minded, lousy, nosy towns . . . I can hardly wait till I go to university in September. Get the hell away from all of them."

Bev glared over behind Lydia. Lydia didn't turn around, she started searching through her purse for her money.

"Yeah, they're just checking you out, 'cos you're new and all. And, of course, because of that house."

"Oh . . . because Tony built the house? They don't approve?"

Bev smirked.

"You name it, they'll gossip about it. Probably post it all over the Internet too." She laughed.

Lydia shrugged. "It's no crime to be new in town, but it sure can be lonely."

Lydia handed over her money.

Bev counted it and returned the change. "You won't be new for long. Soon you'll be gossiping away with the rest of them . . . that is . . . if ya want to. Me? I can hardly wait to get out."

"Well, thanks . . . and see you later," Lydia said as she pushed her cart back out into the sweltering heat.

The alarm system blipped as she turned it off. The heat escaping from the car was intense and she backed away as it rolled out to her.

Quickly, she threw the bags into the car, wondering if she would ever fit in. As she pushed the cart back to the lockup, she caught a glimpse of the boy on the bicycle gliding toward the store. Seeing his face up close, she realized he was more than a Down's syndrome boy. His head was enormous, his eyes far apart and slanted, his nose was really just holes, like a pig snout. He saw her looking at him and waved, grinning a lopsided smile with misshapen teeth. She waved back, a little stunned, and watched him methodically lock his bike to the bike rack. Unable to resist, she watched him longer as he checked and rechecked the lock, and then walked with a strange shuffle step into the store.

She wondered if she would ever have the patience to cope with a child like that, and rubbed her belly. How she hoped that whenever they had their baby, it would be normal. But even if it wasn't, she knew she would still love him. She watched the boy disappear through the glass.

* * *

"I missed you," Lydia said, slipping her arms around Tony. Tony grinned as he put his briefcase on the floor, wrapping his arms around his wife.

"I missed you too." He kissed her full on the mouth.

"Did you get much done today?" he asked, looking around the living room. Books were in the cases, but there were still unopened boxes lying around.

"I went into town for a bit, got some groceries and other stuff," Lydia said, running her hands through her hair. "Boy, it was hot out today."

"I'll say. Time for a nice cool one." Tony went into the kitchen and grabbed a couple of beers from the fridge. He tossed one to Lydia.

She pressed it against her forehead. "I can't seem to cool down. Even with the air-conditioning."

"Well, maybe we just need to go for a swim," Tony said. "Would you like that?"

"Sounds like a great idea. I'll just go get my suit."

"Oh, no, you don't need a suit." Tony took her hand. "Let's live dangerously."

"You are evil!" Lydia smiled, kissing his hand. "Lead away, master."

* * *

Black flies and mosquitoes hovered in noisy swarms above their heads, thick clouds that hummed and circled, relentlessly following, snitching at exposed bits of flesh. The couple swatted their way down to the sparkling water.

Despite the annoying insects, the beauty of the water framed by greenery was inspiring.

"This has got to be the best part of the whole thing," Lydia said as she peeled away her sweat-soaked clothes.

"Which part is the best part?" Tony asked, wriggling out of his pants.

"This private little section of beach. This wonderful little glimpse of paradise. Just you and me and the water . . ."

"And Pilar!" Tony nodded at the dog as she came barreling through the bushes.

"Beautiful Pilar," Lydia said, petting the dog as she panted against her leg. "Go play!"

Pilar ran off again.

Lydia wrapped her arms around Tony, kissing him full on the mouth. She could taste the salt of his sweat on his lips. She pressed her naked body against his, the heat of the day burning down, the hum of flies around her head like a halo, her body aching and straining to mesh with her husband's.

"Mmmmm," she whispered, licking his earring. Tony's hands squeezed her buttocks, rolling them in his strong firm fingers. Lydia could feel him pressing against her belly.

"Last one in the water has to make dinner," she teased and ran into the water. Tony followed, diving after her. They swirled and laughed, gasping and splashing as the heat of the day was washed away.

Buddy stood on the hillside, watching the couple play. He fingered his walking stick, running his fingers absentmindedly over the carved wolves' heads and teeth. Pilar galloped up to him and thrust her head into his hand.

"How are ya, Pilar?" he asked her, stroking her soft long fur. "Not too many burrs on ya today."

Buddy knelt down and pulled at the burrs the longhaired dog had picked up on her frolic. She stood patiently panting while his large gentle fingers picked at the annoying prickles.

"You're a good dog." He sighed. "Such a beautiful animal." Lydia's laughter pierced the air. Buddy watched her breasts bobbing as she jumped, splashing Tony. Tony's muscular body gleamed in the sunlight, his biceps rippling as his strong arms picked up his wife and flung her back into the water.

Buddy sighed.

Life was never that carefree for him. Not since he was a child had he been free, filling his lungs with laughter, real laughter, joyous, wondrous, incredulous laughter. There was no laughter in his world. He spoke with his animals, he felt great joy in the secrets he shared with them, but his heart ached. Loneliness ate away most of it but then there was the darkness too.

There was always a price for everything, and the sheer fact he wasn't dead yet meant he was racking up debt by the minute.

How was it Tony was so blessed? Born lucky, born landing on his feet. And Buddy, born in the same year, seven months earlier, in the same town, yet on the other side of those damn tracks.

Born into a curse, he would die in a curse.

Tony and Lydia were wrapped around each other in the water now, waves swelling out from them in elliptic ripples. Their gentle giggles escalated into moans. Buddy watched them, his stomach knotting, his groin burning as he traced their outline with his eyes. Their bodies connecting and moving, pressed together so tight they could be one, as they stood in the water, the gentle current swirling leaves and twigs around them.

Tony, the golden boy. The up-and-coming executive with his new house, new wife, Tony had it all.

How could it be?

Buddy watched, wondering if Tony had ever told Lydia the truth about the house. About the price he would have to pay one day.

Would a husband keep such a secret from his wife? And yet, how could he reveal it?

Their moans were animal-like now, their movements more frantic. Buddy stood up, holding his walking stick for support. His bones cracked, his body ached. He ran his hand through his beard thoughtfully. Pilar looked up at him with wide brown eyes.

"Come on," he said to her and turned away from the couple.

The man and dog walked through the woods, mosquitoes humming in a black cloud halo around their heads.

Buddy pushed aside branches with his walking stick, carefully stepping over snaking logs and weeds. He knew these woods so well, each tree seemed to speak to him as he passed by. For over twenty years, he had been roaming through these trees, watching them grow and shift, watching their leaves bloom and die, each passing season marking another year where he had escaped death.

They arrived at a bridge that spanned this narrower section of water. A very long steel-and-wood bridge used for pedestrians, bicycles and horses from a path that wound through the properties and led up to the roads. Buddy picked his way through the wild weeds and brush to get under the bridge.

This was one of his favorite places. He liked to sit here where no one could see him, hidden away as secretly as the troll in *The Three Billy Goats Gruff*. He had cleared out a little patch, not too carefully, lest some homeless person wandered by and deemed it his own spot. It was slightly cooler under the bridge, and there was some height here where he could stare down at the swirling water below.

A snatch of song rattled around his head, some old folky melody, and he hummed it as he searched through the gravel for some decent-sized stones. They had to be flat and smooth. Under the bridge, he heard the distant laughter and splashing of Tony and Lydia, echoing down the river bend. The way Lydia was shrieking, he figured they must be finished having sex. His eyes welled up with tears, but he stubbornly blinked them away as his hands brushed through the stones, turning them over, rubbing his fingers along them, watching beetles scurrying away.

Stones had been here so long. Once they had been part of something bigger. Something huge and monumental. Who knows, maybe dinosaurs had walked along them, something big and powerful, something strong and magic. Well, they were still part of something bigger, but now just in pieces, not physically connected. Maybe they would be physically connected once more when they were ground to sand, to the finest of powder. Or was each tiny grain of sand still separate, but useless?

Buddy picked up a pinch of sand and sprinkled it into his hand. He stared at the smallest grains, the tiniest of tiny pebbles. So small it could be a speck of dust. Yet, still, that tiniest of tiny was still separate, still on its own, although it worked better in a team. But that tiniest tiny guy could still fly into someone's eye, could scratch the cornea, could even cause blindness. So despite how tiny that tiny guy was, how invisible he might be to those who were only looking at the big picture, he was still capable of independently creating action and reaction and devastating destruction.

Buddy smiled and brushed the sand from his hands back where he had found it.

Being part of something bigger at least gave one a sense of a role, even though Buddy wasn't sure what that would be. He was part of something bigger. Wasn't everyone?

Weren't all human beings connected by energy, by some sort of electrical charge that ricocheted back and forth beyond time, beyond any sort of a barrier? But that was assuming time was linear.

Maybe time was not linear. Maybe time was chaos or random.

Buddy smiled. Even randomness was fated. Even unconnected events all fit together in some universal puzzle piece.

He picked up a small rock that had an ancient imprint of some kind of multilegged bug. The stone was gray, and as he stared at it, a memory surged into focus.

It was her hair he remembered first. Long, stringy, straggly. That was the style in his teenage years. The sort of antilook, which took almost as long to achieve as a fashionable do. Natalie was blond, she was pretty and he had admired her for months, hell, years really.

She knew it too. Her pretty blue eyes would glance his way now and again from across the classroom and he knew he blushed as he feigned indifference. Meanwhile, he wasn't taking notes at all in the class but fitting together words in the margins of his notebook in a clumsy attempt to describe the turbulence her presence brought to his heart.

So it seemed so strange, so surreal, so very . . . odd, that one day, as he was leaving school, she ran after him and started a conversation.

After his initial tongue-tied shyness was overcome, suspicion lurked in the back of his mind.

Suspicion about what though?

He nudged away his misgivings. It was just the turbulence of his own home life coloring the joyous occasion of this momentous event.

She walked with him for a little while and then as they reached the place where the roads parted, she nervously pecked him on the cheek.

"Can I walk with you tommorrow?" she asked.

Buddy nodded, willing his hand not to touch the spot where her soft lips had met his face.

He watched her walk down the road, her jean-clad ass wiggling, her knapsack low on her back.

He turned the situation over in his mind. He couldn't understand what she wanted from him. Not really. No one wanted anything from Buddy. Even Tony barely acknowledged him these days—he was too involved in sports and the jock crowd.

Natalie didn't seem to want his notes from school. She didn't want to go anywhere that he could see. She had been friendly, shy, nonthreatening.

Once Natalie was out of sight, Buddy allowed himself to smile. He flung his school bag into the air with a whoop. For all intents and purposes, it seemed that Natalie, the girl he had adored, might actually be interested in him.

The next day, Natalie met him after school again.

This time she didn't have to hurry home.

"Show me where you like to go," she said.

"What do you mean?"

"Where do you hang out . . . when you want to be by yourself?"

"I don't know if I should tell you. It's my spot. I don't want anyone bothering me there."

"Oh, come on, Buddy. I know you must go somewhere, all you poet types do."

"How do you know I'm a poet type?"

"Aren't you?"

"I like to read and write, yes. Does that make me a poet type?"

Natalie smiled. "Of course it does. Come on, Buddy, show me where you go to write and think."

Buddy led her along the road, away from the school, away from the subdivision, and toward the abandoned ruins where the house of horrors once stood.

"Oh, my. You don't hang around *here,* do you?" Natalie said as they walked up the long winding driveway leading to the hole in the ground where debris lay rotting.

"Not around here specifically. It's just faster to get to where I wanna go if I go past the house and onto the footpath, instead of trying to get to it by the road."

Natalie stopped and looked at the partially boarded-up pit.

"Do you remember when they tore that place down?" she asked.

"Yes, of course I do. I was there."

"What do you mean, you were there?"

"Me and some friends watched the whole thing from the bushes."

"Wow. That must have been something."

"Yes, it was. Kind of scary. Kind of, like there was some sort of . . ." Buddy's voice trailed off.

"Some sort of what?" Natalie pressed. "Demons? Like they said? Or did you see body parts?"

"No . . . nothing like that . . . well, maybe there were demons . . . I don't know. . . . What possesses people to kill and torture other people, besides madness?"

"Maybe they were satanists? Did you ever think of that?" Natalie asked.

"I don't want to talk about it anymore. The whole thing gives me the creeps," Buddy said, as his arms rippled with gooseflesh. He wondered how much she knew. How much she *really* knew.

Maybe that was why she was being nice to him.

"This isn't the place, though," he said, starting to walk away into the woods. "It's just a landmark. Well, I guess in a sense it provides the place since no one lives here right now so I can wander round as much as I want along this property."

"No one cares?"

"Not that I've noticed."

"And you aren't scared the ghosts are going to get you?"

"Ghosts? What ghosts?"

"The spirits of the murdered people."

Buddy laughed. "I don't think so. I don't believe in that sort of mumbo jumbo."

"Hmmm . . ." Natalie looked at him out of the corner of her eye and started to say something, then stopped herself. She took one more plaintive look at the pit and then followed Buddy into the woods.

After many minutes of walking, they came to the bridge.

"This is where I go," he said.

"Cool." She nodded, looking at the bushes growing wild alongside it. She stared down the hill at the running water.

"I usually go under the bridge. It's cooler and kind of like a secret hideout." Buddy grinned. "Do you want to see?"

"Sure."

Natalie followed Buddy as he left the path and snaked through weeds and bushes. They climbed up the side and crept under the bridge.

"Wow," Natalie said. "It's totally private here. You could party and everything."

"Yep," Buddy said.

Natalie picked her way right under the bridge. The dirt and gravel were dry.

"Come on," she said. "This is cool."

Buddy looked at her sitting in his secret spot. His stomach knotted. Pretty Natalie in his favorite place in the world, was he finally having good luck of some sort?

"Are you going to sit beside me, Buddy? I don't bite." Natalie grinned as she ran her hand along the pebbles and sand.

"I—uh . . ." Buddy looked at those pretty eyes staring up at him. He suddenly felt very tall yet as stupid as a baby. He crawled under the bridge and sat a ways from her. Natalie closed her eyes.

"Listen to the river. It's so quiet here," she said. The river continued to run and a bird called out. Without even thinking, Buddy whistled back to it. Natalie opened her eyes.

"Was that you?" she asked.

Buddy blushed. "Yes."

"Oh, wow. How do you do that?"

Buddy pursed his lips and performed several types of birdcalls.

Natalie clapped her hands. "That is so cool! Do you know what you are saying?" Buddy shrugged although he knew exactly what he was saying. What was the point of learning a new language if you didn't know what you were saying? He thought it was a pretty silly question but had learned long ago to keep most of his opinions to himself.

"Hey, what's that?" Natalie rolled away a large rock that had been sitting awkwardly on the gravel. There was a notebook beneath.

Buddy reached for it. " 'Tis nothing," he stammered, trying to snatch the book from her hands.

"Oh. Is it yours?" she asked, flipping through the pages.

"Yes, it's mine."

"Oh, look . . . is this your poetry?"

"Some . . . can I have it back now please?"

"Only if you promise to read some to me."

Buddy nodded, the butterflies moving up into his throat. "If you really, really want to hear some . . ."

"I do. . . ." She smiled, tossing her hair again.

Buddy studied her face. She seemed to be telling the truth, but he wasn't sure. Couldn't be sure.

He flipped through the notebook. What to read to this . . . this girl that was indeed his muse for most of the poems in the back pages.

He read a couple of what he considered safe ones. Poems about trees and birds and the plaintive sounds of loneliness echoing through the woods. He read a few about wolves, their soft beautiful fur, their ferocious teeth, their ravenous hunger, how they survived on pure instinct. At last, he read one inspired by Natalie herself, though he did not dare tell her that. When he was finished, he saw her eyes were glistening.

"That was so sad," she finally said.

Buddy shrugged. "Just words, is all."

"And beautiful."

The way she was staring at him made him nervous.

"That's it," Buddy said flippantly, shutting the book. He put the notebook back under the rock, telling himself he would have to find a new place to hide it now. He couldn't keep it at home, his mother would destroy it. She thought writing was for sissies, poetry writing even worse. But he couldn't have Natalie know where he kept it, his heart was in that book.

When he turned back from placing the notebook, Natalie was very close to him. She edged nearer, trying to look into his eyes. He avoided her gaze.

"I think you are going to be a great poet one day," she said.

"Thanks, I guess. I don't know what I'm going to be . . . maybe a vet or something."

"You do seem to like animals," she said, putting her hand over his. Buddy trembled, his body stiffened. He didn't know what to do. Her hand was warm and soft. No one had ever held his hand like that before. She was moving her hand against his in a rhythmic motion that reminded him of the ocean.

His heart pounded and to his dismay, he realized his cock was straining against his pants. He shifted his legs around, trying to hide it. Natalie glanced at his lap and licked her lips.

"Am I making you nervous?" she asked, leaning her face closer to his. He could feel her breath warm against his cheek. His heart slammed harder and he wanted her so badly he thought he would die. Yet at the same time, he didn't want her at all. At least not here, not like this. Not in the mud and stones and rubble.

Besides, they barely knew each other.

Natalie ran her hand along his thigh, edging toward the telltale bulge. She pressed her lips softly against his cheek.

"I—I, uh, don't think this is a good idea," he stammered, hating himself even as he said it.

"Don't worry, Buddy. I won't tell," she said, stroking his long hair. She leaned in to kiss him full on the mouth but he turned his face away.

"Hey, like, what's wrong?" she asked.

"I don't know. . . ." A chill surged across him and he saw the hairs on his arms standing on end. "This just isn't right. I—I . . . just want to talk."

The light gleaming in from above the bridge faded as thick dull grayness replaced it.

"I think it's going to storm," he said, a sense of dread coursing through him. He sniffed at the air and detected the hint of something vile . . . something that wasn't quite right.

"Oh, we'll get caught in the rain under the bridge. That would be so romantic." Natalie sighed. Buddy didn't hear her as his senses picked up something more as the wind rose and shifted.

Then he heard them.

He crawled out from under the bridge and saw three boys and two girls standing there with a videocamera, trying to smother their laughter as they held their hands over their mouths. Their faces dropped when they saw Buddy.

"What are you doing?" he shouted at them.

"Just going for a walk, taking some pictures," said Tom, the biggest guy. Buddy recognized him from gym class. They were all jocks. Three fucking smarmy jocks and two bimbo-assed cheerleaders. And they were all the gang that Natalie hung out with.

His stomach lurched.

How could he be so stupid?

Of course she was never interested in him. She was just using him for a setup.

Rage seared through him, the wind picking up, howling in response to his fury. Thick drops of rain began to fall. He stared stupidly at Natalie, finally seeing her with her mask off. He should have listened to his gut. He knew there was something weird about the setup.

"Read us another poem," George laughed. "C'mon, faggot, read us another one!"

Buddy clenched his fingers. He wanted to smash his fist right through that smug pearly white smile, but he dug his nails into his own palm. Three jocks against him were not odds he cared to play.

"Get the hell out of here," Buddy shouted.

"Gonna make us?" Tom asked.

"What do you want from me?" Buddy asked.

"For starters, leave our girls alone." George pushed Buddy back.

"She came up to me. She followed me here," Buddy stammered as he stepped backward. There was a sharp whining sound in his head. Like the high-pitched hum of a television. It throbbed through his head, clouding his vision.

"Don't even *look* at our girls anymore, sissy boy," Bob said, pushing Buddy's shoulder.

The rain was falling harder now.

"C'mon, guys, let's just go," Natalie said. "You've had your fun."

Tom pushed Buddy once more and Buddy fell.

George kicked him in the stomach. "Fucking freak."

Buddy grabbed George's foot before he could deliver another blow. This time George was the one who crashed to the earth. Bob and Tom fell on Buddy, punching him and kicking him repeatedly.

A deafening roll of thunder followed a crash of lightning and the skies let loose as the boys beat Buddy.

The thunder was ceaseless, amplifying perpetual sound. Buddy roared, his eyes shining red as he lashed out at the feet and hands striking him.

Suddenly, there was darkness, as if someone had thrown a blanket over everyone. There was snarling and screaming and when the darkness passed as quickly as it had come, the boys looked at each other in shock. Buddy was unconscious, blood flowing from his mouth, his face cut and bruised, his clothes torn. Tom, George and Bob stared at each other.

"Did you see . . . ?"

"I didn't see it, but I felt . . ."

"It was as if . . ."

The boys looked over at the girls. They clung to each other, their eyes wide, no sound coming from lips that gaped open and shut.

"What was it?"

Tom looked up in the air, waiting for whatever it was to come raging back. "I don't know, but fuck . . ."

They hurried toward the path.

"What about Buddy?" Natalie asked.

"To hell with Buddy," Tom spat.

"Oh, my God," Natalie said.

"What?"

"Over there . . ."

On the other side of the river, they could barely make out shadows. Shadows that shifted and undulated in a gray-black smoke. The rain pouring down created unbelievable fog patterns.

"What is it?" Tom asked.

"I don't know. It's almost as if . . . well, it looks like they have eyes. . . ."

Even as the words fell from her lips, the shadows shifted again and several sets of glowing red eyes were visible even from across the river.

"What are they?"

The shadows shifted again and the teenagers saw that they were now moving over the water, one big rolling mass of rippling smoke with many eyes.

"It's coming for us. . . ."

Buddy shifted and lifted his head, watching the frightened teenagers stare out across the water. He too saw the moving cloud coming for them.

The teenagers ran as fast as they could, but they could not outrun the spectral creatures. As the shifting shapes passed Buddy, he saw they were wolves. Large, beautiful white, faded, angry, red-eyed ghost wolves. They lunged at the teenagers and fell on Natalie. The thundering nearly drowned out the angry snarls and gnashing of their teeth but not quite. They were all screaming now. Buddy sat up, his head swimming, still trying to understand what was going on.

"Off!" he screamed, pulling himself to his feet. He staggered into the throng of the frenzied wolf ghosts.

"Stop it now. Let them go."

The wolf tearing at Natalie's arm paused, looking up at him with a whimper.

"Yes, that means you. Stop it *now*."

The wolves one by one loosened their grip on their victims. The kids stared in disbelief as wild-eyed, bloody Buddy called off the wolves.

"Oh, man," Tom moaned, shaking his head. "Man, oh, man . . ."

"Go. Now," Buddy ordered to the teenagers. "Get the hell away from here."

Buddy watched them run into the trees, the wolves standing guard until they were out of sight. Then, the wolves themselves slowly melded and blended together, rolling into cloud puffs and dissolving as the rain pelted down, until Buddy wasn't sure if they had even been there at all.

Buddy stared at the rock in his hand. Funny how memories came and went. Something as traumatic as that day with Natalie, the traitor, and her asshole friends had been buried for so long, yet the image of Natalie, the muse, still beat within his heart.

He threw the rock into the river and watched it skip along the surface three times before sinking. He grinned.

The assholes would mutter at him under their breath on the school grounds, but there was fear in their eyes even as they did so. Eventually, they grew up, moved on, much as Tony and Jeff had. Much as he had in his own way. He hadn't gone too far, but he had grown up.

Buddy picked through for another rock.

Silly Natalie had gotten pregnant shortly after that incident. She kept the baby, raising it in the comfort of her parents' middle-class home. He had seen the baby, Karey, grow up over the years. She was now a punky, mouthy teenager, much more crude than her mother had been.

Karey was one of those obnoxious girls that was always smacking her gum, always in trouble of some sort and never failing to catcall Buddy when he'd happen into town.

The apple sure didn't fall far from the tree, in either attitude or beauty.

And in their scorn for him.

Buddy threw another rock into the river and watched it skim along the surface before sinking.

It was funny how the universe had a way of balancing things out. Much like the mighty rocks ground to sand, the assholes of the world would get their comeuppance either in this life or the next.

Of that he was sure.

Chapter Six

Lydia and Tony snuggled into each other on the couch, watching a sitcom, sipping red wine.

The doorbell rang.

Tony got up to answer it. Standing there was Sybil, clutching a large box.

"Hey, Mom, what brings you out?" Tony asked as he kissed his mother on the cheek.

"Oh, just wanting to check up on my son, want to be sure he's being taken care of properly and all."

Sybil made a show of adjusting her arms to hold the box.

Tony reached out for it.

"Here, Mom." He took the box. "What on earth do you have in here?"

"Oh, just some this and that. I was clearing out

a few things and ran across this old box. Thought you might be interested in some of your old memories. At first I was afraid of bringing over yet another box for you to unpack, but, well, I see you are taking your time about it anyway."

Sybil's steely-eyed gaze honed in on the boxes against the far wall.

"Tony's been working full-time and I'm doing the best I can getting everything into order. We have the rest of our lives to settle in," Lydia said firmly. She felt herself already stiffening into survival mode against the Ice Queen.

"I suppose. I know that when I move in to a new place, I like to unpack as quickly as possible, getting organized and ready for what's next. You never know what is next," Sybil said.

"We'll just have to see, won't we?" Lydia said, thinking about how Sybil had lived in the same house for over thirty years. What did she know about unpacking?

"Hey, cool." Tony put the box down on the floor in front of the fireplace and plucked out a little car from the top.

"I remember this. It was my favorite car." Tony ran the car along the brick fireplace. Lydia watched Tony, then looked at Sybil watching Tony with that patronizing mom face Lydia so despised, and clenched her teeth.

"Can I make you some coffee?"

"As long as it is no trouble," Sybil said, her mouth curved into a sly grin, as she watched Tony examining the tiny car.

"No trouble," Lydia said, anxious to be gone from the woman's presence. She hurried into the kitchen and set to work preparing the coffeepot. As she ground the beans, she tried to will herself to calm down. The woman wouldn't always be popping in unannounced. She would grow bored of it.

But what happens when the baby comes? Will she be coming by even more?

There was that thought again . . . the baby. Not even, if a baby comes, but when. . . .

Lydia sighed.

Baby.

Sybil. Lydia couldn't imagine the stiff woman cuddling a newborn.

Lydia filled up the cream-and-sugar china set and found their dainty little silver coffee spoons. With the silver tray all set up, she decided to take it out in the living room while the coffee finished brewing.

When she arrived, Sybil was nowhere to be seen.

"Where's your mother?" Lydia asked.

Tony shrugged. "She left."

"But she said she wanted coffee."

"Oh, hmmm. I guess she forgot. No biggie," Tony said.

"I guess. . . ." Lydia scowled.

Tony put his arm around her.

"Aw, don't be all frosty," he said, rubbing her shoulder.

"I'm not the frosty one," Lydia said.

"What's that supposed to mean?"

"Nothing. Forget it. . . ." Lydia walked over to the box. "Anything exciting in your treasure trove?"

"As a matter of fact, check this out."

Tony held up a brick. "Look at this. One of the original bricks from when the house was bulldozed. Me and Buddy and Jeff each had one."

"Cool." Lydia touched the brick, turning it over in her hand.

"Tell me again why the house was bulldozed?" she asked.

Tony looked at her but the way she was staring at him indicated she wasn't buying any bullshit story this time around.

"Well, now that we're here and settled in and you can see what a cool house and great property this is, I will tell you the story behind this house."

"It's about time."

"I didn't want you to freak out. I wouldn't blame you if you did, but now that this place is home, to us, to our future family, we don't have to be afraid anymore."

"Afraid? What would I be afraid of?"

"All sorts of things, really. And yet nothing at the same time. Do memories frighten you?"

"Depends on what they are."

"Other people's memories. Do they scare you?"

"No . . . I don't think so. Why? Should they?"

"They shouldn't, which is what I based my whole theory on."

Tony took her hand and sat her down on the couch. He held the brick. "This house does have a history. I'm surprised you haven't heard about it."

"I don't keep track of every house—"

"Maybe once I tell you about it, you will recognize the story."

"Okay, tell me your story, already."

Tony took a deep breath. "This house, well, I shouldn't say this *house* but rather, this site, since I myself rebuilt the house. When I was a kid, something really horrible happened here."

"How horrible?" Lydia asked, remembering the way the locals gawked at her in the stores.

"It was discovered that there were serial killers living here. They kept their victims in the basement and tortured them."

"Oh, my God, that is horrible."

Tony paused as he let the thoughts sink in. Softly,

he continued his shortened version of the tale.

"When they were finally caught, the town went nuts and had this place bulldozed. It was quite the sight with all the born-agains and TV crews running around."

"Wow, that's wild."

"The killers were executed years ago. We don't have to worry about them bothering us."

"Jeez, no wonder people look at me like I'm insane. I guess in a town this size, something that traumatic isn't forgotten very fast."

"That is what Buddy was starting to tell you that day, but I didn't want to freak you out before we moved in. I thought that I would wait till we got used to the place so that you wouldn't start imagining ghosts and stuff."

Lydia shuddered and ran her hand through her hair. She thought of the basement.

"Do you believe in ghosts?" she asked.

"Heavens no. And I don't believe there are 'evil vibes' here either or I wouldn't have bought the place."

"Hmmm . . ."

"So are you mad that I kept this from you?"

"Not really. I probably would have been freaked out if I had known ahead of time."

"See?" Tony hugged her to him. She pressed into his strong arms, chewing over what he said. She stared at the brick, at the fireplace, thinking about the whole town coming out to see the destruction of the building that stood here before.

At last, she spoke. "I hate to ask what they did to the people they caught."

"You don't want to know. Believe me. Let's forget such stuff ever existed."

"I would love to."

Tony stood, holding the brick. He held it up to the light, turning it over in his hands. He waited, half expecting it to shoot ribbons of color out at him, or entice him into a reverie. Nothing happened so he placed it on the mantel.

"It matches perfectly, doesn't it?" he said.

"Yes, it certainly does."

"Are you sure you're not angry with me?" Tony asked, walking back toward her, his eyes wide as a child's waiting for his father's belt to strike. When he looked at her like that, she could not be angry. She was certain he knew it by now, how her heart melted a little when he gave her that look. She didn't care if he was manipulating her or not. What difference did it make at this point?

"It's a lot to digest," Lydia said. "I guess time will tell."

She looked around the room, at all the hard work he had put into every detail, every molding, the endless sketches he had drawn, the way he had traveled out here constantly to supervise, as much as his job would allow.

"It is a beautiful house," she said, holding her hand out to him.

"This is our beautiful house," Tony said, kissing her hand. "My love poem to you."

He leaned over, pressing his lips against hers. She lay back on the couch, holding him tightly, pushing all thoughts of murder out of her mind. It was twenty years ago. History. What difference did it really make in the end?

The brick on the mantel pulsed, leaking crimson secretions. They dribbled down into the fireplace, then seeped into the floor.

In the basement, the walls breathed as blood streaked down from the ceiling, steaming as it hit the floor in drops. The bloody smoke rolled and billowed, rising up from the basement, back through the floorboards, through the fireplace.

Lydia and Tony were too busy making love to notice the brick weeping, the smoke wafting up the chimney. It milled around above the house, hovering as it gathered into itself before releasing into the scarlet sky.

* * *

Buddy emerged into a field where the last fingers of the setting sun mercilessly bore down on him. He hurried his pace, climbing up a hill, until he reached his sanctuary.

The mouth of the cave yawned open and Buddy stepped inside. Already it was cooler in here. He sat down heavily against a wall, wiping his sweating brow with his hand. Pilar nestled in beside him and he lay a hand on her back.

"Too hot for you too, huh?" he crooned, stroking her back. "Boy, this heat is going to be the death of me, I swear."

Buddy lit a candle, then reached in behind a rock and pulled out a tattered old notebook. He closed his eyes and opened the book. He lay his finger on a passage and opened his eyes.

"Where others have purpose, I am but an outsider, archaic and feeble. Alone, I strive for my own identity yet I crave to be part of the whole."

Buddy sighed.

"Well, if that ain't the truth, Pilar."

Buddy rested his head against the cool stone wall of the cave. He stared at the symbols carved into the wall across from him. Various symbols he himself had found meaning in over the years. A pentacle, a pentagram, an ankh, the ubuoris, the yin-yang . . . all these strange symbols embedded in the wall. He remembered seeing them as a child. They had always been here.

There were other drawings too. Horrible demon-type creatures with furry limbs and long nasty teeth, birdlike with their arching necks and sharp curved talons, chasing after and tearing apart fleeing stick figures.

He could trace those pictures in his sleep.

He dozed off, slipping in and out of dreams like a water snake wriggling through the rushes. His animals, his beloved animals, running and roaming free and easy in a wide open field. He was running too. His body open and painless, his mind uncluttered from anxiety and confusion. He was wind as he flew among the galloping creatures.

Then he saw it. The haze. That huge puff of fog that wasn't fog rolling over the field toward them.

"Run," he cried to the wolves and rabbits, to the dogs and cats and foxes. They turned away, running faster than he until they were long gone from his vision and he was running in place by himself.

"What do you want now?" he cried out.

He raised his hands and the cloud descended, enveloping him in its mystery.

Buddy woke shivering. He peered out of the cave and saw that it was now night. It hadn't been night that long but it was dark just the same.

He nodded, reaching his hands out in front of

him, wiggling his fingers to touch the air.

"I feel it . . . it is time," he sang to himself. Pilar was long gone, presumably home with her owners.

Buddy gathered together some wood and set to work building a fire a short distance from the mouth of the cave. From the shadows, the animals watched.

Fire flames licked the sky as Buddy sang and danced. He drew symbols across his face with a partially burned stick. A spiral, a pentagram. He shucked his clothes, his naked flesh gleaming in the moonlight like fish scales glittering in the depths of the ocean. His hands reached high as he called them to him.

Smoke billowed from the fire, lolling along trees, touching air and grass.

"To the higher power, to the higher being, I command you to give me strength! Give me the vision that I need to see what has to be done. The power running through my body, through my bones. Bring to me my companions of darkness, my lovely obedient creatures."

The fire was hot, orange balls rolled, sparks erupted in a colorful burst. The rumble of the cloud caused the earth to tremble.

The cloud settled in the clearing, turbulently shifting until a pack of wolves stood in its place, snarling and snapping, their gleaming red eyes shining in the firelight.

"My wolves, my beautiful creatures, how I adore you, how I treasure your presence. . . ."

Buddy walked in front of each snapping animal and ran a hand along its ghostly fur. As he touched each one, it whimpered and lay down at his feet.

"That's right, my darlings. Relax. There is still more waiting. Still more readiness before the next chapter unfolds."

One by one the wolves howled, a sound that started low in the throat, like a cough until it rose in painful pitch to hysterical frenzy. Buddy joined in, his call shrieking and piercing the night sky.

Pilar lifted her head. She was lying on the floor at the foot of the bed. There was a tremble in the night. She sensed it at first, and then, she heard it. The call of the wild raced through her blood and she ran over to the window seat to peer out. She stared into the yard, but her limited vision saw nothing. Still, the sounds of the nighttime tickled her ears. She panted, her tongue hanging out as she paced back and forth, back and forth, stifling the whine that wanted to escape her throat, lest her humans lock her out.

* * *

The stairs went on forever today. How could they be so long, so very long? It was only a basement. And since when were these endless stairs covered in a thick slippery moss?

Lydia picked her way down carefully, her sneakers slipping with every step. She held a flashlight, glad now that she had brought it since the basement was so much farther than she remembered, and the light, if in fact it was on, was not illuminating a damn thing.

Then there was the *shssh*ing behind her. It was like being in a wheat field on a hot summer day. All sticky with the wheat touching her, and the noise as the dried stalks rubbed against each other. She kept turning around to see who was behind her, but there was no one there.

The moss was thicker with every step.

She could not imagine how she had forgotten just how many hundreds of stairs there really were. The cold damp air hugged her like a wet piece of plastic settling against her skin, yet she was sweating. She was hot yet she was cold. Shivering yet perspiring, sweat dripping down her flesh in an endless torrent.

How could it be?

The flashlight winked out and she was in darkness.

Her heart pounded.

But why was she afraid?

Why should she be afraid in her very own basement?

Now *that* was crazy.

This was the house that Tony built and Tony would never let her come to any harm. Of course, maybe he shouldn't have put so damn many stairs in. After all, the basement didn't have to be this deep, did it?

Or was it deep to hide the bodies?

She froze.

The bodies were not here. They would have all been removed when the killers were caught.

Wouldn't they?

But of course they would. The victims' families would have claimed them and those left unclaimed would be placed in storage and dissected for clues or evidence or body parts or whatever it was that people were dissected for.

What if the bodies weren't all dead? What if one still happened to be alive, crawling up the stairs while she picked her way down? A helpless creature dragging itself away for help, yet thinking *she* was the perpetrator, and what if that creature had some sort of horrible weapon, something worse then a gun? Something worse than the razor-sharp gleam of a shark bite, something that could feel her flesh yet still leave her alive in screaming agony while the victim prepared for revenge.

"Lydia." She spoke her name loudly. It fell flat against the wall.

Lydia, get a grip.

For God's sake, she was just going down the stairs. So what if her flashlight went out? So what if the moss was up to her ankles and the *shssh*ing behind her was getting louder and her flashlight had winked on again with a dull yellow glow that reminded her of a dying dinosaur's eye for some reason. Yet a dinosaur would be much, much larger and surely a dinosaur's eye wasn't yellow. . . .

Lydia.

She took a deep breath, trying to control her racing thoughts.

Stop.

She surrendered the air from her lungs, not wanting it to leave her body to join whatever else it was that was down there. The release helped to calm her.

Better.

Much better.

Now what was it she had come down here for?

She could not remember. Not for the life of her could she remember why she was even here at all, but no matter, she knew that once she got to the bottom of those stairs, once she was in the tiny room that was too tiny and should have been bigger, that she would see all the boxes piled up and remember what it was that had drawn her here to begin with.

Wouldn't she?

The flashlight glowed with more luminescence and she pressed on. Now she was sure that it was moss no more beneath her feet but something else. Something more . . . liquidy.

She could feel moisture seeping in above the top of her sneakers. Was the basement flooded? Had there been a spring thaw, a creek misrouted and pouring into her cellar and she never noticed before this moment? She was sure she would have noticed piling boxes up in water. Of course she would have noticed. She wouldn't have put boxes in water, would she? As distracted as she could get she surely would not put boxes in something . . .

She realized that there were no more stairs. She aimed the dim beam around the room. The boxes were there, piled high all around. And there was the wall.

That weird out-of-place wall.

She sloshed over to it.

It was so dark, that wall. She directed the flashlight at it, running it up and down in stunned amazement. The wall was throbbing, pulsing like a heartbeat.

No, it wasn't pulsing. There was movement on

the wall. A carpet of blackness roaming, up and down and every which way.

The flashlight fell from her hands as she screamed. The blackness was composed of beetles. Thousands and thousands of beetles scurrying up and down and all around.

Seeing the beetles was repulsive, but not seeing them was even worse.

As she bent over to pick up the flashlight, she saw what she had been wading in and screamed again.

She was ankle deep in dead babies. Fetuses. Baby parts and baby goo and umbilical cords, rippling and squirming as she tried to pick up the flashlight but it kept falling from her hands. Her throat was frozen, more screams lodged inside. She tried to go, run, walk, grab that flashlight, but she was moving in slow motion.

She got hold of the flashlight and almost immediately it slipped from her hands again.

Once more she plunged back into the filthy rot, gagging as she fished around, baby parts brushing against her like cold, clammy fish. Again, she felt her fingers clamp around it, clutching tighter this time.

At last, she held up the flashlight and as she turned to flee back up the stairs, she slammed into something. Some*one*.

She shone the flashlight into his face and, horrified, she saw the wild eyes of Buddy staring back at her.

He grinned with those yellow gaping teeth back at her, and poking between those teeth were little black stringy things. As he opened his mouth, beetles poured forth. Falling like a waterfall they cascaded down his chest and into the water as he tried to tell her something.

She wasn't listening as her screams took hold and filled the cellar. The beetles paddled along the water, circling her, stick legs pumping, antennae twitching, their smooth black beetle bodies shining.

Buddy clutched her arm, spitting out the last of the bugs as he spoke.

"Sometimes at night, you can still hear them scream," he whispered urgently.

"No . . . let me go." Lydia struggled, trying to hit his hand away with the flashlight.

"Hear 'em?" He cocked his head as if listening, his grip iron tight.

"Hear 'em scream?" he asked.

Lydia pulled at his fingers, trying to get them to release her.

"This is just a nightmare, this is just a nightmare . . ." she chanted.

Buddy pressed his face right against hers. "This is no nightmare, honey. This here's the house of pain."

He let go and Lydia fell backward into the mire. She sank, her mouth filling with the vile taste of bile. She flailed, trying to swim up to the surface, but she sank, deeper and deeper into the filth. At last, she managed to turn herself around, pulling her arms in strong strokes as if she were swimming through taffy, heading back to the surface before her lungs were filled with blood and pus, before she lost what little air there was left.

When she broke through, she raised her head as high as she could above the swirling stew, and screamed.

Lydia jerked awake, screams ripping from her throat as Tony shook her.

"Wake up. Wake up!" Tony cried, rattling her shoulders.

"Oh, my God!" Lydia shouted, staring into the darkness.

Tony switched on the bedside lamp. Lydia stared at the walls of her bedroom.

The silent white, still walls of her bedroom.

"Oh, Tony . . . " she sobbed, pressing her face into his chest. "It was horrible. Oh, God . . ."

"There, there," Tony said, holding her close. "It's all right now. I'm here for you. It was just a dream. Just a dream."

Chapter Seven

"I'm afraid I have to stay overnight in the city," Tony explained to Lydia the next morning. She was pale and her coffee cup shook slightly in her hand.

"That's all right. I'll be okay," she said, taking a sip.

"Are you sure? I mean, it's a very important meeting tonight but if you really want me to try to make it back—"

"Oh, no . . . of course not, honey. I'm fine. I'll be just fine," she said.

"You really had some nightmare. I don't think I've ever seen you have one that bad," he said, touching her cheek.

"I don't think I've ever *had* one that bad," Lydia

said, kissing his hand. "I thought you held the prize for the dreams from hell."

"I thought I did too. I guess I shouldn't have told you about the house. About . . . those people."

"Oh, nonsense. I would have found out sooner or later. I'm glad I heard it from you first."

"I hope you'll be okay today."

"I'll be just fine. Now you'd better get going or you're going to miss the train."

"I'll call you when I get into the office."

"If you want. It's really not necessary."

"You know I will. Even if it's just to hear the sound of your voice."

Tony left and Lydia watched as he started the car and backed it down the driveway. With the gunning of the motor, he was off to the train.

Lydia turned and looked around the living room. Still so much to do. Every room still had boxes to unpack, things to organize.

She couldn't even imagine how hard it would be if she had kids on top of it all and had to deal with all of their stuff as well.

Shaking her head, she flopped onto the couch and sipped her coffee. Ignoring the boxes, she grabbed the TV remote and clicked it on.

The familiar chatter of a morning talk show filled the empty house, and for a moment she forgot her dream as she immersed herself into someone else's misery.

Buddy walked along the main road of the little town. Time to get some food and candles and a few other items. He had gone for a swim in the river, washed his hair and body carefully, and picked out a set of clean clothes from the small stack he kept in the cave. It was hot, so all he wore was a T-shirt and jeans and an overshirt. His leg didn't hurt today, but he kept his walking stick with him anyway. There was comfort in having a weapon without having to resort to the knife in his boot.

Going to town was quite a ritual for him. Whether he went once a month, or every day for a week, he had to go through the same process. It was much more difficult in the winter, he barely ever made it into town then, but in summer, it was all right to wander around, looking in the store windows, watching the people walk by, occasionally glimpsing someone he used to know.

He always made sure he looked as best he could before going into town. Just because he liked to live with nature didn't mean he was a total freak, although so many just didn't understand that. He knew how to adapt to society. He knew what the customs and the social mores were. He just didn't want anything to do with them unless he was actually forced to, like today, when he *had* to go into town and *had* to talk to people.

He brushed his teeth and spent quite some time combing the knots out of his long, reddish streaked-with-gray hair. He even had a bottle of Old Spice that he'd had forever to use on these occasions. To amalgamate with the humans, he had to carry their scent, to mimic their mannerisms, just as he did with the animals.

He studied his face for a long time in the mirror. The reddish brown eyes that matched his hair. The worry lines along his forehead and cheeks. The strong chin hidden beneath the beard that he had trimmed nicely.

He could assimilate, he thought.

His eyes grew sad.

His was the face of loneliness. Of life without a mate, devoid of love from the human tribe.

Where others have purpose, I am but an outsider. . . .

No matter.

It was a great day for walking.

He picked up a few essentials at a little corner store and wandered along. The odd person would wave at him or smile shyly. They all knew who he was, that poor child of Tildy's.

Tildy the local slut.

He sighed, pondering the irony. His mother got it too much and he didn't get it at all.

There was a group of teenagers sitting on a picnic table at the corner drive-in ice-cream stand. Still, even though he was thirty years old, the sight of a pack of teenagers made him nervous. It was ludicrous, he knew, but it was like a shell shock he could never escape.

He walked by, glad he was washed and combed and assimilated, maybe they wouldn't notice him.

"Hey . . . bum!" one of them shouted. The rest giggled, high-fiving each other. Three boys, two girls . . . He shuddered.

"Hey, bumbuddy!" another one screamed. This time they squealed with laughter at the pun. Buddy stiffened. He wouldn't let them get to him. He knew what he was. He wasn't a bum. If he lived anywhere but North America, no one would think twice about who he was or what he did.

One of the girls spoke loudly. "Hey, guys, just cool it. He's human too, ya know."

"Oooo, Karey, got a crush on bumbuddy?" one of the boys taunted.

"You're a baby, Jason. Nothing but a big whiney baby."

"Oh, yeah?"

Buddy could hear them bickering but didn't turn his head or even his eyes to watch. Typical teenagers, turning on each other before their mark had even passed.

He was about half a block away when he heard the sound of someone running up behind him. Clutching his walking stick, he turned suddenly.

It was Karey. She jumped as he eyed her.

"Oh . . ." she said. "I . . . I was trying to catch up to you."

Buddy studied her face. This was Karey, Natalie's child. For a moment, he considered how in his fantasies he had children with Natalie. How this child could have been his child.

Well, she was no child. This girl, this teenager standing before him was all woman.

She had short dyed black hair, sticking out in various places. Her face was that of young Natalie's. The face of a blue-eyed angel, with a nose ring and a sneer. She wore a black T-shirt that hugged her large breasts, her belly button peeked over the top of her baggy jeans, glinting with a ring.

"Why would you want to talk to me?" Buddy asked, rubbing his temple as a sense of déjà vu flooded through him.

"Well, like, even though my friends are assholes and all, I've, like, always been curious about you."

"Nothing to be curious about me," Buddy said and turned away, wondering if the others were creeping up on him somewhere, somehow. Ready to beat him and rob him. It wouldn't have been the first time he was jumped. But he would be damned if he was gullible enough to fall for this stuff anymore.

"I'm not a decoy, if that's what you're thinking," Karey said. "No one's here but me."

Buddy kept walking and Karey had to skip to keep up with his long strides.

"I heard you are a witch," she blurted out.

Buddy turned and stared at her. "Huh?"

"Yeah. A witch. Like you can call demons and shit."

Buddy shook his head.

"I don't know what you mean," he said.

"Please, mister . . . mister Buddy . . . I want to talk to you. I think you are cool."

Buddy looked around again, still seeing no one. He stared into her blue eyes. She was wide eyed with curiosity, but he knew she was just like her mother. Hell, he had watched her take half the town boys, one at a time, to various spots in the woods. If she didn't watch it, she'd be a teenage mom just like her own mother.

But what did she want? What did she really want . . . ?

He sniffed. "What on earth do you think I can possibly help you with?" Buddy sighed.

"I just wanted to ask you some stuff," she said.

"What kind of stuff?"

"Well, I've heard some things, and wondered if they were true."

"Things . . ." Buddy stared off into the distance. "Things come in all shapes and sizes."

Karey shifted from foot to foot. "If you think that I'm trying to trick you or something, why don't you pick a place for us to meet? I want you to teach me how you do it." Karey arched her back a bit as she toyed with her hair.

"Do what?"

"How you conjure the demons."

Buddy laughed.

" 'Fraid you got the wrong information, missy," Buddy said and started to walk off.

Karey grabbed his arm. "No, I don't. . . ." This time her eyes bore into his with grim determination. A slow burn swelled in his groin. Fire and ice, just like her mother.

"I have seen you," she whispered. "You didn't know I was there, but I was. I saw you call the white wolves."

Buddy's eyes grew wide and his heart skipped a beat.

"Calling white wolves?" He shook his head. "There are no wolves in these here parts. Maybe a wild dog or two, but no wolves, and sure as hell, none of them white."

"Maybe you don't want to admit it now. Maybe I can meet you . . . I'll meet you. . . ." She looked down the road.

Buddy followed her gaze. The river snaked along the edge of town. It was not nearly as wide as over by Tony's place, but still wide enough and deep enough to have a substantial bridge built over it. The bridge shimmered in the heat, almost an illusion in the distance. Buddy figured that walking quickly would be about ten minutes to get there, maybe more.

"The bridge in twenty minutes. Alone . . ." Buddy glared at her.

"I appreciate it, mister Buddy. My mom talks about you sometimes, says you have more juju in your little finger than the rest of us can stumble across in a lifetime."

Buddy narrowed his eyes and walked away.

"I'll be there," Karey said, not even sure if he heard her.

He stewed over what she had said. Sure, she may have seen him call the wolves, hell, who knows how many wasted teenagers may have stumbled on him when he was knee deep in ritual? He could barely remember anything at all sometimes. He just knew that he was a tiny bead on a long string of pearls. He knew when to shine and when to just blend into the background.

Buddy was glad he didn't have too much stuff to get. He looked into his bag. Hell, he had enough stuff. The candles and matches had been the most important so that he could see in the cave. Everything else was secondary.

He would get to the bridge first. Make sure that history wouldn't repeat itself.

Satisfied that no one was coming, he crawled underneath. This bridge was a local party hangout, still broken beer bottles and debris from a badly made fire. He stared at the water, wondering what it was Karey really wanted. Her mother had probably told the story about the wolf attack when they were teenagers.

He rubbed his hands together and examined them.

More juju in his little finger . . .

He grinned. It was true. He may not have much in the world but he had juju and he could use it.

There was the sound of branches snapping and gravel spilling into the water below. Buddy looked toward the noise as Karey clambered down to join him. Her forehead glowed with sweat and she was panting.

"I ran, I didn't want them to see where I was going," she said.

Buddy stared at the water, stroking the walking stick, never letting it leave his hand, just in case.

"I—I . . ." She gulped, looking at Buddy. Buddy didn't look at her, but . . . *my God, can it be?* he thought. *She* was nervous. Nervous talking to him. To Buddy. To the outsider.

"So, what's it ya want ta know?" he asked softly. "Don't know much . . . but maybe somethin' . . ."

"How did you do it? Call them like that? Are they demons? Angels? Ghosts?"

"They . . . they exist as we do. I can just bring their time merging with our time. Maybe they are here in our reality. Maybe we are there in theirs for that moment."

"Huh?"

"A shadow . . . a wrinkle . . . ever read that book *Wrinkle in Time*?"

"No."

"S'good book. Tells you a bit about jumping 'round in time. Been years since I read it, but it was a good analogy."

"I don't read much," Karey stated.

Buddy sighed.

"You *have* to read. That's how you learn. You can't build on the foundation if there is no foundation. You have to dig through the rock, firm up the sand. . . ."

"Man, I sure don't know what the hell you're going on about." Karey sighed and pulled out a cigarette. She offered one to Buddy. He took it and rustled through his bag for matches. She already had her lighter out and held the flame toward him. He stole a look at her face, at her mother's face.

His stomach clenched with dormant hurt. It had never gone away. They say time heals, but does it really? His heart ached as if the betrayal that day had just happened.

"So . . . like, how do you do it?"

Buddy took a drag on the cigarette. He watched the smoke form in lazy circles.

"Years of study," he said.

"But what kind of study?"

"Just . . . study . . . can't really explain it."

Karey pouted. "But I want to see it. I want to be part of it."

Buddy looked her over. She was staring at him in earnest. The way her mother had stared at him when he read her his poems. His heartfelt poems, written for her, and only for her. And for what? To make a mockery out of him? To tease and torment him? As if his life didn't suck enough, coming home day after day to a screaming, slurring mother and the banging against the wall all night long as man after man slipped between the sheets . . . and for what? A shitty little home full of rats and roaches, and a half-pint of whiskey for her, and a couple of coins for lunch money, dinner, breakfast . . . for him. . . .

Hatred swelled up inside of him.

She wanted something for nothing. She wanted him to spill the secrets that had taken him years to cultivate. Wasn't that typical?

"Be part of . . . it. You want to be part of it," he mused.

"Yes . . . is there a way?"

Buddy hummed and took out his carving knife. He whittled away at his walking stick. Karey watched him.

"Uh . . . mister Buddy . . . " she said after a moment as flakes of wood fell curling to the ground. She watched in fascination as the sharp fangs of a wolf took shape under his skilled fingers. He hummed and whittled, as if she were not there at all.

Karey looked around uneasily. The rush of the river was suddenly too loud, the secret place under the bridge suddenly too secret.

She slowly started to stand. Buddy looked up sharply and grinned. It was not a pleasant look.

His eyes clouded over. "Yes. There is a way."

Karey studied his face. If she wanted to learn the secret, she had to trust this man. After all, someone who could pull creatures from the air, could speak with the animals, couldn't really look and act . . . sane . . . could he?

* * *

The river was enticing today, Lydia thought, as she hung her towel from a tree branch. A nice dip would cool her off, maybe inspire her to do some more unpacking.

She dove into the water and relished its embrace as she swam along. She went very far, beyond the tickle of underwater weeds, out to where she could see the bottom no more.

She wondered just how deep it got out here. It couldn't be too deep, could it?

An image from her dream flashed through her mind. The clammy sensation of baby parts bumping against her. The smell of rot and filth and decay. She shuddered and pushed it from her thoughts.

Taking a deep breath, she dove down, down, down as far as she could. Her hair trailed behind her like a mermaid's, and she opened her eyes in the greenish yet clear water. As far as she kicked, she still could not see bottom. Not a rock, not a weed, there was nothing there to indicate the depth.

Her lungs were straining so she returned to the surface. She casually treaded water, catching her breath, wondering if she could go deeper this time, if she could find the bottom.

Once more, she dove, pushing herself farther and

farther, yet her lungs were protesting before she could tell if she was close.

She paddled to the shore and found a large rock, about the size of her hand. She swam back out to where the bottom had disappeared and dove down as far as she could go. She dropped the rock and watch it sink until it was swallowed up by murky darkness.

As she swam in long easy strokes back to shore, she thought about going into town to pick up a mask and some flippers. Maybe a bit of propulsion would get her nearer to the bottom.

She took her towel from the tree and wrapped it around herself. Funny how she was shivering with cold yet she knew it would only be minutes before she was hot and sweaty once more.

There was a twig snapping in the distance and she turned to look at the noise. She didn't see anyone. It might not be anyone anyway. The woods were always snapping and popping and she was never sure if it was birds or squirrels or Pilar or animals or something else.

She felt as if she were being watched, so she hurried back up the path. If there was someone there, she didn't want to meet them. Not while Tony was out of town.

* * *

Buddy watched Lydia return up the path. He was alone again. His once clean T-shirt had smears of blood streaked across it, his hair was tangled, his knuckles were cut as they gripped the walking stick, a burlap bag with a rabbit in the other.

He was suddenly tired in this hot sun and continued along his way, closer toward his cave, where he could enjoy a nice dip in the river before the darkness came.

Lydia took a long, hot shower. Everything was so quiet with Tony gone. Not that he was much of a talker, but just his presence filled up the emptiness that now seemed to rattle around this big house.

As she poured shampoo onto her hair, she thought about how she hoped that he wouldn't be upset that she had gotten nothing done yet again. It was the nightmare hanging heavy in her bones all day. She couldn't seem to shake it, and every moment spent in the house seemed to bring it back.

Most of all, she couldn't face taking boxes down to the basement.

The shower pounded away the stress of the day and she relaxed under it.

What were the people like that had lived here before?

Tony was very closemouthed about the whole

thing and she was sure that he knew way, way more than he was letting on.

Was the story that horrible?

Well, anything to do with murder surely was. Especially murderers that had people in their own homes.

She rinsed the shampoo from her hair, watching the frothy white foam bubble down the drain.

When she was done, she wrapped her hair in a towel. She walked back into the bedroom, tying another towel around her as she went.

The murders.

What about the murders?

What about the people that had committed them?

She kept walking until she was standing in front of Tony's computer. It was on, the screen saver dancing. She sat down, and dialed up the Internet, using her own name and password. As the computer hummed and whirred, she thought about where she should search first.

Newspapers seemed the obvious choice.

With only a couple of clicks, she found a plethora of articles on the murderers, the victims, the house.

As she scanned through them, her stomach rolled. Despite the most grisly details being kept from the press, she was able to glean the sheer horror of sexual abuse and maniacal torture those poor people had been subjected to, in this house, in the shackles in the basement. It was unbelievable how humans could do that to one another.

And for what?

What was the motive? Was it for kicks?

What a sick and twisted way to get kicks.

There were photos from the day the house was destroyed. She was relieved in an odd sort of way, that the original house had been much smaller, and not much like the one she lived in now.

She studied the anguished faces of grievers, the fervent eyes of the religious zealots, the dazed look of onlookers. Then there were pictures of the murderers, Donald and Debbie. Donald, square jawed, handsome, blond with piercing blue eyes. He looked as if he could be a model or a politician except for those creepy eyes. And then there was Debbie, a pretty woman with long blond hair, held back in a clip, wide angry eyes glaring out at her.

Monsters.

Chapter Eight

Buddy threw a handful of herbs into the pot bubbling in the middle of the small fire. The rabbit was roasting, gleaming succulently on a spit, juices dripping down, steaming as they washed the flame. Smoke billowed up in the darkness, snaking along the treetops, writhing along the air, until it reached the house, where it wormed its way down the chimney, down into the basement.

The walls pulsed and breathed, splitting and rolling. In the fireplace the brick throbbed, spewing liquid that dripped through the rafters, into the basement and spattering the walls.

Buddy sang. His wolf pack howled. He crawled along the ground, sniffing and tasting the dirt, the twigs.

The pot bubbled and steamed, a putrid odor filling the air. As last, Buddy reached in with a giant spoon and scooped a ladleful into his bowl. He breathed in the pungent aroma, wrinkling his nose in distaste.

After the soup cooled a bit, he sipped on it. The taste was bitter and foul, but he slurped it down, ignoring the shivering contractions his throat and stomach made. As the liquid fanned through him, he shuddered, his body quivering, jittering as he fell to the ground. The wolves sniffed and pawed at him as he rolled, crying as the foulness burned his stomach. He lurched up and vomited.

His head felt lighter and warmth spread through him. A comforting warmth, like a tender caress. He stared at the white wolf pack, their ghostly forms undulating, their fire-red eyes flickering.

A sound started deep in his belly and worked its way up along his throat until it was out of his mouth, echoing through the woods like the rest of the pack. They sang and howled with him, this strange man, on his hands and knees in the dirt, his wild eyes flickering in the shadows.

Buddy's body was heavy, too heavy. He felt the weight of material holding him down, tying him up. He could never be free with all this bondage.

He pulled at his clothes, tearing and ripping at them. The confinement was too much. At last he was naked, feeling the heat of the night, of the fire steaming against his flesh. His sweat rolled as he danced and howled, the wolves running in a circle around the fire, faster and faster, until they were an albino blur.

The energy of the pack sizzled into him, inching under his flesh and into his bones. He was still too dressed, too cumbersome for his creator.

He pulled at his hair, grabbing it by the roots, pulling and tugging until he heard ripping as his scalp released its hold. With a yowling howl, he tore away the skin, relieving his bones and nerves from the heavy burden of flesh and hair.

He shucked away his body like a snake, until he stood gleaming and bloody in the flickering fire flame, his eyes now shining green as emeralds. He raised skeletal hands to the sky. The wind whipped up, fanning the smoke higher, puffs of greenish black belching toward the myriad of stars twinkling in the heavens.

Buddy, now Walking Bones, sang and whistled, his body playing like some kind of flute as he danced.

"Walking Bones, Walking Bones, I do your bidding.

"Walking Bones, Walking Bones, I will guard the living.

"Walking Bones, Walking Bones, bring them all to me.

"Walking Bones, Walking Bones, I am your destiny."

He laughed, marveling at the sounds his sharpened hearing detected, how they amplified down into his body, vibrating sinewy veins and bones.

The wolves stood at rapt attention as Walking Bones continued his strange dance.

"I can hear it . . . the sounds of all and nothing, I can feel the tide shifting, changing, trembling, encompassing all I know and all I don't know."

Walking Bones danced over to the cooking rabbit. He picked up the end of the spit and held the steaming meat high into the air. Juices dripped to the ground and wrapped around Walking Bones's arm.

"The sacrificial lamb," Walking Bones said. He held the rabbit up to his mouth and began tearing into it. The wolves watched obediently. After a few bites, he tossed it over to them. The alpha wolf went to it first, nosing around and then nibbling daintily at it. One by one, each wolf approached the rabbit and took a tiny bite.

Walking Bones clapped. "Good for you. Good for all of you."

The wolves calmly returned to their places.

"And now, let the darkness reveal to us what the sun hides."

An impenetrable fog rolled through the house. Thick as cotton, real as smoke. Lydia waved it away as it hovered in her bedroom.

She watched the news. There was that anchor lady, Connie Bellows. Connie was in her late forties, one of those coifed and affected reporters. Her story tonight covered the mysterious disappearance of a young man. When his picture appeared on the screen, Lydia did a double take. It was the boy she had seen on the bicycle that day.

Her eyes welled up as she watched footage on an earlier interview with his mother, pleading for Timothy to come home, asking anyone who had seen him in the past twenty-four hours to let the police know.

Pilar whined, running to the window and back. She stared out across the yard, howling.

Lydia looked over at the window and saw the fog rolling outside too.

"Might as well be living in Maine with all of this," she mused, as she poured herself another glass of wine.

The boy had never returned from running an errand. Just disappeared. No trace of him or his bike.

Lydia frowned.

The poor child. Even though he was a man, he was a child. An eternal child. Born into this world with a million strikes against him.

Was he lost?

Or had some asshole lured him off?

Lydia sipped on her wine, her mind churning. She couldn't even imagine the grief his mother must be enduring.

The news quickly moved on to cover something else. She lost interest again, her mind still reeling over the boy. How could it be, in such a small town, that a person could go missing?

A sound caught her attention. At first, she thought it was part of the news footage, but she realized that it couldn't possibly be. Over the television, she heard a wailing. A hysterical sobbing as if someone's heart would break.

She threw off the covers and opened the bedroom door a crack.

It was there. Racking, hitching sobs.

Lydia swallowed.

She was awake this time, she knew it.

She walked down the stairs to the kitchen and grabbed a flashlight.

She didn't have to even wonder where the sound was coming from, she already knew.

Lydia opened the basement door and flicked on the light. She peered down the stairs. There was nothing there to match the sobbing. Even though the light was working, she held tightly to her flashlight. Each step down, she wondered what the hell she was doing, why she was purposely going down here at night, alone. She licked her lips, wanting to return to the safety of her bedroom, but she couldn't. She had to see.

Once she reached the bottom step, the crying stopped.

The silence was almost worse than the noise and she looked anxiously up at the door. It remained open.

"Hello?" she called out. "Hello? I heard you crying."

There was no answer.

She walked around the room, looking behind boxes, but the room was small and the boxes were neatly stacked. There was no place for anyone to be hiding.

She walked over to the wall. It didn't seem right. It seemed somehow different today.

A different color?

Were the bricks brighter?

She wasn't sure. The images from her dream haunted her and she couldn't remember what the wall looked like before or how the dream may have changed it.

Although she really didn't want to, she touched

one of the bricks. To her surprise, it was warm. Almost soft.

As she brought her hand away, she saw that it was smudged with rust. Maybe somehow the grueling heat of the day had caused it to sweat. Even as she thought it, it seemed ridiculous. The cellar was cooler than anywhere else. Maybe it was just dampness. She would have to get a dehumidifier down here if she didn't want all her storage things to get moldy.

But the crying.

Who was crying?

The wind?

A wild animal?

Even as the thoughts rolled around in her mind, she could sense the despair, feel the terror of the unseen mourner.

A ghost?

Were there ghosts in this house?

Lydia laughed out loud. Crazy. As if there were ever ghosts anywhere. Ghosts were a fairy tale. A story made up like the mystery novels she so adored.

Something touched her hair and she put her hand up to it.

"Stop it," she said, turning quickly, hoping yet not hoping to see who was teasing her. There was nothing. She looked up at the light and, sure enough, it was swinging, a foggy spectral image emanating from it.

"If you are a ghost, then I want to see you," Lydia said. How she hoped she would see nothing as her hand tightened its grip on the flashlight.

A wave rippled through her, warmth like an August current, and she sank back into it, feeling as though she were in the river again. It undulated through her, around her like a hug. She couldn't see anything but it cocooned her like a blanket. A blanket of sorrow and grief. A blanket of fear and then sharp stabbing pain.

"Stop!" she cried out, shaking her hands, pushing at nothing as it clung tighter to her. The sadness leeched into her, a bone-wracking sorrow; then tears spilled from her eyes.

"I'm sorry. I'm so sorry . . . " she sobbed. "I don't know how to help you."

Lydia sank down onto the cold cement floor, not feeling it as she lay her cheek against it, the oppressive weight of sentiment pinning her down.

At the top of the stairs, Pilar barked. Roused from her reverie, she felt the sensations slip away. Relief swelled through her, she was herself once more.

"Pilar!" Lydia called. "I'm coming."

Lydia ran up the stairs and slammed the door behind her.

* * *

"You have to return to work soon," Tony said, as they sat on the couch, sipping wine.

"Next week." Lydia reached for a piece of cheese on the coffee table in front of them.

"Do you think you'll have the house unpacked by then?"

"The house unpacked . . . hmmm . . . it *is* going slow, isn't it?" Lydia looked guiltily at the pile of unopened boxes still in the corner.

"Quite." Tony nodded.

"It's been kind of hard, you know. I'm just trying to get used to living in a new place, a new town, on top of trying to figure out exactly what to do with our stuff. It seems, well, a tad overwhelming."

"I know it's a bit of culture shock."

"Total culture shock. I'm used to the constant blare of sirens and horns, of watching every step I take from freaks and traffic, of grabbing that morning coffee from the café two doors down. . . . Gonna take more time than I thought to reprogram this brain of mine," she half joked.

"I suspect if you get more unpacking done, you will feel more at home. Maybe you're putting it off because you don't believe you are here yet. Maybe you don't want to be here. . . ."

"Oh, Tony . . ." Lydia turned to him and stared

into his eyes. "I do want to be here. I really do. I just need some readjustment time, that's all. I promise, I'll get more done tomorrow."

"I'm not your boss, Lydia. I'm your husband. And I guess I should have really taken some more time off too, but I just couldn't. We have such a big account right now. So big, in fact, that we may be building onto this place sooner than we thought!"

"It's big enough already," Lydia said.

"We can go bigger, my dear. A solarium or something. A covered swimming pool. Things like that. I plan to have it all." Tony grinned.

"Don't kill yourself, I want you around to enjoy it all."

"Oh, I'll be around, don't you worry."

Tony took a piece of cheese and laid it carefully on a cracker. "I have some work to get to. A couple mails to send. I'm going up to the study." He stood, wiping his hands on his leg.

"I guess that's my cue to do something," Lydia said.

"Not at all. It's late. If you want to hit the hay, go right ahead. I'm going to be a while."

"All right."

Lydia watched him go and returned her gaze to the dreaded boxes of stuff. Why was it so hard for her to deal with this? She was so efficient at work, but this domestic stuff, it just wasn't happening for her. Was it laziness? Was it a sense of finality when it was done? She just couldn't put her finger on the block.

"All righty then . . ." She sighed and stood up, making her way over to one of the boxes. There weren't that many left in here, she could unpack what was necessary in a couple of hours. So what was the big deal?

She opened a box and a soft gasp of surprise escaped her lips. There sitting on top was a tiny knitted baby bonnet and coat. They were hers when she was a baby.

Carefully she lifted them out, feeling the soft white yarn against her fingers. She pushed her hand into the bonnet, marveling at just how tiny her head had been. She held up the tiny jacket and tried to imagine herself in it. Why was it that no one had much memory of being a baby?

She sniffed the jacket and wasn't surprised it smelled mostly of moth balls.

Would her own baby be this tiny? She couldn't even imagine it. A little human being totally dependent on her for every single thing. Every mouthful of food, every diaper change, every bath, every breath of air would be monitored by Mommy in some way or another.

She put her hand in the little hat again. That little head had to come out of her. That whole body had to come out of her. She couldn't imagine how much that would hurt. She couldn't imagine how the human race continued to exist, how a woman would have a baby, knowing the agony. Yet she had run into people who spoke of childbirth with a gleam in their eyes. Saying cryptic things like it is meaningful pain, it is pain that has an end and the most wonderful result, unlike something like a broken arm or heart attack. Still others, very few others, insisted it was mere discomfort, you forget it as soon as it happens when you see that wonderful bundle of joy in your arms.

That little bundle of joy that is totally dependent on you, not just for that moment, not just for that year, but for the rest of your life, on some level.

She thought about her own parents. They had flown up from Arizona for the wedding. They had only met Tony a few times and, their being quiet people, she couldn't tell what they really thought of him.

But that was her parents.

Secretive.

There wasn't much she really knew about them. Was there anything to know about them? She wasn't even sure. They kept their opinions pretty much to themselves, didn't seem to want to venture too far past their little circle of friends. They were content with the way things were, never liked to rock the boat.

She tried to imagine them as new young parents. Were they scared or happy or some combination of both? Had she been wanted or was she an inconvenience? She had never felt too much in either direction. She had the sense that they had a child because it was expected of them. She didn't know why there had not been others, if they had wanted others.

She put the little outfit back into the box and quickly looked through it to be certain that it really was a memento box. It seemed as though so many boxes were mementos. But of what? She had such an unremarkable life and probably always would. She never aspired to fame and fortune although she always did intend to earn enough to have a house no less than this and the furnishings that went along with it, husband or no husband.

Maybe she felt out of sorts because she wasn't at work, didn't have a real focus. She was purposely not even thinking about work. There was so much to be done and she dreaded the pile growing higher on her desk. The e-mail alone must be horrendous and she had to keep willing herself away from the study. She hadn't even set up her own computer yet, in fear that she would start working on one of her accounts and then never stop and if Tony thought the house wasn't happening now . . .

Lydia pushed the memento box aside. She opened another box. This one was easier to deal with. Books and knickknacks, both of theirs. She set to work putting the books on the shelves and figuring out where to put the odd assortment of little statues of animals and bowls. People collected the weirdest things, she decided as she put things on the shelves. At the time, it always seems like a good idea but then years later, looking at a little red bowl bought on impulse on some trek to China-town, just really didn't make that much sense. Yet she put it out. She would worry about rearranging later, or putting things back into boxes if she didn't like them out after all.

See, it was easy, she told herself. One box emp-tied. One pushed aside. No biggie.

She opened another box. This one had kitchen stuff in it, so she dragged it into the kitchen. As she set to work putting the glasses on the shelves, she had the distinct feeling she was being watched.

She looked over at the window but there was nothing there. She continued to put the glasses up and felt the hairs on her neck stand on end. There was definitely someone watching her.

Putting down the glass she had in her hand, she walked over to the window. The yard was a maze of shadow and moonlight. Nothing there.

Boy, living in the country sure could be creepy, she thought. *Whoever would have imagined it?*

There was a crash from upstairs and her heart jumped.

"Tony!" she called, and raced up the stairs. Tony looked sheepishly at her from the office door.

"Sorry," he said. "I just knocked these books over."

He knelt down to pick them up.

"You scared me." Lydia nervously laughed.

"Got the heebie-jeebies?" he asked.

"Sort of. I was having this feeling I was being watched."

"Probably the raccoons," he said. "Why don't you just go to bed. I'm almost done here."

"What are you working on?" she asked, glancing over at his computer. His messenger was blinking.

"Oh, just that account."

"I see you're talking to someone," she said.

"Yes, just one of the guys from work. I was looking up something for him when I knocked all this over."

"Oh . . . well, I'll let you get back to it then," Lydia said, trying to make out the name on the messenger, but she was too far to see it.

"I'll be right there," Tony said. "Honest."

"Okay." Lydia left and was about to go into the bedroom when she remembered all the lights were still on downstairs. She returned to the kitchen, and as she was flicking the switch, there was movement in the backyard. She went over to the window, and witnessed Buddy walking into the bushes.

Damn creepy guy was spying on me, she thought. *I really have to tell Tony to have a word with him.*

Three teenage boys hovered around a campfire.

"You go first," Jeff said to Tony.

Tony looked at him with wide eyes.

"I don't want to."

"Someone has to be first."

"Why not you, why not Buddy?"

"Because it should be you."

Tony shrugged and nervously removed his clothes. His thin teenage body glowed in the flickering firelight. He looked over to his friends for approval.

"So?"

"Okay . . . I'll go next," Jeff said. He pulled off his T-shirt and yanked down his jeans. With a laugh, he slipped off his underwear, nearly tripping.

"Here I am," he said, arms outstretched. Tony looked enviously at his body. Jeff was more muscular than he, and had the blond hair to match.

The two naked boys turned to Buddy, who was

already shucking his clothes. Now the three of them stood pale in the moonlight.

"So what is next?"

"I guess we should mark ourselves somehow. Some sort of preparation for the ritual," Jeff said as he leaned toward the fire and picked up a piece of charred wood. He ran his hand along the end. It wasn't hot but the burned part of it smeared along his fingers. He walked over to Tony and drew a pentacle on his chest and belly.

Tony held still while Jeff solemnly drew. Buddy was next, and he giggled as the wood tickled his flesh.

"Now do me," Jeff said, holding out the stick. Tony took it and carefully drew the pentacle. He looked at the boy's nipples, hard little nuggets that framed the top of the design. Jeff's tummy was hard and flat and Tony saw that he was getting an erection. Seeing that, he in turn felt himself growing hard and he tried to think about other things. Yet, all he could think about was Jeff's cock swelling before his gaze. He looked over at Buddy and saw that he too was hard.

"There," Jeff said, placing the wood back into the fire. "Now we are marked."

"Are you sure we should be playing around with such things?" Tony asked. He looked up at the full moon. It was bright as day out here in the clearing.

He wondered if anyone was watching them. He would be in such shit if he were caught. Namely from his parents. He thought he was more afraid of pissing off his mother than any cops.

"I've been reading. . . ." Jeff smiled. He went over to his knapsack and pulled out a notebook.

"I know what it is we have to do."

"What is it we are trying to do anyway?" Buddy asked. He was standing close to the fire, watching the flames dance and dart, curling into shapes. The shapes of animals. He could see a bear, a dog, a flying bird, a wolf. Buddy grinned, the fire glow giving his face an elfin quality.

"We want to talk to the killers, don't we? Isn't that what this is all about?"

"Shouldn't we be at the graveyard for that?"

"How can we get in? You know they are guarding it. For this very reason. At least we are near where they did the killing. That should count for something."

"What if we end up calling all the victims instead?"

"Then that is what happens. Whatever happens, don't you think it would be cool?" Jeff asked, his eyes glittering earnestly in the firelight. Tony nodded, his eyes unable to leave Jeff's handsome chiseled face. How could a boy be so strikingly handsome? Square jawed, square shouldered. He already had biceps and rippling abs. Tony put a hand on his own stomach and felt his thinness, his bony little body, skinny little Tony. He looked at Buddy and Buddy was still young-boy skinny too. He laughed. Buddy looked so at home, playing naked around the fire. His shoulder-length hair flying around as he danced and whooped, the pentacle on his chest already smudged as he added more designs up and down his arms.

"Tony, here." Buddy came up to him and smeared stripes along his face. He went over and did the same to Jeff.

"I feel so . . . primitive," Tony said.

"Get in touch with your Indian heritage." Jeff laughed.

"I don't know if I have any." Tony shrugged. "I think my family is all from Europe."

"I know there's a tiny bit of Indian blood in me somewhere," Jeff said. "I'll have to ask Mom again. What about you, Buddy?"

"I think my dad was an Indian. So I guess that makes me at least half. Don't know if Mom remembers what she is, she never talks about it. But she does talk about how she was in love with some Indian dude and that he was my dad. Sometimes she just stares at me and then says junk like I look just like him."

"Cool. So with all the Indian blood here, and

whatever Tony has, maybe some gypsy blood or something, we should be able to work some magic somehow!" Jeff smiled.

"Get the juju flowing!" Buddy howled.

"That ol' black magic!" Tony shouted.

"Shhhh . . ." Jeff put a finger to his lips. "We don't want anyone to hear us. Who knows who else might be trying to do what we're doing tonight. We don't want them bothering us."

"Or the cops."

"Like they aren't going to see the fire." Buddy smirked.

"Shh . . . guys . . . let's try to do this. . . ." Jeff waved them closer. He pulled a knife and a couple of bags of dried plants from his knapsack.

"What's that? Pot?" Tony asked.

"No. It's for the ceremony. You'll see."

Jeff then pulled out a goblet, a bag of salt and a bottle of water.

"Gonna make some soup." Buddy giggled.

"Okay, guys. We have to get serious if we're gonna get anything done. Here's what we gotta do. Buddy, you pour the salt where I dig the knife in a circle. Try to make it last, that's all we've got. Tony, you follow us."

Jeff walked around the fire in a half crouch as he dragged the knife along the ground. Buddy followed him, throwing pinches of salt into the trough. Jeff was humming, a toneless buzz, which Buddy and Tony imitated. As they walked in the moonlight, Tony was watching Jeff's firm butt. It barely jiggled as the boy knelt and stood, slicing the ground with the blade, his eyebrows furrowed in concentration. Tony kept humming, willing his cock to stop rising again but unable to tear his eyes away from Jeff's butt, his thighs.

They reached the beginning of the circle again.

Jeff took the goblet and filled it with the water.

"I call upon the powers of north, south, east and west. I call upon the four elements, earth, wind, water and fire. I call upon the all-mighty energy. . . ." He took a sip and passed the goblet to Tony. Tony took a sip and passed it to Buddy.

"Bring us the spirits of Donald and Debbie."

Jeff took a pinch of each of the herbs and threw them into the fire. The fire rose higher, crackling as the herbs burned.

"Bring us the spirits. Bring us the spirits," the boys chanted as they walked around the circle again.

A thin wisp of smoke curled up from the fire. It rolled, growing in immensity as the boys' walking turned to dancing, their toneless humming evolving into chanting.

The cloud hung heavy in the air. Tony saw it take form. The form of a face. He hitched his breath in.

He wanted to ask the others if they saw it too, but when he looked at them, he could tell by their feverish eyes that they did.

The face was huge, skeletal, with glowing red eyes. The mouth opened and an unearthly moaning filled the air.

"Tell us, why did you do it?" Jeff asked. "What was it like?"

The face looked angry, glaring as its mouth moved, a howling amplifying into a wind.

There was a screeching sound, and high above them, another cloud was taking shape. This one was huge and they could feel anger in the air.

"This was not a good idea . . ." Tony muttered.

"Shhh . . ." Jeff hissed.

The new cloud rolled and shifted, another face taking form. This one didn't seem human at all. Its eyes were huge, its mouth ugly and long like a beak with rows of sharp gnashing teeth. It swooped down toward them and Buddy screamed, jumping out of its path.

"Shit!" Buddy screamed and broke the circle. Tony was right behind him. The two boys scrambled to grab their clothes, while Jeff stood staring up at the monster, his arms held wide.

"Jeff, get the hell out of there!" Tony screamed.

"My master . . . " Jeff said. "I will do your bidding."

The creature screeched again.

Tony and Buddy ran. Buddy tripped over a log, his knee cracking on a rock as he fell.

"Shit!" he cried, scrambling back up. The pain seared through him, but his fear was greater. He followed Tony into the darkness and left Jeff alone with the demon.

Tony woke in a pool of sweat. He was gasping as he fumbled for the bedside lamp. Lydia was still asleep beside him. He didn't blame her. She was used to his nightmares by now. Besides, she seemed to be having her own share of them lately.

He sat up, staring around the room.

It was only a dream.

It was only a memory.

It had happened so long ago.

The next morning, Lydia set to work really giving this house-unpacking business the old college try. She forced herself to stop reminiscing and instead played her Faith No More CD at maximum volume. As she sang along, she was able to make the work go at a much faster pace.

Soon, she had an empty box. And shortly after that, another one. She thought about the last time she had gone down to the basement. How there was such sadness in the room. Could a room really retain the energy of those that had gone before, even though it had been totally redone?

She went down the stairs with great trepidation.

"Are you here?" Lydia added a box to the stack. The basement seemed foggy today, but she wasn't sure if the haze was her eyes or the room. Sleep had not been a friend to her in a while.

The sensation of something being here was present, as always, and she hoped that by acknowledging it, she would feel less spooked.

"Hello?" Lydia called. A sense of despair washed through her in a wave, and the hairs stood up on her arms. Her vision swam, more blurred, as if she were caught in a dense fog. She could almost make out forms swirling around her, gaps in the haze that let in the room light.

She saw images on the floor. As she squinted her eyes, she thought she saw shackles bolted to the floor. She leaned over to touch them and they evaporated as if an illusion.

Over on the wall, she saw more shackles, and long chains hanging down from them. She walked over, pushing aside the swimming forms with her hands like seaweed. When she got to the wall, again the image disappeared.

Her hair was standing out on end and she tried

to push it down but she couldn't. It was as if someone were hanging on to it.

"Are you here today?" she asked. "I want to help you."

The room seemed to sigh, another wash of anguish flooded her and then she felt a sudden stab of pain, as if she were being gutted from her neck to her belly.

She screamed, holding herself, staring down at the red slice that split open, watching her own guts and blood spill out.

"No!" she cried, watching the steaming, throbbing organs slip to the floor. She stumbled up the stairs, holding her chest.

Once in the kitchen, Lydia slammed the door, leaning back on it, sobbing and hitching her breath.

At last, she allowed herself to look down at her chest. There was nothing there.

"Thank God." She sighed as she trembled. Pilar came into the room, and looked at her and then at the door. The dog whined.

"I know, I know . . . I'm not going back down there today," Lydia said.

Pilar wagged her tail and licked at Lydia's hand.

"Jeeze, what is happening to me?" she asked, wiping at her chest. She could still feel the echo of the pain, and she unbuttoned her blouse. There was a faint line running down from her neck to her stomach.

Chapter Nine

"Break out the champagne!" Tony said as he marched through the door. Lydia looked up from the couch where she was watching a talk show.

"Why? What happened?" She stood up as Tony put down his briefcase. He swept her up in his arms, swinging her around.

"We did it. We did it!" He laughed.

"What? What did you do?"

"The deal. We closed the deal. We're going to be *rich!*"

"Oh, my God. I don't believe it!" Lydia laughed. "This calls for a celebration!"

Lydia ran into the kitchen to get the champagne. Tony followed, finding their best flute glasses high up in the cupboard.

"We are on our way now!"

Lydia popped the cork with a giggle and poured the bubbling brew into the glasses. It frothed up and over the rims. Tony took the glasses and handed one to her. He linked his arm through hers.

"To us!"

"To us!" They laughed as they sipped.

Tony stood back.

"Oh, it won't be long now. We will have everything. Everything we ever dreamed of and more . . ."

"I'm so happy, Tony."

Tony kissed her. "So am I, Lydia. We have almost finished paying our dues, and then the world will be ours!"

"I don't even want the world," Lydia said, kissing his neck. "I just want you."

Lydia hurried through the grocery store, grabbing just what she needed, keeping her eyes on a narrow track between list and shelf. She had been here enough times now to know that there would be stares and whispers and she just was not in the mood for that game today.

As she pondered the potatoes, she thought for a moment of the missing boy. That poor child that she had seen riding the bicycle on her first visit to this store. She hoped they would find him soon, but something in her gut told her that he was gone. Gone for good. The weak go first. That was the order of the hunt, wasn't it? Thinning the herd, weeding out the gene pool . . .

She shook her head. Some of the thoughts rattling around in there freaked her out sometimes. It was this place. Not just this store, but this place. The whole country thing. There was something kind of creepy, lurking and sinister in the underbelly that just wasn't right.

Was it the trees, the field?

The whisper of the leaves?

The buzzing of mosquitoes on a hot summer night?

Weren't those supposed to be friendly things? Homey things that city folk longed to embrace?

She reckoned it wasn't her style.

The more she looked around at these slow-moving women with their judgmental sneers and flabby arms poking from brightly flowered shirts, the more she yearned for the black leather punks with their nose rings and attitude. At least they were up front about where you stood, and they didn't waste time with idle gossip.

She put several potatoes into her basket, still not accustomed to buying things by the bagful. After all, most of the time it was just she and Tony. They ate on the run, or picked things up from the multitude of fruit stands and delis on the way home. She wasn't used to this driving a million miles to grab a bite to eat.

One day she'd get used to it. She'd have to, wouldn't she?

She eyed the bright juicy strawberries. She hoped Tony's boss liked what she was preparing. There was no way to know. She didn't think she had ever entertained a boss in her home in her life. But there were no fancy restaurants out here, none to take a big New York executive to, that she had found so far. Yet for some reason, Tony had insisted on bringing this man home. She still couldn't figure it out. Something about liking the country, or maybe Tony wanted to show off the house he had designed, or maybe the boss was also looking for a small town to live in.

"Why, Lydia. . . ."

Lydia froze, recognizing the sickly sweet salutation before she lifted her gaze. "Hello, Sybil." Lydia's smile felt as plastic as one of those hideous clown doll's.

Sybil's grimace was just as insincere as she lifted up her sunglasses, beady eagle eyes picking up every hair out of place, every wrinkle in Lydia's quickly thrown together outfit.

"Picking up a few things today?" Sybil asked.

Lydia wanted to scream, *no kidding, duh. . . .* But she was an adult now. A married lady and this shrew was her mother-in-law . . . forever. . . .

"Yes. Tony invited his boss for dinner." She regretted the words the second they slipped out, but once they hung in the air, there was no way to retract them. She busied herself with the berries again.

"Oh, the boss is coming to dinner, is he? Isn't that lovely."

"I think it's to celebrate the new account," Lydia added quickly. "They've been working very hard."

"Well, maybe you'll find time in your busy schedules to have us over for a housewarming dinner."

"Of course we will. We just aren't moved in yet, that's all. It was unexpected of him to invite his boss, if truth be known. I was hoping for a little more warning. . . ."

"Yes, well, I have a busy day planned myself. No time for chitchat, have to get to the gym and a million other things before Walter gets home from work. You know, just because one is slender doesn't mean one is in shape," Sybil said, slipping her sunglasses over her eyes. Lydia ignored the quip.

"I'll see you later, Sybil," Lydia said, pushing her buggy away from the woman.

She resisted the urge to wipe away the essence

of her by rubbing her hands against her clothes, but that was ridiculous. You couldn't really feel people's essence. It was just a gut reaction. Some people you liked, some you didn't.

Yet, maybe you could feel someone's essence or spirit or whatever it was. After all, there was some really wild shit going on in the new house's basement. And she was positive it was tied to the murders. The ghosts of the victims, unable to break free. Or was it just their essence, trapped, suspended in a void of grief, never able to move on?

Would the basement always be that way? So creepy and weird?

She had hoped by now that it, or she or whatever the problem was, would have settled down.

Against her better judgment, she glanced around the store to see where Sybil went. As she expected, Sybil's lips were flapping a mile a minute to some huge sunburned woman in an expensive dress and a New York hairstyle. Where did the people get the money out here?

Years of commuting and low house prices were all she could guess.

It wouldn't be long before this little snatch of the world was caught up in the clawing jaws of the housing boom. Almost amazing that it had been missed this long. Almost . . .

* * *

As the power chords from the old rock-and-roll album *Who Are You?* shook the house, Lydia organized the breakfast nook. The sun shone brightly through the windows. If only she had gotten it together to order a new dining room set. But the kitchen would do, it was big and bright and the cushioned breakfast nook would be fine for entertaining Tony's boss.

She pushed all the unpacked boxes into the closets, and what didn't fit in the closet she stacked against a wall and placed a cotton woven throw over it.

The chicken and potatoes were cooking nicely, filling the kitchen with a warm homey smell. The way the sun poured in the window gave her hope that the evening would go well.

It wouldn't be long before they arrived.

Lydia poured herself a glass of red wine, realizing how nervous she was. She had never met Mr. Greenspan before, wasn't even really sure what to expect. Tony had only been working in his department a short while. She imagined he was a silver-haired man in his sixties, with three-piece suits and a formal manner.

He'd better not be expecting a very formal dinner. She sighed. But he knew they had just moved here, surely he wouldn't expect the house to be set up perfectly just yet.

Pilar barked and Lydia ran to the window. With a smile, she saw Tony's sports car creep up the driveway, Mr. Greenspan a shadow in the seat beside him.

She glanced around the living room one last time for anything strangely out of place. There was nothing. She checked herself in the oval mirror she had hung on the wall that afternoon. Her hair and makeup seemed fine. She hoped she was dressed all right in a black pantsuit that showed off her slender figure.

Tony entered the house. Pilar bounded over, tail wagging. Tony held her collar.

"Lydia?" he called. "We're here."

Lydia turned to face him. "Hi, honey."

She stopped and stared at the man who was with him.

This was not some older man in his sixties. He wasn't even in his forties.

"Lydia, please meet William Greenspan."

Lydia extended her hand, staring into his dark brown eyes.

"Lydia, so very pleased to finally meet you." William smiled, his warm hand clamping hers firmly as he laid his other one on top.

"I—I'm thrilled you could join us."

She tried not to stare at his handsome face. A square firm jaw, those brown eyes, blond hair combed back executive style, all wrapped up in a semicasual jade suit. He looked down at Pilar, who was staring at him. Her tail had stopped wagging and her ears were back.

"What a beautiful dog," William said. "What breed is that?"

"She's a Belgian Tervuren," Lydia explained, taking the collar from Tony. "She's sometimes a bit skittish around strangers." She could feel tension sweeping through the dog, and patted her.

"It's okay, Pilar. It's a visitor."

Pilar's ears perked back up, but she was still wary.

"Go lie down," Lydia said, pointing to the dog bed by the fireplace. The dog whined as she slunk off to her cushion with a sigh.

"Boy, she's obedient."

"I've had her for years. We've been through a lot together."

"Gorgeous animal. Dogs don't usually like me, so I'm not surprised." William smiled.

"That breed is known for sticking to its humans anyway," Tony said. "It took her forever to warm up to me too. A one-woman dog, that one."

"Please come in, may I get you a drink?" she asked.

"Certainly, what do you suggest?"

"We have pretty much everything. Scotch, wine, brandy . . ."

"Make it scotch then." He grinned.

"Same for you, honey?" she asked Tony.

Tony nodded. "I'll show William his room while you get them."

"Certainly."

She heard them speaking softly as they ascended the stairs. Damn, but that man was handsome. And familiar-looking too. As she poured the drinks, she tried to think of where she had seen that face before, but it would not come to her. Maybe his chiseled good looks were reminiscent of a movie star of some sort.

She put three scotches on a little silver tray and went up to the spare bedroom.

The men stopped talking as she entered.

"Oh, I'm sorry. Am I interrupting?" she asked.

William laughed. "Not at all." He reached for one of the scotches.

"I was just telling William here that this will probably not be a spare bedroom for long." Tony slipped his arm around Lydia. Lydia blushed.

"We'll see. It might be quite a while before anything happens," Lydia said softly.

"Where there's a will, there's a way." William grinned, and raised his glass. "To baby."

"To baby." Tony smiled.

"To baby. . . ." Lydia clicked the men's glasses.

"Would you like a tour?" Lydia asked, changing the subject.

"Certainly."

Lydia walked out of the room and the men followed. She went into the office.

"We both have our desks in here. As you can see, we're still unpacking everywhere," Lydia said.

William looked at the two desks and two computers surrounded by boxes and piles of papers. "I can see that."

"The bathroom goes in between the two rooms," Lydia pointed out.

"That's a good layout." William nodded.

They left the office and went to the master bedroom. Lydia walked in and as William followed, a low growling came from the darkness of the room. Lydia switched on the light to reveal Pilar crouching in the window seat, her hackles raised.

"Enough!" Lydia snapped at the dog. The dog silently showed her teeth, eyeing William warily. As he stepped across the threshold, Pilar growled again.

"Maybe we should just leave her to her space," William said, stepping back out into the hall. "A lovely room you have there."

"Sorry about that dog. I guess that's why they call them bitches," Tony joked.

Lydia scowled and shut the door. "We'll just keep her locked up in there for now, where she won't bother us."

Lydia shepherded the men back down the stairs. "Dinner should be ready soon."

After dinner and a few more drinks, they retired to the living room, where Lydia brought out slices of chocolate mousse cake and coffee.

"My, oh, my, you are spoiling me." William winked as he took his piece.

Lydia giggled. It had been a lighthearted meal. William held court, telling tales of his travels to various places, some deals he had made, dropping just enough celebrity names to be intriguing yet not boasting.

"So, tell me, William, why is it that a handsome man as yourself hasn't married?" Lydia asked.

Tony furrowed his eyebrows at Lydia and she pretended not to notice.

"I guess I just haven't found the right person yet. Or maybe I've just been too busy to even look. I'm quite enjoying myself these days." He grinned and winked at Tony. Tony looked into his coffee cup.

"Nothing wrong with that." Lydia smiled.

"So, how do you like it here, in a small town?" William asked. "Must be quite a shock from city life."

"It is. I've never lived like this before, but I'm getting used to it. How about you? Are you a city person?" Lydia's eyes were growing heavy. Too much food and scotch, she figured. But William was so charming she wanted to keep talking to him. She sat back in her chair.

"Now I am. I grew up in a small town, though, like Tony. Maybe if I ever get married and settle down, I'll be lured back. In the meantime, I love New York. So much to do and see."

"I love the shows. And shopping." Lydia stared at the fireplace. It was rippling. Were the ghosts coming up here too now? She blinked and shook her head.

"I like to catch shows too," William was saying. "Maybe we'll all go see something together."

"Sounds great," Lydia said, the words coming out of her mouth almost automatically as she continued to stare into the fireplace.

The men watched her and looked at each other.

The clock on the mantelpiece chimed midnight.

"How did it get so late?" Tony said, stifling a yawn. "It's been one helluva day."

"I guess it's time to get some shut-eye." William

nodded. "That's one of the drawbacks of living in such a pretty place. The commute."

"It can be exhausting by the end of the week," Tony agreed. They both looked again at Lydia, who had shut her eyes.

Tony poked her and she startled.

"Huh . . . ?"

"Honey, you go on up to bed. I'll put away these dishes," Tony said. Lydia looked around the room, blinking rapidly.

"Oh, okay . . . sure," she said. She stood up and a wave of dizziness consumed her, knocking her back to her chair.

"Whoa . . . stood up too fast," she half joked.

"Are you all right?" Tony asked, taking her arm.

"Yes . . . I'm fine. Just didn't realize how tired I was, I guess." Lydia stood up again. She still felt woozy but was able to focus.

"Should I help you to bed?"

"I'll be all right, honey," Lydia said, stumbling toward the stairs. Tony held out his hands to her and she waved him off.

"I'm fine, really."

Lydia pulled herself up the stairs, hanging on to the railing. She made a concentrated effort to appear more normal than she felt, she didn't want to embarrass Tony in front of his boss. But her head was swimming, she couldn't focus on anything. The stairs swam when she looked down, the picture at the top of the stairs morphed in and out of the wall. She felt so strange, but not in a drunk way. She'd been drunk a thousand times in her life, and maybe drunkenness made her dizzy and tired, but this was something else combined.

She opened the bedroom door, barely noticing Pilar, who ran over to lick her hand. Lydia flung herself facedown on the bed and in seconds, was out like a light.

Standing around her bed were three figures in hooded robes. She tried to reach for the bedside lamp but she was too weak. Staring groggily at the hooded people, she vaguely wondered who they were, yet she already knew. Dreams were funny that way. How things happened with such logic and clarity, yet if you ever tried to explain to someone in your waking state about what was going on, you wouldn't find the words.

No. She sighed deeply. You wouldn't find the words.

Gentle lips touched her cheeks, hands stroked her body and she thought about the ghosts in the basement. How they liked to pet her. Maybe they had wormed their way into her dreams now too. The heavy scent of incense filled her and she reached up to stroke a face. Her eyes were so heavy, she had no desire to even try to open them again. Instead she concentrated on the delicious sensations undulating along her body.

A rainbow of colors shimmered behind her eyelids. Purple and red snaked and wove into each other, yellow and orange fluttered and rippled like streamers on a kite.

She realized that the sensations were sliding into her. It was just a dream so she spread her legs wider, welcoming pleasure deeper into her body.

It was good to feel someone that wasn't her husband. A fantasy yet it was only a dream. He filled her with rhythmic thrusts and she met them eagerly.

More lips touched hers, a warm, moist tongue licked her neck and she arched into it. Hands cupped and kneaded her breasts, rolled her nipples and still, inside of her, pleasure. Delicious pleasure.

She smiled, small moans escaping her lips. She locked her legs around the man, clenching her fingers into his ass, pulling him in deeper.

She opened her eyes and dreamily saw Tony, William and Buddy lying naked around and alongside her. Funny how in dreams, there was always the glimmer of reality. How weirdness happens yet it is so normal. How she was lying here with three men, two she barely knew, and didn't even complain, no, actually relished the sexcapade unfolding. She watched through the red and blue shimmering that flashed around her eyes as Tony kissed William. Two handsome men, lips meeting and parting, hungrily. She realized it was Buddy inside of her, so big, so hard, so exquisitely animal-like. She reached up to pull at his hair, bring his face to hers, realizing how in the dream he was a nice-looking man, underneath all the hair. She wrapped her hands in his hair, pushing her hips up to meet him.

She watched her husband kiss William's neck. In real life, she would be so jealous. No, more than jealous. She would be utterly freaked out that the man she loved, the man she *married*, was holding another man's cock in his hand.

But this was just a dream, so it was okay. He could play with William's cock. Make it all hard and maybe he'd put it inside of her too. . . .

Buddy thrust wildy now and Lydia felt her body tingle and surge with floods of pleasure. He came with a groan and she held him closely, savoring every last pulse of him releasing into her.

She gasped as Buddy pulled out and William turned her on her side, sliding into her. It took a moment to get used to him, but only a moment.

Before long, she was matching him thrust for thrust.

Hands and mouths, fingers and chests entwined. She was writhing and rolling between them, among them, the pleasure surging and building, ebbing and flowing. She moaned and sank back into the blackness.

Chapter Ten

It was another beautiful summer day. Lydia stretched, feeling every bone in her body aching. Tony still slept beside her. She watched him, thinking about the dream, wondering how much she must have thrashed around and if she had kept him awake half the night.

She hugged the pillow, and wondered what it would really be like to be with three men at once.

Tony's eyelids fluttered and he turned his sleepy-eyed gaze toward her.

"Morning, handsome," she said.

"Morning. Are you feeling any better?" Tony asked.

"Much. Boy, I had the weirdest dreams. Guess it's been a while since I had so much scotch."

"Nothing too scary, I hope?" Tony asked, sliding an arm around her.

"No. Amazingly enough, no real nightmares. Just . . . weird . . . can't even explain it," Lydia lied. She thought about the men again and shivered with pleasure.

"I guess I should go put on some coffee. William might already be up," Lydia said, sitting up. She felt as if she had been through the wringer. She looked sideways at Tony, wondering if he had made love to her while she slept. If he had, he didn't give it away. She smiled to herself. Of course he had, she could tell. But that was all right. She pulled on her bathrobe and hummed happily as she went into the bathroom.

Lydia waved good-bye to Tony and William. They were going into the office again today for a while. More work. It never stopped anymore, it seemed.

Well, that was all right. She didn't have much time left to finish unpacking and try to figure out exactly what was going on in the basement before she too was back in the rat race.

She was full of energy and in no time, succeeded in unpacking a few more things.

She called Pilar and took her up to the bedroom.

"Come on, honey. That's a good dog." Lydia enticed Pilar toward the dog crate with a treat. Pilar bowed her head and entered the crate. Lydia locked the door behind her.

It was for the best when she was dealing with whatever was going on in the basement. She didn't understand it, but she also knew that the dog was growing more nervous every time she had to go down. If Pilar was safely locked in her bedroom with the TV on, then she would be none the wiser.

Lydia went into the study and unpacked a couple more boxes of books and files. She made every effort not to get caught up in reading the files, pushing out of her mind the thought of all the work that was surely piling up. She looked at her computer, all set up and ready to go. But she would not turn it on. No sirreee. She would just have to wait. She would be back on the fast track soon enough.

She folded up the empty boxes. Taking a deep breath, she readied herself for God knows what would be happening next in the basement.

Pilar whined. The television wasn't soothing her. There was something going on. She could smell it. She scratched at the corner of her cage. A shadow fell across her and she looked up at the person standing there. She barked.

The cage was opened and she ran out. She

wagged her tail, smelling a familiar friendly smell, but when she looked at the person in front of her, even her dim doggie vision could see that this was not whom she smelled.

This was a walking skeleton. A half man. Bones with sinewy ropes of muscle and veins wrapped around him. He lowered a hand to pat her head and she cowered.

Walking Bones grinned, and a hissing kind of laugh escaped from his teeth.

Pilar lay down at his feet.

Walking Bones took a little flask from his satchel and unscrewed the lid. He poured a small amount of the contents on the floor. Pilar looked at it.

Walking Bones patted the ground.

Pilar cautiously lapped at it. The red substance was deliciously salty. She couldn't help herself as she drank every last drop, lapping repeatedly at the carpet long after it was gone.

Walking Bones held the flask up and wiggled it in front of her. She stood up, tail wagging. He left the bedroom and picked his way carefully down the stairs and out the front door.

Pilar happily followed.

Lydia braced herself as she walked down the stairs, but this time the basement seemed to be a normal everyday basement. The fog was gone, there were no chains and shackles. Even the sense of sadness was not here.

She put the folded boxes over with some others, and smiled.

Thank God, she thought. *Thank God that maybe I'm not insane after all.*

She went over to the wall and knocked on it. It was solid brick. She ran her hands over the bricks and they felt as they should, cold and clammy.

Basement bricks.

Wasn't it funny though that she had never noticed that there was a space just above her head where it seemed a brick was missing?

She stood up on her tippytoes, to try to see in the hole where the brick was missing. Of course there would be nothing to see, this wall was surely thicker than one brick. She slid her hand up there, trying to reach into or beyond the crack.

Nothing happened to illuminate her.

"Oh!" She suddenly remembered and ran back up the stairs. She walked over to the fireplace and took the brick that Sybil had brought over that day.

She rolled it over in her hand, studying it. It was just a brick. An old musty brick.

She went back down the stairs with brick in hand. Just as she suspected, it slid perfectly into the hole.

"You're home now."

The wall seemed to sigh. Lydia put her hand on it, and now it pulsed beneath her touch. She could feel it breathing.

"Oh, great, here we go again." No sooner were the words out of her mouth than there was a loud creaking sound. The wall suddenly opened inward, like a door, and she fell through with it.

"Oh, my God."

She was in another room, just as she had always suspected. This room was empty and looked much as the other room had before she had started to stash her stuff in it. The only light was pouring through the door and she could see shackles on the floors and walls, forms wafting and undulating.

Hands stroked her, and there was crying. Sobbing and shrieking. Fear and hopelessness echoed through her bones, memories that were not hers flitted through her brain.

She stood up, wiping her arms as if she could wipe away the sensation, but knowing it was coming from the inside out.

There was a hanging light in this room too and she reached to pull the string. The light burned bright for a moment and then the bulb shattered. Glass flew and she averted her eyes in time to avoid being hit by the splinters.

The door behind her swung shut and she was

trapped in the dark. Moans were louder and she ran to the door, trying to push it open, running her hands along the bricks to discover a spring or a handle.

Hands ran along her body. She could feel them feeling her, grasping at her ankles, at her shins, at her waist. Pulling at her as if she were a life buoy that would rescue them as they drowned in desperation.

"Leave me alone!" she cried.

Gasping and sobbing filled her ears and she ran from the door, blindly in the dark, as if she could somehow tear herself away from their grip.

She tripped over some chains, heard clanking rattles, then slammed into one of the walls. Her shoulder burned and she was grateful she hadn't met the wall with her teeth first. The sharp slice of pain seared down her arm and right through to her baby finger in a tingling, numbing sensation.

"Goddammit," she spat. There was no light at all, no casement windows, no leaking from the other room. Complete and utter darkness.

She shut her eyes and it was the same.

What was she going to do?

She heard barking. It must be Pilar.

But of course, she had had the wise idea of locking her only hope in her crate two stories up.

That was just brilliant.

Even that creepy Buddy wouldn't hear her down here if he was skulking around the yard.

In the dark, no one can hear you scream, she taunted to herself.

Her shoulder throbbed. Every pulse of her heart sent a new nerve screaming. She must have really whapped that wall but good.

She didn't even want to think about what beetles there might be crawling along this floor.

"Help!" she called out. But only once. It was pointless to scream right now. No one would hear her. And Tony wouldn't be home for a long, long time.

In the darkness, mist hovered. The floating shapes that were so familiar in the other room were in here now. She could make out hands with long fingers, reaching toward her. She pulled back in fear. The hand caressed her shoulder and she felt warmth ebbing through her. The cloud was closer and in its shifting form she could almost make out the face of a young girl, and just as quickly it was lost. Another hand morphed into view and stroked her hair, losing shape almost as soon as it touched her. Hands ran along her body lovingly and her fear was soon lost in their gentle touches.

She writhed against them, as they ran along her breasts, down her belly, between her legs. The touching was warm and erotic and she was aroused. The hair on her neck and arms stood on end, yet soon she was lost in the pleasure.

She moaned, pushing herself against the unseen hands, so many of them now, stroking her, every inch of her body warmly touched.

She gasped.

The door creaked open again. Light spilled in and she had to close her eyes against the intrusion. She didn't want to leave.

But she didn't know if the door would be slamming shut again.

Lydia clumsily pulled herself up, the hands now pushing her toward the door. She felt as if she were floating as she returned to the other section of the basement.

Once she was back out in the light, her legs trembled as she raced up the stairs. She kept running until she burst into the bedroom.

She stopped, blinking in disbelief.

The crate door was hanging open.

"Pilar?" Lydia called, glancing around the room.

There was no jangling of tags in response.

Maybe she hadn't clicked the latch all the way when she put her in there.

"Pilar?" Lydia called louder. Her heart raced. If Pilar had gotten out, surely she would have come to Lydia when she was in the cellar, or at least when she was running through the house like a crazy woman. She spotted the wet spot on the carpet and knelt to examine it. It wasn't pee, there wasn't enough dampness for that. There was a faint scarlet tinge to the rug. Blood?

Was Pilar hurt?

Lydia ran into the other rooms, calling her dog's name.

Her voice echoed back to her. There was no Pilar.

Lydia sat on the couch, tears drying on her face, when Tony returned from work that evening.

"Oh, my God, Lydia. What's wrong?"

"It's Pilar. She's missing."

"Missing? Are you sure?"

"I think someone must have stolen her."

"How do you know? Maybe she just ran off for a while."

"No. She was locked in the crate. And when I came back for her, the door was standing open, and she was gone."

"Someone was in here?"

"They must have been."

"And you didn't hear her barking?"

"No, I was in the basement."

"Why on earth did you have her locked up if you were here?"

"I told you how freaked out she gets when I go down there. I was just taking some boxes down. . . ." Lydia didn't even know how to explain what had transpired down there that day. Part of her didn't even want to tell him that she had found another section. Surely he knew such a section existed, he had designed the house. And if that section existed, why was it blocked off? Why had he kept it from her, and from the blueprints he had shown her?

There was something that didn't quite add up about all this and she wasn't in the mood to get into it now. Her dog was missing. And that's all she could think about.

"Did you call anyone?"

"Like who?"

"Well, the police, for instance. If there was someone in the house . . ."

"It is all so weird . . . so very weird," Lydia said and broke into tears. "I can't even explain it . . . and no, I didn't call the cops."

"Maybe she just somehow opened the gate herself. She's a very smart dog."

"Maybe. . . ."

Lydia sobbed and Tony put his arm around her.

"There, there, honey. She'll turn up. I know she will. You just wait and see."

"I hope you're right."

"Maybe I should call the cops."

"No . . . no . . . let's just wait and see," Lydia said, not wanting the police in her house. For some reason she just did not want them poking around. She wasn't sure why, but she just didn't.

"Why don't I make you some tea," Tony offered.

"Okay." Lydia sniffed. "You make some tea. . . ."

While Tony was in the other room, Lydia thought about the basement and about Pilar. Things were very strange in this house. Haunted for sure, and telling a cop about her haunted house just didn't seem like something she had the strength for right now. She hadn't even really said much to Tony, and she wasn't sure why that was, either.

Lydia dragged the large wooden contraption behind her as she made her way through the woods, toward the swimming hole. Tony had gotten this raft float thing from one of his friends who had recently built a long dock. The float was more awkward than heavy. It kept getting caught on tree stumps and rocks, and she would have to stop and jiggle it loose again before continuing on.

By the time she arrived at the swimming hole, she was sweating and exhausted.

"Time for a swim," she said, and then quickly realized there was no one to tell. Pilar was gone. Still.

She pushed the thought from her mind. She would come back. She knew she would come back. She *had* to come back . . . if she could.

How she hoped that Pilar hadn't gone running off to someone else's property. Belgians were often mistaken for wolves despite their golden coats. It was their long beautiful fur, their regal stance, their manes. She had heard stories of other Belgians being shot in the belief they were vicious animals instead of loving pets.

But she would not think of that. She couldn't think of that.

Lydia took a long thick coil of rope from the knapsack and tossed it on the ground. Then she looked out at the river. Where to put this floating thing. Well, she could always move it around if she didn't like it.

She pushed the float some more until she got it into the water. Then she flipped it sideways. She took the rope and tied one end securely to one of the metal rungs bolted into the side. To the other end, she tied the heavy anchor that Tony had brought down the day before.

She put the anchor on top of the float, then tossed her towel on top of it and pushed it out. When the water was too deep for her to stand, she swam, pushing it out even farther. She looked back at the shore. There were no trees shading the float from here. It would be a nice sunning spot.

Lydia tossed the anchor down, waiting until it hit the bottom. She wasn't in the mysterious too-deep part yet and the anchor glided a bit until it lodged against a rock or some debris at the bottom.

She tugged on the rope to make sure it was wedged good. Satisfied, she hoisted herself up onto the float.

The sun was hot on her and the wood was already heating up beneath her feet. The float was about six feet long and four feet wide. Big enough for her to sunbathe on. She spread out her beach towel and lay down on it.

She knew she should be unpacking. That damnable endless unpacking. What the hell was wrong with her? It should have taken two days, tops, to empty out those boxes. Then she could have set to work figuring out what they needed, ordering furniture, adding dashes of this and that to make it truly home. But she couldn't do it. She just couldn't do it.

She wanted to do it. She yearned to do it. She dreamed of it already done.

But the physical act of dealing with those last thirty or so boxes was almost too overwhelming to contemplate.

And she knew Tony was pissed.

The sun was delicious on her eyelids. She stared

at the pretty patterns of red and orange. Was it flesh? Was it her blood? Was it her eyes reflecting into her skin somehow? She didn't know, she just knew that there were no boxes here out in the middle of the lake.

And where there were no boxes, there was no basement.

No basement where those poor girls still stayed.

Tony must have known she would look up the incident eventually. Of course she would. And he could say he didn't remember details all he wanted, but who could ever forget such a story once they heard it?

No wonder he had nightmares.

And yet . . . he had bought this house.

That was the part that she found so strange. Maybe that was the part that kept her from sharing her experiences in the basement with him.

Who, really, honestly, would buy the home of serial killers, child molesters, sex torturers, no matter how cheap?

No one had in twenty years.

No one . . . despite this lovely piece of property, this wonderful swimming hole, the woods that led to that walking bridge and the field beyond. On a cooler day she would explore that field.

What tied him to this place?

She realized that even though they had been together for a few years now, she really didn't know him.

She didn't know where he went when his eyes were far away.

She didn't know what he had seen that day the bulldozers came.

She didn't know why the basement was half a basement.

She knew what he would say if she asked. He would say too many horrible things had happened in the house and that he only had the most minimal basement he could get away with.

Of course he would say that, what other explanation could there be?

Yes, indeed, what other explanation could there be?

Lydia concentrated on the dancing dots behind her eyelids again. She didn't want to think bad things about the man she loved.

This was a happy time, even if her dream house was turning out to be haunted.

A dog barked in the distance. Lydia's eyes snapped open, the sun blinding her for a moment. She sat up, looking toward the woods.

Nothing.

She sighed.

There were tons of dogs. Why would it be Pilar?

She looked expectantly toward the swimming

hole, hoping to see the mahogany-furred dog sitting there, but of course, she wasn't.

Sadly, she jumped back into the water. It was cold now that she had been sweating in the sun so long.

She swam with long lazy strokes back to shore, and made her way back up the hill to face the daunting endless task of unpacking.

When she arrived back up at the house, she gathered up all her strength and marched down into the basement, flashlight in hand. She pushed the secret wall and it sprang open. Waving her flashlight around, she illuminated each brick, inch by inch. They were here, playing around her, teasing her hair, sliding between her legs, stroking her goose-pimpled flesh. After a few moments, she realized they were pushing her, pulling her toward the other end of the basement. Their urgency filled her, dread, apprehension, yet she was powerless to resist their efforts.

She was standing at the far wall now, and they took her hands, forcing her to push.

"All right. I hear you," Lydia said, trying to swipe them away like annoying flies. She pressed her hands against the wall and wasn't surprised at all when it slowly creaked open. The flashlight lit up the space behind the false wall.

"Oh, my God . . . " she said.

There was a tunnel, at least it seemed to be a tunnel. The flashlight beam didn't go far enough to tell. Glints of white refracted off the dancing beam as she waved it back and forth to see exactly what this was all about.

The ghosts were encouraging her to keep moving, to dare to go into this tunnel. She didn't want to, but then again, did she really have a choice? She had come this far, and who knows, maybe the next time she looked for this place, it wouldn't be there.

She stepped into the tunnel with great trepidation. The temperature must have dropped ten degrees in the space of one footstep. Cool musty air filled her lungs, the smell of centuries of rot and decay permeated her senses. As she cautiously stepped down the tunnel, checking for beetles and bats, puddles and God knows what else, she could feel them with her, encouraging her to go on.

The sides of the tunnels glimmered every now and again. After a few minutes of painstakingly slow walking, with a fear so great she swore her heart was going to explode, she realized that there were decorations on the walls. She illuminated the patch she stood beside. It was like a maze of bones, pressed into the dirt and rock of the tunnel. Little designs of bones, patterning along the sides as far as she could see. Bones of all sizes, bones from animals and birds, and then, a human skull.

She dropped the flashlight in shock. It smashed to the floor and the light went out.

"No!" she cried, as she fell to her hands and knees. Why the hell was she so damn clumsy? And why was she always so startled when she should be used to all this weirdness by now?

Did Tony know about this tunnel?

He must. He did the floor plans. He said he had inspected every inch.

And just what the hell *was* this tunnel?

She hit the flashlight a couple of times with the heel of her hand and it snapped back on again. She stared at the human skull grinning at her.

She did not want to go any farther. She did not want to know what lay just beyond the next bend. If this place was never to be found again, she wasn't sure she would be sorry.

Chapter Eleven

Lydia stared out the smudgy window, her Styrofoam cup of coffee untouched in her hand, watching the trees whip by.

Beside her, Tony clicked away on his laptop. She looked over at him, his glasses perched on his nose.

She sighed and took a notepad from her pocket. Her mind swam with so many images. The dog, the basement, the dreams, the ghosts.

As her mind drifted, her pen doodled images along the page. She barely noticed what she was drawing as her hand moved back and forth, and round and round. The sound of Tony's clicking stopped and she flushed as she realized he was watching her.

"What is that?" he asked.

"This?" Lydia stared down at her paper, startled to see what she had drawn. Part of the catacombs, Pilar's head, flames and ethereal creatures floated on the page. She was no artist but the renderings were true.

Tony frowned, scratching his chin thoughtfully.

"Does this look familiar to you?" she asked.

Tony shook his head and shrugged. "Kind of reminds me of that catacombs place . . . where is that? Mexico?"

"I guess there are millions all over the world," Lydia said, tapping her pen nervously on the paper. Tony turned his attention back to his spreadsheets and started clicking again.

"Do you ever wonder . . . ?" Lydia asked, after a moment.

"Wonder what?"

"How they died?"

The question hung in the air.

"Huh?" Tony asked.

"You know, Debbie and Donald."

Tony stopped working again and looked at her quizzically. "Been reading up on it, huh?"

"A little. How come you told me they were executed instead of found mysteriously dead in their solitary prison cells, hundreds of miles apart?"

"It's a horrible enough story without all that

weirdness thrown in . . . I mean really . . . how would you ever explain that?"

"They never did explain it. Not even the cause of death."

"Didn't they say heart attacks? Some theory that first one died, then the other heard and that one died too?"

"I thought that was a bullshit story the minute I heard it and so it would seem that it is."

"What do you think happened then, Miss Marple?"

"I don't know the case as well as you. I was curious about your theory. You were there. . . ."

"Hmmmm." Tony looked off into the distance, his blue eyes clouding over as he turned a variety of thoughts over in his mind. At last, he looked at her.

"Well, I always wondered if they didn't have some weird secret pact. Took cyanide pills or something like that."

"Interesting . . . but how would they have smuggled those into prison? They would have been searched a million times for such stuff."

"Maybe, maybe not. Maybe whoever searched them would rather see them dead. After all, it would save the taxpayers millions."

"That would be one hell of a conspiracy. They would have to fool or coerce more than one set of guards at two different maximum-security prisons. Or somehow, someone snuck in and got it to them."

"So, then, what do *you* think happened?" Tony asked.

"Are they really dead?"

Were they ever really alive . . . ?

"Of course they are dead. And they are buried and that is that. It's over and has been for a very long time."

"Is it?"

"Lydia . . . what is wrong with you?" Tony asked, searching his wife's face. Lydia turned away, unable to vocalize what she wanted to say. Afraid of what can of worms she would be opening next.

They parted ways with a perfunctory kiss and Lydia walked the few blocks to her office.

How she had missed New York. It felt as if she had been away forever. She went into a Starbucks and bought herself a real coffee, a large mochachino with enough caffeine and calories to make her feel truly alive.

She didn't even mind the people jostling against her as she sipped on her scalding drink. The only thing she missed was Pilar walking regally on guard by her side.

She breathed in the smells of traffic, food, dust, dirt, sweat . . . yes, she was in her beloved city once more.

The security guard was happy to see her as she signed in. "Missed you around here." He grinned.

"I missed all of you as well," Lydia said.

"Where's Pilar?" the security guard asked, looking at her legs. Lydia's face dropped.

"She's missing. Don't know if she took off or was stolen. Either way, it really sucks."

"Sorry to hear that. Hopefully she'll turn up."

"Yes, hopefully." Lydia nodded and hurried toward the elevator that was spewing out rushing people.

She watched the buttons light the way to her office. It seemed so surreal to be around all these people, all the murmurings and buzzings of people and electricity. She stepped from the elevator and took a moment to get her bearings in the hallway. The lights flickered and hummed down at her. She felt as if they were quivering through the finest of hairs on her arms.

It felt as if she had been away a lifetime. She had left this place, not that long ago, to move into her new home. . . . Now that she was back, it was as if she had never been here at all.

Her feet led her automatically to her office, but even as she entered and closed the door, the room did not feel familiar. This was someone else's place from another time.

After she hung her coat on the stand, she approached her desk and stared at the neatly stacked files. Files that needed to be opened and read and dealt with. A photo of Tony, Pilar and herself graced the corner. She picked it up, stroking the silver frame.

"Oh, Pilar. . . ." She sighed. "Why did you leave me?"

She touched the dog's face, then looked at the picture of herself and Tony. They were smiling. It had been a fun day, that day. They had gone for a picnic a couple of months ago and asked a stranger to snap the photo. She stroked Tony's face. His eyes stared out at her. So blue and vibrant. So alive and happy. Yet, even there, she could now see a veil of mystery.

What was the mystery?

She sighed, tears welling up in her eyes.

There was a knock at the door, startling her from her reverie. She put the picture down and, wiping her eyes, let in her assistant Miriam.

"Lydia, I'm so happy to see you back." She smiled, her hand clutching yet another folder.

"I'm glad to be back."

"How is the new house working out?"

"Fine. A lot of work, moving. I never thought it would be so hard."

"It must be very pretty there."

"It is. So unlike the city." Lydia looked at the folder in Miriam's hand. "What do you have there?"

"A new account. I started it while you were gone, but of course, you really need to look at it."

"Of course. I'm sure you did a fine job while I was gone. You're the best." Lydia smiled.

"I tried," Miriam said.

"Well, show me what you have and let's get this show on the road."

The women sat down and Lydia reentered the rat race.

She was running through a bright green field. Pilar bounded and barked beside her. It was so sunny and warm out. She felt she could run forever.

She came to a cave. Pilar ran in first, sniffing around, tail wagging happily. This cave must be safe, Pilar would have told her if it wasn't.

The cave was dark and she clicked on the flashlight that was suddenly in her hand. All around her were primitive drawings on the cave walls. Drawing made with paint and chalk. Drawings of little stick people doing little stick people things. Somewhere a baby was wailing.

The cave was hot, the air was too thick. Although the entrance was right there, she couldn't get out. It was too small in here. The walls touched her, spongy, sticky, shrinking in closer until she was like a bug in a bowl of jelly. She couldn't breathe air anymore, just sucked in mud and dirt.

She vomited.

Lydia sat up quickly as vomit flew out of her mouth, spraying the bed.

Tony burst awake as she heaved again. "Oh, my God."

He tried to pull her from the bed and she puked again, this time on the rug.

By the time he got her to the bathroom, she was dry-heaving. He drew water over a washcloth and patted her brow with it.

"Lydia, are you all right?"

"Oh, my God . . ."

Lydia stared down at her soiled nightgown in disgust. She retched again, this time diving for the toilet, but nothing came up. She was spent.

Nausea roiled and rumbled through her, she was hot and cold at the same time.

"What is wrong with me . . . maybe I have the flu or something?"

Tony wiped her mouth and pushed back her hair. "You poor thing."

"I had the most horrible dream. A cave, and it was too small, and the baby was crying and crying and wouldn't stop but I couldn't find it."

Tony lifted her nightgown over her head, trying not to smear the mess any more than he had to.

He rinsed the washcloth and wiped her again, dabbing at her chest and belly.

He looked at her nipples. They appeared darker and more swollen than he had ever seen them. He stared at her belly, usually so flat and taut but now perceptibly swollen.

He put his hand on her tummy.

"Lydia . . . " he said, softly. "I think you might be pregnant."

Lydia stared at him with large dark eyes. Suddenly she grinned.

"Of course, that's it. I bet I am."

She started to laugh. "That's all. I'm not crazy or sick. I'm just pregnant."

Tony wrapped his arms around her. "We're going to have a baby!"

The constant hammering was getting on her nerves and she hoped they wouldn't turn the power off while she was on the Internet. How quickly Tony had started the second phase on their house. It was as if the minute she found out she was pregnant, it had given him permission to proceed with more construction.

He wanted it done quickly, so even though it was Saturday morning, here they were, hammering and sawing away at the extension. She wished she could be as excited about the building as he was, but she had more things on her mind.

There was yet another girl missing from the town. A pattern that eerily echoed events from years gone by.

Lydia craved a cigarette, but she restrained herself. It wouldn't be good for the baby.

She scrolled down the news articles, she had seen them so many times now. The whole idea of Debbie being an abused wife, coerced into torturing and raping the victims, even her own sister, just did not ring true to Lydia. Maybe she had been Svengalied, lured to the darkness for some other reasons. After all, this had gone on for many months, surely the woman would have been able to escape or tell or something. She had family nearby and many friends, which was more than Lydia had, it seemed, sometimes. She felt that Debbie had to have been the most coldhearted murderer, worse than her husband even.

Yet, she testified against her own husband. The whole idea seemed ludicrous, yet who was she to question it? The proof had been there all along.

What was there to testify about? Even now, the house ached with sorrow, even up here in this office. It seeped up from the floors, ebbed through the walls, and this wasn't even the original building. She couldn't imagine how horrible it must have been before the house was destroyed.

How many were missing now?

How many were missing then?

On a hunch, she checked the newspapers back even further, another twenty years.

She was not surprised to discover another series of disappearances. Another round of abuse and torture, by a husband-and-wife team. There wasn't as much information on this case, apparently there were more important things going on in the world at that time, than to worry about a tiny farming town and missing people. Troubled teens and single mothers. Society's castoffs.

Lydia leaned back in her chair, craving a cigarette even more than ever. She thought about this town forty years ago, more than forty years ago. What had caused the cycles?

She stood up and paced. Crazy husband and wife teams. Maybe the first case imitated the second case?

They had thought it sounded cool and copycatted?

But why?

Surely they would have known they would be caught.

She wanted to know, to ask the killers what they were possibly thinking while torturing those people. Why *this* town?

She didn't dare look any further back in history today. The constant noise of the construction was giving her a major headache. Tony wouldn't be home for hours, as usual. The more successful he got, the less he was home.

Lydia grabbed her purse and left the house.

Lydia drove along the back roads, staring at the fields and woods, the rolling hills in the distance. Such a pretty part of the country, yet she found no comfort in its beauty. All she could see were the faces of all those people, missing and dead, staring out at her from the Internet. Faces that depleted the town's population, yet, the town itself was strangely silent on it.

Well, what did she expect?

Hysteria and panic from every eye? Freaked-out children and psychotic store clerks? New York had tons of missing and murdered people and life went on. Why shouldn't it here?

Lydia pulled up the long narrow dirt road. The car creeped along until she was in front of the wrought-iron gates. She slid out of the car and tried the gate. It wasn't locked. She flipped the latch and let herself in.

The graveyard was very old, and run down. Crumbling headstones and pockmarked angels stared at her as she waded among the thigh-high weeds. No one came here. This was not the graveyard of the rich, or the loved.

This was a graveyard where people were best forgotten.

She had never been here before, but Tony had pointed it out to her a couple of times when they had driven past it.

On one of the cult pages dedicated to Donald and Debbie, there had been a map of the graveyard.

Bees and flies swarmed about her head, humming in that annoying heat-induced fever pitch. Overgrown grasses scratched at her, as she wandered through the markers, glancing now and again at names crumbling and forgotten.

Despite the rumor that this was a paupers' graveyard, a place no one cared about, there were some exquisite stones, lovingly carved, with pictures of children on them. There were little stone angels, broken and blind, and matching stones of husbands and wives.

The faded, peeling paneling of the church that bordered this place of rest and the sagging roof confirmed the abandonment of those that rested here.

Once Donald and Debbie had been buried here, superstitions abounded and business moved to the newer, larger church on the other side of town.

That was fine by Lydia. That meant no weddings, no funerals to dodge.

The grass was musky in her nose, dirt and rot the only perfume with the odd whiff of wildflowers.

At last she found it.

Amazing that it was in as good a shape as it was. Amazing that they hadn't been unearthed and scattered by an angry mob. Maybe the fear was prominent even in death.

The stones were destroyed, broken beyond recognition. No grass grew where they lay. A small mountain of religious icons, crosses, rosaries, holy water, little Marys, was piled on the dirt. Water-damaged pictures of victims in little frames stood sentinel over their killers.

The air grew thicker as Lydia stood at their feet, staring down at the earth.

"Who are you?" she asked them. "What was your purpose? What did it all mean? Did you really think you wouldn't get caught?"

A wave of sadness rushed across her as she looked at the eyes of the young girl in the frame. She walked over and knelt beside the artifacts. Trembling, she picked up the picture of the teenager, one of many victims. She closed her eyes, wondering what it had been like. To be abducted, or coerced, or lured to such a fate. What had they done to this child?

She thought of the shackle-ring marks still in the basement, the energy of despair that seemed to cripple her every time she set foot down there. Whether the ghosts were real or in her mind did not matter. The pain of this evil, these unspeakable acts, was trapped in the walls, in the soil and now trapped in her.

"How can I make it better?" she asked the girl, carefully setting the picture down. She picked up another picture, another teenager, blue eyed and fair haired. A cheerleader type. Perky and pretty on this photo day, but just a mountain of sliced-up flesh by the end. She tried to imagine the hooks through her back, how this petite, pretty thing had been hung like a slab of meat, and carved up until they could only recognize her by her dental records.

Lydia put the picture down, tears streaming down her face.

How could she live there? How could Tony have built this place on top? Was it really the cheap price, a foot in the door of his hometown? They were rich now, they didn't need any bargains. But he was in love with the house, the house he had dreamed and designed.

But was there more?

Had he been drawn to the horror for some reason? The myth of the evil that dwelled there, some macho instinct proving he could conquer the rumors?

After all, the past was past.

A house itself was not evil. The ground was not evil. Even the energy left behind was not evil.

She rubbed her hand along her belly.

There must be ways to turn the house into a happy house. A home where she could raise her baby without fear of the basement, fear of the past coming back to haunt them somehow.

She stared at the twin bare dirt mounds where no grass grew. Even grass did not want to take hold in such evil.

With every ounce of courage she thought she might have in her body, she reached down to the grave of Donald. She touched it, closing her eyes, expecting a surge of evil to sizzle up her arm.

She saw his face. The face from newspaper clippings. That handsome chiseled face with the piercing, beckoning eyes. His blond hair tousled, hanging boyishly over his forehead. She could see why his wife would do anything he asked. His charisma embraced her even in death.

She saw him smile, holding his hand out, his lovely wife taking it as they walked up the stairs of the little church on their wedding day. She knew it was a memory from old news footage but she watched the vision unfold behind her eyes, wondering if she would see something new.

The ground trembled and a darkness swept across their faces. They gazed up to the sky, their faces frozen in horror, eyes dark with fright. Then a ray of light broke through, illuminating them, and their smiles shifted from fresh-faced bliss to secret cynicism. Lydia shuddered and felt the ground rumbling again.

She opened her eyes, and pushed herself back from the graves.

Prepared for the worst, she was surprised and relieved to realize that the rumbling was only from the trucks on the road passing through the town.

She returned to her vigil, running her hands through the dirt of the graves. It was so loose, no wonder no grass had taken hold.

It must have been recently raked. Maybe there had been some horrible things there, something burned or an animal sacrificed.

She looked around the graveyard.

Who was she kidding? No one ever tended to this place. She bet that even the parents of Debbie and Donald never bothered coming by. She wondered if she would. If her child turned out to be the epitome of evil, would she still visit the grave?

She rubbed her tummy. Her baby. What would he or she be like? What would being a mother be like? What would giving birth be like? She didn't want to think about the birth part. Maybe she could get them to just knock her out and cut the baby out without her having to deal with it.

She stayed by the graves a few minutes longer, but nothing else came to her. At last, she stood and walked slowly back to the car.

Chapter Twelve

Tony and Lydia were watching the news, eating their dinner on TV trays in the living room. That reporter, Connie Bellows, was covering yet another disappearance of a local citizen.

The phone rang, startling them. Tony answered it and as he talked, his face grew pale. Lydia watched him expectantly.

He hung up, his hands trembling so badly he missed the receiver. He fumbled for the phone again and rested it in its cradle.

"Oh, my God," he said, his voice so quiet she could hardly hear him.

"What is it?"

"There's been an accident." His eyes glistened,

and he blinked rapidly to keep the tears from falling.

"Where? Who?"

"My parents . . ."

His face was ashen as he sank into the couch.

"We have to go to the hospital right away," he moaned.

"What happened?"

"I'm not sure . . . something about a car crash." He sat up suddenly and then ran for the door. Lydia followed.

Lydia scrutinized Sybil and Walter sleeping in hospital beds. The white of the room was so glaring and the stench of antiseptic made her tummy rumble.

"I don't understand. How did this happen?" she asked. As much as she had her differences with Sybil, she never meant her any harm. The woman wrapped in bandages was so small, so helpless. Lydia looked over at Walter, also wrapped up mummy tight. Blood seeped through from a head wound. Both of them had blackened eyes.

"This is unbelievable," Tony said softly. He stared at his parents as if he were having a bad dream. He walked over to his mother and stroked her hand.

"Mom?" he said quietly. "Mom. Can you hear me?"

"They are both unconscious still," a nurse said as she entered the room. She looked at Tony and Lydia and shook her head.

"It's so sad . . . I hate seeing things like this. I feel for you both."

"Thank you," Lydia said.

"They will be able to stay together," Tony said.

"For now, yes. I see you have requested it here on the chart."

"It is important they stay together," Tony stated firmly. Lydia saw that his mouth trembled as he spoke, his eyes glistened with tears.

"Yes, sir."

"What is the prognosis?"

"You have to wait for the doctor for that. I am not at liberty to discuss anything like that with you right now."

"We understand," Lydia said.

"I will let the doctor know you are here," the nurse said as she left the room.

"Thank you," Lydia said.

She watched Tony, hovering over his mother.

"Mom . . . " he said softly.

There was no response except the constant whooshing of the oxygen. She could see Tony trying to keep it together. The poor man was shaking.

She patted him on the arm, and he winced.

"Tony . . . I'm so sorry," she said.

"So am I. . . ."

The doctor entered the room. Nervously, the couple watched as he looked over the patients and consulted the clipboards at the ends of their beds.

He shook his head. "Car crash . . . boy. Lucky they had their seat belts on."

"How does the situation look?" Tony asked.

"It's too soon to really tell. They are lucky to be alive. We'll know more by morning." The doctor continued to read the notes.

"Is there anything we can do for them?" Lydia asked.

The doctor looked at her with dark eyes that seemed oddly void of compassion.

"You should go home and get some rest. They'll need you more tomorrow," he suggested. With that, he put the clipboards back and left the room.

Lydia stared after him.

"Boy, nice bedside manner," she said.

"Yeah . . . " Tony said disinterestedly. He walked over to the window and stared out at the moon. Lydia tried to put her arm around him but he brushed her away.

"Why don't you go home? I'm going to stay here a while," he said.

"Leave you here?"

"It's okay. I'll call a cab or something," Tony said.

Lydia studied his face, but he was far away again. She wished she could break through to him somehow. Sighing, she turned and headed for the door.

"All right, honey. If you need anything, call me," she said.

Tony continued to stare out the window as she left.

Lydia navigated the dark narrow roads, her mind racing. The shock of seeing her in-laws laid up like that really threw her. It seemed like one more thing in a growing mountain of "things."

Things that stirred uneasiness in her bones.

The moon was bright, a glowing orb, a telescope for some giant being to study the weird rituals of the tiny, inane human race. How insignificant she was in the scheme of things. Her life, her dog, her family . . . the baby growing inside of her. They meant nothing. Just another little human eking out that time between birth and death. Filling it with pockets of mystery and excitement, of boredom, of possessions.

Each little life grinding along. Her in-laws grinding through theirs, now faced with new hurdles, new hoops to jump through, as if learning the dance all these years wasn't enough. As if eking out a living, raising children, making coffee in the morning, doing the laundry and shoveling the snow weren't enough to fill the hours. Now they were facing days, weeks, months with plastic tubes snaking through their flesh, every breath a reminder of an ache that hadn't been there before, every step a painful reminder of a moment's inattention, a moment's . . .

What had happened?

What had really happened?

Freak accident . . .

But what did that mean?

Was Sybil nagging at Walter about something and he turned to retaliate and lost control?

Was a car driving toward them, the headlights too bright, blinding him momentarily?

Was he dreaming of a happier time, when he was young and handsome, a single man on the brink of adulthood, a whole future to fill?

Was Sybil reaching her hand over to his lap, stroking his thigh, worming her fingers through his pants as Lydia so often did to Tony?

The last image made her cringe, though she knew it shouldn't.

The idea of Sybil sharing warmth of any kind, with anyone ever, just seemed ludicrous. Yet there was something there. Of course there was something there. That is why they were married, stayed married, had the affection of Tony and each other.

She was nearly home now, right by the field on the other side of the woods that framed her house.

She swerved as an animal ran out into the middle of the road. Eyes glowed in the headlights and she slammed on the brakes. The ghostly figure of a dog stood staring at her.

"Pilar?"

She opened the door and the dog ran off into the brush.

"Pilar?"

Her heart slammed against her chest as she ran from the car following the animal. It looked like Pilar, kind of. Or like the essence of Pilar. Whatever it was, she could still see it ahead of her, could hear it crashing through the weeds and bushes. She ran, trying to keep it in sight.

It bounded along, slowing now and again, as if urging her to follow.

The dog ran into a cave and Lydia ran after it.

She didn't notice the hieroglyphics on the walls, nor the recently used fire. She ran past the first chamber and down a narrow tunnel that sloped downward, growing more and more narrow as it twisted and turned, burrowing into the earth.

The cave suddenly branched into two narrow paths. She wasn't sure which one to take, and the sudden realization of where she was started to take hold.

The dim moonlight couldn't reach any farther and the thought of continuing on blindly frightened her. She stood paralyzed, the pounding of her heart invading her ears.

As she caught her breath, she grew aware of a noise over the thumping of her heart.

Voices.

She crept along quietly, wondering who would be talking down here in the dark.

Her only guide now was her hearing. She kept one hand against the wall, the other reaching out in front of her, trying not to consider the bats and bugs that surely lived here.

She reached a wall. She ran her hand along it, feeling that it was not the mud and dirt of the cave, but a doorway. As she groped farther, she realized there were no more paths. This was the end.

The voices were coming from the other side.

She pressed her ear against it, trying to hear what was being said.

Voices were raised in anger. Men arguing and complaining but she could not make out about what. The bass sounds were muffled just enough that she could hear tones but not actual words.

After a few minutes, the voices dropped down again. No matter how hard she strained, she could not decipher a single clue. Hell, they might not be even talking in English.

Then, the voices boomed once more. More fighting. They must have moved closer to where she was.

Now there were just snatches of words, but not enough for her to truly understand what the arguing entailed. There was one voice, though. One voice, nearly right by her ear, that rang familiar. Then as the other voices drew closer to the door, she realized that they too had a familiar resonance.

But from where?

"It just isn't right," a voice said loudly.

A cold sweat broke out on Lydia's forehead.

She knew that voice.

It couldn't be. No, it just could not be.

They were so close to the door now that she realized they were going to be coming through.

And what if they found her here?

"The time is near. You will see . . . " another voice said.

Lydia had had enough. She ran back through the winding tunnels, panic urging her on. Whoever was there, she couldn't afford to get caught. She didn't want to think about it.

She burst out of the cave, panting in the moonlight.

In her anxiety to follow the dog, she hadn't realized just how far the car was. And now she had to walk back from the cave to the road, in this creepy, unfamiliar terrain.

Where there were lost dogs and strange voices . . .

Where people mysteriously disappeared every twenty years.

And it was happening again.

She ran as fast as she could, blindly tearing across the field, thinking about monsters and slasher movies. Praying that she wasn't going to become yet another statistic.

It seemed like forever before she got to the car. And even longer as she fumbled with the car keys, shaking fingers neurotically missing the lock.

At last, she was safely inside with locked doors, motor humming.

She gunned the engine and sped toward home.

When she arrived home, Tony was sitting in the living room, looking tired and disheveled. He was fragile and drawn and there was a strange smell emanating from him. Not a hospital smell, but something else, something . . . darker.

"Tony . . . " Lydia said, sinking down beside him on the couch. He was staring into the fireplace and didn't turn to look at her when she spoke.

"It's going to be all right, Tony," Lydia said, putting her hand over his. She kissed his cheek.

"You smell . . . musky," she said.

"What do you mean?"

Lydia wrinkled her nose. "Like incense or damp or something."

"I do?" Tony sniffed at his shirt.

"Never mind. . . ." Lydia stared at him, trying to penetrate that armor.

"How were they when you left?" she asked.

Tony sighed. "The same. I'll go back in the morning, I guess. Maybe one of them will be awake and can tell us what happened."

"Yeah. Boy, it must have been so scary. . . ."

"I really don't feel like talking about it right now," Tony said.

Lydia nodded, resting her head on his arm. He was so tense.

But it was to be expected. She couldn't even imagine how she would feel if she had seen her own parents laid up like that.

They sat in silence for a while, both deep in their own thoughts. Outside, distant thunder rumbled.

"I thought I saw Pilar on the way home," Lydia finally said.

"Really?"

"I nearly ran her over. I called her . . . but she wouldn't come. She took off."

Tony patted her leg. She could tell he was trying to bring his mind back from wherever it had wandered, back to her.

"Oh, I'm sorry, honey. Maybe she's confused," he said softly.

"Or hurt . . . she didn't . . . look right. . . ."

"How do you mean?"

"I—I can't explain. . . ."

Lydia stood up. She wandered around the room, touching a figurine, moving a book, adjusting the pictures on the mantelpiece. At last, she stood still and looked at Tony.

"Tony?. . . ."

"What?"

"Don't you think it is odd . . . ?"

"What?" Tony furrowed his eyebrows.

"Everything," she said, waving her arms. "All of it. . . ."

"Huh?"

Lydia took a deep breath, not even sure she wanted to go down this path, but here she was, one step down that yellow brick road already.

"Look around us, Tony. I may be living in a fantasy but still, I catch on eventually. There's a lot of weird stuff going on around here. A *lot* of weird stuff."

"What on earth are you talking about?"

Lydia's eyes welled up with tears. "For starters,

that creepy basement. That basement that is but a half basement, and I don't know why, and you have yet to tell me."

"Huh?"

"The basement, for God's sake. What's the deal with the basement?"

"I don't know what you mean. Jeeze, I never even go down there."

"And I wonder why that is? Could it be that you feel it too? That you know this house is haunted but don't want to admit it?"

"Haunted . . ." Tony shook his head. "You better sit down, Lydia, you're hysterical."

"Damn fucking right I'm hysterical. I've pretty much had it. I want to know right now, what is going on?"

"What is going on . . ." Tony reached his hand out to Lydia, remaining cool. "I think what is going on is that you are having a hormone surge. Maybe you are imagining things. . . ."

"You know . . . I thought at first I was. Even before I knew the history of what went on here, I felt things. But now, with Pilar gone, your parents in an accident, people missing and a basement that is not a basement . . ."

"There's only one way to deal with this," Tony said. "Take me down and show me just what the hell you are babbling on about."

Lydia dragged him down the stairs and there they stood, in the small basement. She knew *they* weren't here. She didn't think they would be. But she could show him the false wall, the other room, and he couldn't deny that.

"Here, right here is the spot," Lydia said, pressing on the wall.

Tony stood watching her. "The spot for what?" he said.

She pushed on it again, but nothing happened. "Figures . . ." She started slamming at the wall with her fists. "Open, damn you."

"Whoa, baby. You'd better just chill out," he said.

"Chill out? Is that all you can say? Chill out? Yeah, like hell I'm going to chill out. Look around you. Does this look like the proper size basement for a house? Why is there a false wall? Why . . . ?"

Tony gave a little half smile. "You don't want to be looking at furnaces and pipes and all that shit, do you?"

"I don't really care. I just don't understand."

Tony took her hand but she snatched it away.

"Come on now, Lydia, you are in shock. Overtired, in shock and raging from hormones. Let's get you up to bed."

Lydia looked at the face of the man before her. There was no warmth in it, no concern, just a veiled layer of moderate interest. Interest, no doubt, in getting her to shut up and leave him alone.

She wanted to punch him, to kick and scream, to throttle the truth out of those lying eyes, but there was an air in his countenance that chilled her. So she choked down the rest of her rage, and silently marched herself to bed.

Lydia watched the little red sports car zooming toward her. It was a warm day, like spring really, with the scent of musky grass pungent in her nose. The clouds swirled above her, a gray mass rolling and turning slowly like a beast lumbering across the sky. Where the clouds parted, slashes of sunlight flowed through, illuminating stones on the road.

The trees swayed, bending in the growing wind, their leaves rustling with a noise so loud it made her ears hurt.

And the little red car continued to come toward her.

She looked over to the lake, a swelling mirror rippling, shards of sunlight bouncing up to the sky like breaking glass. Shadows moved along the shore, four-legged creatures running but seemingly not making progress.

Much like the car that continued to approach, but still hadn't arrived.

Among the leaves, she could hear buzzing. At first, she thought it was a hive of angry bees. Then the sound shifted and seemed to be of a cat screaming in distress.

Still the car hadn't arrived, yet she knew she must wait for it. She didn't know why. She just knew that she was supposed to stand here and wait for the little red car while the clouds whirled and swirled above her, the lake glittered and the sound of rustling leaves and hitching protests of an infant grew louder.

She touched her belly but it wasn't swollen, it was flat, and she panicked for a moment, wondering when she had lost the child. But her child wasn't lost, he was screaming from his cradle way up high, where rockaby baby would be safe in the treetops.

At last the car was here and it pulled to a stop beside her. Smiling from the convertible were two beautiful blond people in sunglasses and big toothy grins. The woman wore a red kerchief, to keep her hair from flying.

"Are you coming?" the woman asked, opening the door. Lydia saw her little halter top and white shorts, a tiny woman, very lovely to behold.

"Do you think I should?" Lydia asked.

"Of course." The woman grinned. "We came all this way for you."

"I know, I just wasn't sure if you really wanted me."

"Oh, we want you," the man with short blond curly hair said. He lowered his glasses, and peered over the rims at Lydia, raising his dark eyebrows. "You are, after all, part of the plan."

"What plan?" Lydia asked.

The woman giggled. The sound was very child-like, it didn't even seem to be coming from her lips. Lydia realized that the baby had stopped crying, that the leaves had stopped rustling. Even the lake had stopped glimmering.

"The plan for fun, of course," the woman said, reaching her long pale hands toward Lydia. Lydia saw that her nails matched the car. How did she do that, make her nail polish match the car like that? How did she find the time to grow them so long and file them so perfectly? Long perfect claws reaching out toward her.

Lydia took the woman's hand. It was cold, but the wind was blowing stronger, so of course the woman would be cold. She was riding in a convertible with only shorts and a halter top.

"Squeeze in, honey," the woman said, and shifted to the middle of the tiny car. Lydia squeezed in and shut the door.

They sped along the highway, trees whipping by,

yet they never seemed to actually progress. The distant landscape never got closer.

"I know you," Lydia said suddenly, not even sure where the words had popped out from.

"Of course you do," the woman said, stroking her arm. "You wouldn't get into a car with strangers, now, would you?"

"I know you," Lydia said, turning and studying their blond hair, their strong chins, their strangely California looks, although this was about as far from California as one could be, without living in Maine.

"Of course you do." The man laughed. "After all, we are famous."

"More famous than Bonnie and Clyde." The woman giggled.

"No, we aren't that famous . . . yet," the man corrected. "History will tell. Time will tell. After all, time is on our side." He started to sing.

"We will outdo Bonnie and Clyde," the woman said sharply.

"Bonnie and Clyde were bank robbers. I don't think you are bank robbers," Lydia said.

"That's all there was to do back then. Now there is so much more!" The woman was aiming a small videocamera at Lydia. "Now smile pretty, you don't want the history books to see you're not having fun."

"Where are we going?" Lydia asked, as the car continued to speed along going nowhere fast.

"Going on a picnic . . . leaving right away . . ." The man sang the old children's rhyme, chanting it as the wind snatched away the words as fast as they sprang to his lips.

"Maybe I need to go somewhere else," Lydia said, jiggling the door handle, wondering if she could possibly jump from the car without killing herself. But why did she suddenly want to leave? She had known them when she got into the car. She had known them and the path of destruction they were carving out for themselves. No, she was supposed to be along for the ride. She had a reason, though she couldn't think of what it was now. She had a reason, yet it eluded her mind, had slipped away like a soap bar from wet fingers. There was a reason she had delivered herself unto this couple. Her hand patted her belly, now swollen again. But she couldn't think of what the reason had been.

"We are here!" The man grinned as he stopped the car.

Lydia looked around. They were back where she had started. In the middle of nowhere, with the rolling gray clouds and the glittering lake. She opened the car door and was sucked into a vortex.

She spun and whirled, tumbling head over heels,

wondering if this was how Alice felt falling down that rabbit hole.

At last her body was still, but she was not standing. She wasn't exactly lying down either.

She was floating. Somehow.

How could this be?

She stared down at the ground. It must be raining, for droplets of rain were beating down to the distant floor.

Her back hurt. She felt her shoulders, her back, her butt, all burned as if a bunch of wasps had crawled under her skin and were pricking her ceaselessly. She tried to move her hand to scratch at it, but they were chained, Christ-like, as she floated like some weird human airplane. Every time she moved her hand, her back would hurt more. She couldn't figure it out.

She screamed but she couldn't scream. There was something in her mouth, hard and rubbery, preventing her from saying a word.

The more she moved, the worse the pain was, so she tried to relax.

She watched the ground swirl and shift below her. It wasn't the ground swirling, though, it was her rocking, swinging back and forth, on the chains that held her. She saw the chains looping through her hands, right through her palms, and she wondered why they didn't hurt. No doubt because the pain in her back was far worse. She saw the chains loop around and up, but couldn't turn her head far enough to determine where up was, what there was to see. Her neck ached with the sheer weight of her head. How much did her head weigh? she wondered. She thought about some weird show she used to watch, *Kids in the Hall*, and of some annoying little boy character that would chatter on about useless facts and how he went to a butcher's shop one day and prattled on about his head and how much it would weigh.

She saw beneath her, a little dark-haired boy walking slowly, carefully. She wondered who he was. If he was afraid. Did he know why he was here?

He looked up at her with wide-eyed wonder. She wanted to scream, to flail, but all that happened was that blood dripped onto his face, which he wiped off with his finger and stared at it.

When he looked up again, he had a grin on his face that nearly stopped her heart. It was a look that stirred an echo in her soul, an elusive sense of familiarity, and then it was gone.

He reached small boy hands up toward her. She cocked her head, trying to see what he was grasping. It was a small, bluish gray bundle, swinging lazily back and forth between her and the child.

Slowly, she realized what the bundle was.

Tiny arms and legs hung limply, tiny head flopping as the baby swung from its umbilical cord.

The baby.

The dead baby.

The child was trying to catch it, jumping as if it were a ball or a toy.

Lydia grew aware of the pressure between her legs, of the cramping pain throbbing there that she had been unaware of because of the pain in her back.

The baby.

The poor dead baby.

Her poor dead baby.

Her body could not take the pressure anymore and she felt him slipping, slipping away from her. With a sickening squelch, the placenta was released and the baby fell . . .

. . . falling

. . . falling to the boy's outstretched hands.

He cradled the child as there was sudden darkness.

Lydia jerked awake, her hands folded around her stomach.

The bulge was still there.

"Baby?" she whispered. "Baby, are you still there?"

She rubbed her belly, poking and prodding until at last, there was the fluttering kicking.

I'm here, Mommy.

I'm here safe and warm inside of you.

Lydia sighed with relief and turned to face Tony. His side of the bed was empty.

Lydia frowned. She peered at the clock.

Four in the morning.

Where the hell would Tony be at four in the morning?

Goddamn him and his secrets. Did he really think she didn't notice his increasingly frequent absences?

Lydia swung her legs around. Cramps snaked up from her calves to her thighs. She jiggled her thighs and the cramps surged down to her toes. She cried with the pain, the spastic nerves, watched as her feet tremored with a mind of their own.

She remembered something she had read in one of her maternity books, and with tears pouring down her cheeks, slowly pulled her legs back up to the bed, and turned around until she was walking her feet up the wall. She rubbed her thighs, trying to get the blood moving again. Her toes were splayed and she couldn't get them back together again.

"Oh, God . . . go away!" she cried. The paralysis seeped away but the burning pain remained. She stamped her feet, her head thrashing from side to side.

It is only temporary pain . . . it is only temporary pain, she chanted to herself. *Totally normal. Ligaments stretching, that's all, that's all.*

At last the cramps eased and the blood flowed normally through her veins once more. Exhausted, she fell back to sleep.

Chapter Thirteen

Snow. Why was there snow so early?

Lydia watched out the window as Tony drove the snowblower down the long driveway. The way it had come down in the night, you would think it was February, but it was still fall. She couldn't believe it. But then, the weather had been odd for years. Her whole life. She knew her parents had talked about how when they were kids, four seasons were four seasons in this part of the world. Snow in winter, relentless heat in July. In her lifetime, though, the weather had always been odd. You could see snow in May, T-shirt weather at Christmas, it seemed that weather was always a surprise, nothing you could count on.

Despite how deep the snow was, she knew it

wouldn't last. By next week, the most stubborn flowers would still be in bloom as if nothing had happened at all.

Tony was putting away the blower and she went into the kitchen to pour him a cup of coffee. She heard him come in, stamping his boots.

"Man, it's cold out there today."

"It looks like it," Lydia agreed, bringing the coffee to him. "It's going to take forever to get into the city."

"Maybe we should consider staying there for a couple of days, get a hotel. It looks pretty brutal."

"I guess we could." Lydia organized her briefcase, snapping it shut. She looked over at Tony. "You know, we won't have that kind of luxury when the baby comes. We'll have to come home every day, at least one of us."

"Lydia, we've been through this before," Tony said impatiently. "Once the baby comes, you can stay home with it."

"What if I don't want to? What if I need to work, to get out of the house . . . ?"

"You don't need to work, I'm making fantastic money now."

"But it isn't the money, we've been through that. I like my job."

"You will like being a mother," Tony said disinterestedly as he checked his briefcase, riffling papers around.

"I'm sure I will like being a mother, it's the loneliness that gets to me. We've been here a few months now and I still have no friends."

"And that is my fault?"

"I'm not saying it's your fault. I'm saying I have no friends. I can't seem to meet people."

"Maybe if you didn't act so . . ." The words hung in the air.

"So, what?" Lydia prodded.

"Well, so big city."

"Huh?"

"Well, face it. You think you are too good for most of the people in this town, and let me tell you, people like that work on instinct, from the gut. They can tell you aren't even trying."

"Tony, that's not fair. I've tried like hell to fit in."

Tony stared at her, his blue eyes glassy and cold. In that look, Lydia felt as if she had just fallen from a thousand feet. She did not know this Tony. This Tony who had grown as cold as the snow outside.

His words were still the same, yet there was something more. Something higher than the wall that had been building brick by brick between them.

"I'm not crazy, you know," Lydia said. "I have seen and felt things in this house, and I'm sure as hell not the first nor the last person on the planet to sense ghosts or spirits or any other thing like that. Believe you me. How do you think mediums stay in business?"

"Here we go again. Look, if I had known you were gonna go loopy just because of the history of the house . . ."

"Tony, think about it. Any normal person would. I don't know if anyone on the planet would feel comfortable making a home in a place of so much grief."

"I'm sorry I dragged you into it."

"Look, I'm not being ungrateful, I'm just saying what I feel. I love the way you've built this house, it's just that it isn't at peace. There must be a way to settle it. To rid the tormented ones . . ."

"Lydia, it's late. Can we talk about this in the car?"

"We don't have to talk about it at all," Lydia said as she put on her coat.

"I know this psychic . . . she's only a few blocks away," Miriam told Lydia. Lydia sipped her tea thoughtfully.

"Hang on, let me look up her number." Miriam searched through her purse.

Lydia watched her. Such a tiny girl, so pretty. So

smart. She was a good worker too. Lydia would be lost without her.

"I should have thought of this ages ago, when Pilar first went missing," Miriam said.

"Who would think of it, really? I mean, I don't think of consulting psychics for anything, they aren't even in my realm of existence."

"She's good. I've only been a couple of times. But I tell you, she's been pretty accurate. Do you want me to go with you?"

"No. It's okay." Lydia didn't want Miriam to know the true reason she wanted to consult a psychic. It seemed weird enough that she even considered finding her long-lost and probably dead dog through one, let alone asking advice on how to rid the house of spirits.

Lydia checked the address and put the card in her purse. She put on her coat. "I'll be back in an hour or so, just keep working on that file while I'm gone, if you don't mind."

"Sure thing. Good luck."

Lydia nodded and left the office.

It was still snowing and bitterly cold. They would definitely be spending the night downtown. Lydia pulled her collar up over her face against the wind that tore through the buildings.

How had it come to this so quickly? It wasn't that long ago they were newlyweds, so happy, so sickeningly in love that they couldn't keep their hands off each other. And now, she found herself not even trusting her own husband. She couldn't even remember the last time they made love.

She wondered if it was the pregnancy that was building the wall between them. Maybe now that the baby was nearly a reality, Tony was having second thoughts. As his wife changed shape, maybe he wasn't attracted to her anymore.

Tears welled up but she dismissed them. It wasn't the baby. He wanted the baby. Was practically obsessed with the baby. No, things had been weird since they moved into the house. If only he would meet her halfway on the idea of the ghosts. Or even of the very nature of why the house stood empty for two decades. Everyone at work had shuddered when they heard the history of the house. Any normal person would.

Why didn't he feel it? Was it because he had worked so hard to build the dream house that he was blocking his own discomfort?

And why was she now the one with the foul dreams? She hadn't seen him toss and turn in ages.

Damn, it wasn't fair. She had finally met the man of her dreams, had married him, was bearing his child, and life was so full of shit she could scream.

She would have thought lethargy would settle in after a few years, not months.

Lost in her thoughts, she almost missed the address. A tiny door in between a café and a junk store. She rang the bell, shivering.

There was the sound of someone thumping down the stairs inside and then the lock turned. A pair of dark brown eyes stared out. "Yes?"

"I'm here to see . . . uh . . . the psychic," Lydia stammered, suddenly nervous.

"That is me. Come on in." The girl opened the door and Lydia slid past her so she could lock it again. They marched back up the stairs. Lydia stared at the girl. She didn't look as she had expected. One part of Lydia thought it might be some ancient gypsy woman with a thick accent, the other part thought it might be a punky, multiply pierced and tattooed punk. But this girl was neither. She had shoulder-length red hair, and was dressed in a colorful woolly sweater and slacks. The modest apartment opened at the top of the stairs and the girl led her over to a small area in the corner. There was a tabletop fountain with gargoyles, a couple of slabs of crystal clusters and an incense holder burning incense. Lydia stared around the rest of the apartment. Pretty normal. This must be like the living room, a couple of small couches and a coffee table, then doors leading to God knows where. It was one of the strangest setups she'd ever seen, but then again, this was New York and homes were created out of the weirdest spaces.

It made her homesick for the loft she had left behind.

"I'm Cassandra," the girl said, indicating a chair that was positioned in front of a round table. Lydia sat, clutching her purse in her lap.

"I'm Lydia." Lydia held out her hand. Cassandra took it, and shook it, nodding as she felt whatever it was she felt. Lydia took her hand back, not wanting her to feel it for too long. She wasn't sure why, but she just didn't.

Cassandra sat across from her. On the table were a crystal ball and several tarot decks.

"What is it you want? A reading? Tarot?"

"I need some information, actually. I don't think I want a reading. I'm not sure I really want to know about my future and all."

Cassandra narrowed her eyes and rubbed her hands. "I guess first we should discuss rates. I charge eighty dollars an hour. You can ask however many questions you want, with whatever oracles you care for me to consult."

"That sounds reasonable. I'll have an hour. I have a couple of questions. As for what tools you use, whatever you want, it's all the same to me."

"You have lost something . . . or someone. You can't get them out of your mind."

Lydia stared at her. "Yes. You are right. I have. Will I find her again?"

Cassandra picked up one of the tarot decks and shuffled it. She fanned the cards and held it out. "Pull three cards."

Lydia pulled three and put them down.

Cassandra flipped them over, shuddering visibly as she did so. "She is not lost, but she is not found either . . . hmmm . . . she is very near."

"Near . . . do you think she is dead?"

Cassandra shook her head slowly. "She is not dead, yet she is not alive. This is so odd. I wish I could be less evasive for you, but that is what I see. Can you tell me something about the situation?"

"Well, there's nothing weird about it, I don't think. Well, with her anyway. I mean what I'm going to ask you in a minute *is* weird . . . but she . . . it's a dog. I moved into a new place and my dog went missing. I haven't seen her since."

Lydia thought for a moment. "Do you think it's something like she got hurt and crawled under the porch to die?"

"I don't think so. But, the situation will be clear very soon. You will find her. I cannot say if she will still be alive."

"At this point I just want closure, the poor thing."

"I understand."

Lydia sighed and watched as a little black cat peeked out from under one of the couches.

Cassandra leaned down and wiggled her fingers. "Here, puss puss," she cooed.

The cat stared with round green eyes.

"She's a funny one, that Agatha." Cassandra grinned. "Sometimes she's shy and sometimes she's a mush ball."

"She's cute." Lydia looked at the crystal ball. It was beautiful, round and clear. How did one see anything in there? Her gaze fell upon several pentacles on the table, woven into the cloth, and upon the dainty necklace and ring Cassandra wore.

"How is the devil better than God?" Lydia asked.

Cassandra looked puzzled and then reached her hand to her necklace. She toyed with it. "This isn't a pentagram, this is a pentacle. There's a difference. A *big* difference. The pentagram—actually, an upside-down pentagram—is devil worship. The point of the star faces down. A pentacle is spirit, God, witches. It represents the four elements, earth, wind, fire and water, which combined bring us the fifth element, spirit. Or God as some call it."

"Really? Hmmm." Lydia pondered that, suddenly realizing that she had seen many things, many people, in her life all wrong.

"Witches aren't devil worshipers. If we worship anything, it is nature. Cycles. Our own strength and weaknesses as humans on this earth plane."

"I can see that now. I'm glad I asked." Lydia watched the cat still staring at her.

"Well, I guess I'll get to the real point of my visit." Lydia sighed. "I'll keep it short. I got married in June and moved into a house that my husband had built for us. It's a pretty house and since then, we've added onto it. But the thing is, this house was built on the site where horrible things happened long ago. There were murders there, and when the murderers were caught, the original house was destroyed. But we are living on the foundation."

"So the house is haunted."

"Yes and no. You see, it seems to be only the basement . . . I go down there and feel them. The victims. They don't try to scare me or anything, well, not really, it's like they are trying to talk to me or just want me to do something, but I don't know what it is."

"They need to pass over."

"Yes. That's what I think. So what do I do?"

Cassandra closed her eyes for a moment. She shook her head. "It's very sad. They are so frightened. They think it's going to happen again."

"But they are dead."

"Are the killers dead?"

"Yes."

"Maybe the killers are with them. Or maybe . . ."

Cassandra opened her eyes. "What you need to do is sage the basement. I'll explain to you how in a minute. And you need some crystals."

Cassandra gathered together some crystals and sage and explained to Lydia how to perform a cleansing ritual. When she was done, she looked at Lydia with a serious expression.

"You must be careful. Things are not what they seem. If you think you are in too deep, please come back and I will help you find someone who knows how to do this."

"All right." Lydia paid her and stood up. She put the supplies into her purse.

"Be very careful. I send you and your baby my blessings."

Lydia smiled. "You can see my bump."

Cassandra grinned. "No, I see him, around you. His birth will not be easy, there are challenges ahead. But he wants to be with you."

"A boy?"

"Yes, he's a boy. A very special boy."

Cassandra's face grew dark again. "Be careful. You are being misled. You must be on your guard at all times. Your road is not an easy one, I'm sorry to say."

Cassandra took her hands and held them tightly. "Blessed be."

"Blessed be . . . " Lydia echoed.

* * *

Tony and Lydia sat on the bed, each with a laptop, working away. The hotel room was nice and as Lydia glanced again out the window, the snow was still coming down.

She was so eager to get back to the house and try some of the things Cassandra had told her, but she had to wait. Wait until she could get back, and wait until Tony was gone.

"What are you thinking about?" Tony asked her.

"Nothing really . . . just dreaming, I guess."

"About the baby?"

"Yes," she lied. "The baby. What do you think it will be?"

"It doesn't much matter to me," Tony said.

"As long as it's healthy, right?" she asked.

"Of course." He started clicking again.

"You know, we've never even discussed names for the baby," Lydia said.

Tony looked over at her. "No, I guess we haven't."

"Well, do you have any preferences?" she asked.

"Not really at this point. I haven't thought about it, to be honest."

"No?"

Lydia pretended to return to work, but her mind was racing. How could someone not have preferences for what to name their baby? Every day she imagined the phantom child running before her and what name she would call after him to bring him back. Him . . . She smiled. Was it really a little boy?

"Do you like traditional names or something a bit unusual?" she asked.

"Like I said, I haven't really thought about it. Haven't had much time to think about much," Tony said.

"Yeah . . . I know," Lydia replied, trying to keep the edge out of her voice. She tried to work for a bit but was unable to concentrate.

"Have you talked to your parents lately?" she asked him.

"Not since we saw them last week."

They both fell into silence, thinking about the visit. Both Sybil and Walter were unable to walk freely, both relied heavily on the use of canes. Outside of the house, they needed to be transported in wheelchairs. Tony was able to hire a private nurse for them and a person to come clean the house now and again. Sybil was slowly regaining her spirit, bossing the nurse around and complaining about the cleaning lady, even making comments on how Lydia should look after herself better with the baby and all. Walter, on the other hand, had all but given up the ghost. He seldom laughed and he was so gaunt that he looked as if he might fly away at any given moment.

Both of them had suffered brain trauma and were unable to remember exactly what had happened that night.

It was a mystery and, at this rate, one that was unlikely to ever be solved.

Tony was immersed in his work again. Lydia turned off her computer.

"I'm going to try to get some sleep," she said, as she placed the laptop on the table beside her. She snuggled down under the covers, feigning sleep. But all she could think about was what she needed to do next.

Chapter Fourteen

Lydia laid out all the ingredients. The sage stick, the clay bowl of sand, the little crystals. She stared around the basement. The lightbulb swung as it always did, and she could almost see shapes and forms shifting expectantly in the corners. Maybe they were illusions. Maybe they had always been illusions and this ceremony would be good for pacifying her rampant paranoia.

She thought of what Cassandra had told her, hoping she wouldn't forget anything. It seemed so very simple, too simple. She really didn't think anything would happen. Was this how they got you? Little pockets of hope, until you were willing to do crazy things like fork over thousands of dollars to the "professionals"?

Cassandra didn't seem like a huckster, but who could tell these days? Lydia tried to push the girl from her mind and focus on the task at hand.

She lit the sage stick. It winked out before she even stood up, so she lit it again, fearful of burning it too much and burning the house down. The thick smoke burned her eyes and she thought it smelled like pot. This time it stayed lit, and she stood, holding the bowl underneath it to catch little pieces that might fall off. She walked around the small room, waving the smoky wand up and down along the walls, paying special attention to the corners. She said the simple words the girl had taught her, over and over again.

"Go into the light."

The wisps floated around her, dancing through the smoke, circling her, until she wasn't certain where the ghosts started and the smoke ended. Maybe it was all smoke, had been some sort of damp fog all along.

Then they started to touch her. They tugged her hair, gently playing with it, as children would braid and toy with their mother's hair. They fiddled with her shirt, stroked the bump of her belly, leapfrogged between her legs.

She stood still. "None of you are taking this seriously."

She didn't think she would get around the room

three times with the ghosts teasing her the way they were. But then, the room grew very cold and the movement stopped.

She could almost see it, a new form, over in the corner. How did she know it was new? She was no psychic. She was just a woman, a pregnant woman, who might be losing her mind.

But this . . . this thing . . . it had some sort of power over the others. She could feel their fear in the goose bumps crawling up her arms. She walked faster in her little circle, and when she came to smudge the corner with the new entity in it, she paused. The ghost did not move. It did not strike out to her, it did not grab her stick and shove it in her eye. All she felt was confusion and anger. A lot of anger, and a hopeless sense of loss. She ran the smoking stick over the being, her words trembling as they barely left her mouth.

"Go into the light."

The ghost suddenly struck out at her, grabbed her by the wrist. Lydia screamed, dropping the stick and bowl. The stick landed in the pile of overturned sand. Lydia was pulled by the new ghost, pushed by the others, to the room behind and the room and beyond. She was whisked down the corridors so fast, she thought she was flying or dreaming. They sped down corners and caverns, past mountains of bones embedded in the walls, past drawings and words scratched into the dirt, the floor, the walls, until they dropped her in darkness.

Lydia lay dazed, staring into nothingness. Not even the dim spectral images were there. Just blackness. Complete and total blackness and their sadness. The ghosts were urging her to do something, but she didn't know what it was. She stroked her belly for a moment, willing her heart to stop racing as she tried to figure out why they didn't let her continue the ritual.

As her eyes grew more accustomed to the dark, she made out the faint outline of a doorway. At least, she assumed it must be a doorway, since it was large and rectangular. She sat up slowly, waving her hands all around her as she did so, in case she bumped her head on anything. She crawled over the rectangle and felt between the light. It felt like wood. Wood pressed into a dirt and bone wall. She reached up, sliding her hands carefully along the surface until they found the knob. Lydia frowned. How very strange to have a door in the middle of a cave. Or was it the end of a tunnel?

She slowly, carefully turned it. She waited for someone to say something, for someone to notice, for who knew what was on the other side?

There was no answer.

Taking a deep breath, her heart pounding, she turned the knob until the tumblers clicked.

"Please don't let there be anything creepy . . ." she prayed, and slowly pushed the door open.

Her jaw dropped as she saw what was on the other side.

How could it be? Where was she?

Now she knew how Dorothy had felt landing in Oz.

This room was huge. Almost like a dome. There were pillars and archways of golden metal, maybe they really were gold. This door opened behind a pillar, like a secret passageway. She peeked out, heard echoing male voices arguing. There were other sounds. Plaintive mewlings, moaning . . . those sounds were closer.

She leaned out a tiny bit more and saw the source of the cries.

If her heart had been pounding wildly before, now it just stopped.

She could not in a million years believe what she was seeing.

Goose bumps rose on her flesh as visions from a thousand nightmares came slamming back.

The light in this part of the room came from torches fixed into pillars on heavy brass pentagram holders.

In the alcove, not far from where she was, there were several people, young people, chained and ball-gagged. Two young men hung from the ceiling, suspended on meat hooks through their backs. They were the first to see her and turned wide frightened eyes toward her, shivering at what fresh new horror she would bring with her.

On the floor were two young girls and the missing deformed boy. One of the girls was the cashier from the grocery store that Lydia remembered had gone missing a while back.

What was her name? Oh, yes. Bev.

She recognized their faces, the lost people of the city . . . Timothy, Jason, Karey . . .

They watched her watching them.

There was a long wooden table filled with gleaming silver and polished black leather items. Creeping closer, she examined the instruments of torture. Whips, crops, chains . . . things she didn't even recognize. Clips and clamps and knives. A small videocamera and a stack of tapes, both new and used, beside it.

The floor was stained with blood, the prisoners bleeding and filthy, open wounds glazed with seeping pus. Lydia put her hand to her face, the stench unbelievable as she drew nearer to them. They sat, nearly naked except for rags. Not only blood, but urine and feces were smeared along their legs and backs.

"You poor, poor people," Lydia whispered.

A dog barked. Lydia froze. The chains clanged

as the prisoners huddled. The deformed boy, Timothy, moaned, spit leaking out the sides of his ball gag as he rocked back and forth.

The dog barked again and a man's voice impatiently told it to shut up.

That voice . . .

Lydia was riveted. She knew that voice. But from where?

The dog whined but didn't come bounding over. She expected it was on a leash or in a cage. Who knew what was happening to a dog if *this* was happening to people?

Satisfied that no one was coming over to inspect, she started to creep over toward where she had heard the dog. There was a jutting in the wall that separated the prisoners from the rest of the room. She was glad there were so many pillars, they were wider than she was, and she could use them to peer from.

On the other side of the room, some sort of meeting seemed to be in progress. Three men sat in huge carved wooden chairs, plush red velvet backings and seats. Several torches flickered, casting wavering light over the people, black robes and hoods hiding their faces. They sat around a huge mahogany table. It could seat twenty, she imagined.

What the hell kind of place was this? It was part church, part Gothic castle, part dungeon. Yet it was underground, tunneled from her basement.

Was this where the tortures had truly taken place all those years ago?

Then what were the shackles right beneath her house? What of the traces of what had gone before?

Maybe the rounds before the recent one. Maybe further back in the cycle. The cycle that even now was repeating and she still hadn't been able to figure out the most important piece of the puzzle.

Why?

Did people just lose their minds every twenty years and go on torturing sprees? Or was there more to it?

One thing she did realize, her ghosts weren't with her anymore.

The men were talking, and she strained to hear what they were saying. Their whispers were swallowed up in the cavernous chamber. They were seated in front of a set of long wide stairs, maybe five or six of them, leading to another door. On the stairs, she could make out forms of some sort. They glowed, much as her ghosts had flickered in and out of her vision, but these were oblong. Reclining on the stairs. She stared just past them, blurring her eyes, trying not to look directly at them, as she had with the spirits. Misty shapes took form behind her eyeballs and suddenly, one of them pulled into focus, then snapped out just as fast.

It was a wolf. A huge white wolf, with long white teeth, gazing disinterestedly at the men. All the forms were wolves. How many of them could there possibly be?

Five, six, seven?

Her view was blocked by the table, the men, the pillar.

Who the hell were these men and why were they in her basement?

One of the wolves raised its head and stared right at her. Red eyes glowered through the ghost mist. It growled lowly, a rumbling sound that she swore she could feel in her feet.

"Would you tell your damn dogs to settle down?" one man snapped to another.

"Probably just nervous today," the other man grumbled. "He senses our stress."

"Damn right we're stressed. There's not much time left." Lydia's fingernails dug into her palm. If the first voice was elusively familiar, this third voice she could mimic in her sleep.

Tony.

What the hell was Tony doing here? Dressed like that?

And those people . . .

A wave of nausea swept through her.

Tony . . . It had been Tony all along.

Tony lying . . . lying about staying in New York when he was right here.

Tony . . .

What the hell are you up to?

Lydia hugged her tummy.

Don't worry, baby boy, I won't let Daddy near you after this.

Lydia didn't know what to do next.

Should she run? Should she stay?

She had to stay. She had to find out what was going on. Gather more evidence.

But weren't the prisoners enough evidence that something sinister was going on here?

It was more than that.

She had to know just what the hell her husband was up to.

She watched as the three men joined hands. They were chanting softly, words she couldn't make out. Well, she figured even if they were shouting, they were no doubt speaking some ancient devil worship lingo.

The firelight flickered and shifted, yet she still could not make out their faces. The hoods were pulled so far out, their faces would be far inside. The one she was convinced was Tony brought one of the other men's hand to his face. He pressed it to his cheek, stroking the long fingers tenderly before bringing the large jeweled ring adorning the index finger up to his mouth. He tenderly kissed the ring, pressing it against his lips for many moments. Then, he held the hand before him as if studying it, the dark head cocked to the side, faceless as a nightmare. All the while, the men softly whispered words in unison.

The ringed man held his hand out to the other robed figure. That person too kissed the ring, without breaking the chant.

A perfumed smoke rippled from an urn on the table. It smelled like frankincense or a similar sweet musky scent. She watched the smoke billow to the ceiling, and for the first time, noticed the ceiling itself. It glowed in the dim light. Not from light, not from a phosphorescence, but as stained glass would refract the torches. She could almost make out a design in the perfect circle that domed the room. How did the walls all slope up in such a way? How long did it take to build such a place and how long had it been here?

The rattling of chains reminded her of the prisoners here. How she too was a prisoner here until they left, for she could not even tell where she had come in. Maybe there were several secret entrances, but she didn't know.

It was dark, and as thick as the frankincense was, it did not cover the rotten odor of decay.

She looked back over to the ghostly wolf pack. They all stood, alert now. They all had their ears pricked at attention, their long lolling tongues hanging between ghastly teeth.

They all were staring at her.

Lydia gulped.

One by one, they started to whine, pacing in place, anxious to leave their post.

The prayer over, the men slipped their hoods back.

Lydia gasped.

Not only was her husband there, but his boss. And Buddy.

Confusion consumed her more than ever now as she tried to understand what this meant.

William walked up the short set of steps and took his place on what could only be described as a throne. Tony paced. Buddy went over to the agitated wolves.

"What is wrong with you?" he asked his beasts. One of them howled, another snarled and snapped. Buddy took his staff from where it leaned against the wall and waved it over the wolves.

"Settle down . . . " he cooed. The wolves whined and paced, one of them throwing a forlorn glance over to Lydia.

"Get those damn things settled down, or they're going outside," William barked.

"Okay, that's enough," Tony said, running his hands through his hair. "We have to think. Time is running out."

"Time has been running out since we started this whole business," Buddy muttered. "Even all the time in the world is never enough. If the universe expanded forever outward, it could never fill the empty space in man's heart."

"You aren't helping, Buddy," Tony said sternly. "Focus on the task at hand. Jeff, what do you think?"

Lydia frowned. Jeff?

But wasn't his name William?

She thought back to stories that Tony used to tell her, about growing up. The little bit that she knew, that she had gleaned.

Jeff had been the friend that moved away.

He had come back too.

But why?

Just so the three of them could tie up people and torture them?

She started to creep backward, when one of the wolves barked. She startled, turning toward the sound. This one was smaller, one she hadn't noticed before. It must have been nestled in among the larger ones. The wolf wagged its tail, the ghostly hue shimmering back and forth. This wolf wasn't as translucent as the others. This one was almost more solid, more real. And had a golden hue.

The wolf barked again and bounded over toward her. She shrieked, and the men turned astonished faces toward the sound.

Buddy called out. "Pilar . . . get back here."

Pilar jumped up on Lydia, putting her paws on Lydia's shoulders, her tail wagging, her long half-ghostly tongue warm and wet against her face.

"Pilar . . ." Lydia hugged the dog, tears streaming from her face. "My Pilar . . ."

"Lydia!" Tony stood before her. Lydia was frozen with fear, but she could not let them know that. She had to be cool.

"Tony, what the hell is this?" Lydia asked. Pilar wriggled around her legs and she put her hand on the dog's head to settle it.

"You finally figured it out. Took you long enough," Tony sneered.

Lydia stared at him, wondering who this man with the cold eyes and sneering lip was. Surely this wasn't her husband.

"I haven't figured out a goddamn thing," Lydia said. "All I see is some kind of . . . shrine . . . and three men who have been going through a lot of trouble to trick me."

Jeff smiled.

"Oh, there is so much more to this delicious story," Jeff said.

"You, Buddy . . . you have been here all along. . . ." She stared at Buddy. He was not the ratty, raggled man skulking along the trees. He was scrubbed as clean as the rest of them, from his combed hair, to his shaved face and shiny black shoes peeking out from under his robe.

"Yes and no. The real fun didn't start until Tony and Jeff came back." He grinned.

"Came back for what? What is it that you do here?"

"So many questions, ah, but did we expect no less?" Jeff mused. He nodded to Tony and Buddy.

"You could have found out sooner or later or never. But you are here, and so the last cycle begins."

Jeff motioned toward Buddy and Tony. They each took one of Lydia's arms before she even knew what they were doing. She struggled but she was no match for them.

"We expect great things from you, Lydia," Tony soothed.

"What the fuck are you doing?" She kicked Tony in the shins but his grip was iron tight. "Goddamn you."

Tony's arms were like steel, restraining her, his chest and belly rock hard.

She might as well have been a rag doll as Tony and Buddy dragged her over to the prisoner's part of the room. Her struggles were in vain as they shackled her to another set of chains embedded in the floor.

"You bastard!" she screamed at her husband. "What the fuck are you doing?"

"Shut up."

"Nosy people always end up in trouble. Haven't you ever figured that one out?"

"What is this?"

"This is the place where everything begins and everything ends." Buddy grinned. "Like a circle. The ubuoris . . ."

Lydia followed Buddy's finger as he pointed to the ceiling. From this angle, she could see that the circle of the ceiling was in fact the ubuoris. In the center, the pentagram, and in the center of that, a beast of unimaginable wretchedness. The same beast that was manifested all around the room, in brass, in gold, in silver, with red garnet eyes and a long serpent tail.

"What is beginning and ending?" Lydia asked.

"Life. The eternal circle," Jeff said, staring up at the ceiling.

"The time is soon. It will begin again," Buddy said, his eyes shining.

The shackles secured, the men turned and left her there.

"What the hell are you doing? You can't leave me here."

They did not respond to her screams. One by one, the torches were extinguished. The prisoners moaned and cried, their wretchedness muffled by their gags.

Before the last torch was out, Jeff looked at Tony.

"You know what you have to do," he said. Tony nodded.

Tony walked across the room, his shoes echoing in the large chamber. He approached the table and stood thoughtfully at it. At last, he picked up a ball gag, and turned to Lydia, his eyes gleaming with a look she had never seen before.

"Tony, what are you doing? It's me. Your wife. The mother of your child."

Tony looked at her as if she were a stranger.

He held her head, and try as she would she could not move her head from his grip. He slipped the ball gag into her mouth. She gasped, trying to spit it out, but the harness was strapped against her head. Once he buckled it up, he roughly threw her to the floor.

He walked away.

The last torch was extinguished and the men, and the wolves, left.

* * *

The sound of screaming filled her ears.

She was in that dream again. The dream where she was hanging by the flesh on her back.

Only this time when she opened her eyes, it was no dream.

The ball gag muffled her screams as she bore witness to the atrocity being performed below her.

Tony was whipping one of the boys with a long leather strap. The naked boy, dark haired and thin, had his hands tied on either side to a pole. Blood spilled to the floor, the boy's eyes rolled back into his head as he clung to the last semblance of consciousness. She saw two videocameras mounted on tripods, red eyes glowing as they recorded the flogging.

The pain in her back was excruciating. She couldn't imagine how her skin didn't rip, how she even was conscious. Maybe she had been floating in and out of consciousness for days, weeks. Who knew how much time had passed? She tried to remember, to tug at the darkness, but her mind refused to rewind. It could only shriek with the screams of nerve endings.

She closed her eyes and for some reason, thought of something she had seen on TV months ago. Some show, one of those daring believe-it-or-not shows, where all these young adults drove hooks through their backs to create the world's largest mobile.

She remembered how queasy she had felt watching that, wondering about the people who did it. How they claimed to find another form of consciousness. How some claimed visions, epiphanies, claimed God.

All she could feel was pain.

And beneath the pain, anger.

She had to get past the pain, get past the anger if she was ever going to get out of here.

The boy had collapsed, his back a mound of raw meat. She could see where the flesh parted and gapped, where the blood seeped, where the muscle was escaping. The poor boy didn't understand.

Hell, she didn't understand.

Her husband, her loving, giving husband, betraying her all this time.

When did it start?

When he bought the house?

When they moved into the house?

When they were children . . . ?

Chapter Fifteen

Tony wandered into the graveyard where Debbie and Donald lay. The moon was a sliver in the sky and he had a flask of rye in his pocket. Soon he would be leaving town, off to the university and then a job somewhere. He'd get married, settle down and maybe never set foot back here again except for Christmases.

The idea depressed him and he sipped on the flask thoughtfully. The graveyard was old, so old and nearly forgotten, which is why the bones of the killers had been laid to rest here. The theory was that no one would bother them here. No one would want to wade through tangles of weeds and burrs to gawk at or deface a piece of rock or land marking one of the worst crimes of the century. Certainly the worst that this town, or any for miles, had ever experienced.

He had always liked to come here because it was so lonely. It gave him time to think, away from anyone else, away from the wild philosophies of Buddy. And now that Jeff was gone . . . he found he didn't make friends very well.

Jeff had been gone a long time now, and the loss of his friend still ached in his heart. He thought of the fun they used to have as kids. Swimming, fishing, building forts, getting into some sort of low-key trouble, smoking pot, even dropping acid a time or two, though both found that just a bit too intense for their already overactive imaginations.

Tony found the tall weeping willow by the murderers' markers and sat down under it. He lit up a cigarette and sucked on it thoughtfully, the smoke winding itself around his head.

Sometimes the graveyard at night made him nervous, but not because of ghosts or demons. It was more because you never knew what drug-addled wackos might be lurking around. Not many, in this town, but it only took one to wreck a lovely late summer night.

Yep, he was all packed, his boxes and suitcases in the lobby of his parents' house.

He would be glad to finally have a chance to spread his own wings, but he would miss his parents. His mom could be bossy but he guessed that was what moms did. She still did his laundry, sewing on stray buttons, matching his socks, making his bed each day.

He hoped he could figure out how to deal with all those mundane rituals on a regular basis. Or at least score a chick who would do them for him.

His life lay before him, a vague shadowy road for the next few years, but then, he could see what lay next. He would find Jeff, somehow convince him to come back to town.

The pacts they had made over the years haunted him.

Did Jeff mean them too?

Did Jeff feel the energy they created when they were together?

He took another drag of the cigarette.

Yet, it was even stronger when Buddy was there too. Somehow, the three of them together created a triad of vibrations, he could sense it tickling his flesh. That was how the bricks had bled that day. That was how they had called whatever it was they had called those few times they had dared. He was sure the others knew it too.

If they had a way to use that energy, to create some kind of powerful empire . . . it would all be worth it. It could not be now, there was so much to learn. He had to fill his brain with ideas and theories, learn the best and quickest way to market himself and his work, find his knack, what he was good at. He had to get strong, make his mind, his body, his life strong and filled with possibilities. Then the way to have ultimate power would be clear, and he would seek out Jeff.

He took another slug from the bottle, another drag from the cigarette.

Money was the ultimate power. Money gave you the ability to control others in so many ways. You could buy almost anything, everyone had a price. He had seen it in his own family for generations.

Fame didn't interest him. People didn't interest him except as a way to help him achieve what he craved.

A wife, who was smart, but not too smart, pretty but not too pretty, someone who could look after him but was independent too. His parents would be expecting a wife, and he would have to provide one, at least at first.

The tree he was leaning against seemed to be vibrating. He put his hand up above his head and pressed it against the trunk. There was rumbling and he could feel it in his feet, in the ground.

His hand trembled as he knocked back another large gulp of rye. The rumbling was familiar and he knew what was next.

He fought back a scream as a blinding sharp pain

pierced his right temple. Automatically he put his fingers up to rub it, massaging it, to no avail. His head throbbed, the pain blinking with every beat of his heart.

He opened his eyes and there they were. Just as they always were. Debbie and Donald.

She was smiling that smile that flashed too many teeth yet was a sneer at the same time. A smile that even in the videos flashed on the television did not reach her eyes. Her blond hair was swooped back from her face, dancing along her shoulders. Yet, she was not solid. Just a mist that really had no color, but he could see the honeycomb color of her hair just the same.

He was nearly the opposite. His eyes did smile, smile with the maniacal glee of a man who loves his job, a man who serves only himself. His mouth was a straight line, yet the tiny tug on the left side gave the hint of the slightest of grins. His short light hair was a bit curly at the front, falling over his face almost like a kewpie doll from the fifties.

When this charming couple had been on the news and in the papers for the horror they had caused, no one could believe it.

Not this model couple.

Not these beautiful specimens of God's work who should be creating more little beauties instead of smearing the world with blood.

They stood before him, grinning, flickering like an old movie. The pain in Tony's temple had now sent him into an almost Zen-like state and his ears were ringing.

He knew what would happen as his ears rang. They throbbed too like the pain in his temple. A pulse, reminding him that he was alive even if they were dead.

His ears rang louder, until the crickets were nearly drowned, pulsing until they reached that sensation of sound where he was surely trapped in a bell jar.

It was then that Donald spoke.

"We are waiting for you," he said.

"I know. I am working on it. When the time nears, I will be ready. Very ready."

"You had better be. You are the chosen one, no fuckups allowed."

"No, there will be no fuckups."

"We trust you, and those that you pick."

"I will be ready."

"We are saving the house for you."

"I have to go to school before I can buy it. It has to be done in order, or it will look funny."

"It will be fine. We are saving it," Debbie said firmly.

"You must bring back a bride. For the sacrifice."

"Yes." Tony nodded, hypnotized now by the

voices in his ear amplified in his head, yet as he stared at the ghosts in front of him they did not appear to speak.

"The cycle will be here before you know it."

"Don't worry. You have chosen well. You will see," Tony said.

"And you will not falter when the time of sacrifice comes?" Donald asked. "The pain will be great. Your first . . . we couldn't provide it in time . . . so we were caught."

"I still don't understand how you were caught."

"Circumstances. It wasn't our time to enjoy. *She* is a tricky one. She is everything and nothing. She is all of us connected, yet she is careless and flippant. She *will* sacrifice all your hard work, so be aware."

"Why are you warning me?"

"Don't you see? We are part of you. We are all connected. Everything and everyone. We are all nothing yet we are all everything. Each vibration in the energy carries us on the path. Though we cannot reap the material rewards anymore, of money, cars, clothes . . . there are other goals in sight now. Other rewards we desire, and in helping you, we help ourselves."

Debbie's smile was pure evil now and Tony felt a chill climb up his back. "What rewards?"

"It is impossible to explain until you cross over.

Your mind could not imagine the sights we see, the pleasures we taste. Your time will come to follow us down this path, for your destiny has been set. But first, you must follow your dark passions on earth." Her breath was cold on his neck as she sat down beside him under the tree. Her hand ran along his thigh.

"Strength draws on strength. Power is strength. Strength is power. Never falter." Donald sat down on the other side of him.

Tony shrugged, not understanding half of what they were saying, but the words stayed with him.

Their hands stroked him, like a wind dancing along his body. He shivered, their touch cool and elusive yet deliciously sensual. Their images flickered, forms shifting as they wove around him and each other like ribbons. She kissed him, her tongue darting in and out of his mouth like a snake as he laughed, trying to taste it, but it never seemed quite solid enough to catch. He felt Donald's hands on his head, holding it firmly, pushing him toward the ground, until he was on his hands and knees, his face mashed into the earth, his butt in the air.

His heart thumped as he felt helpless yet powerful at the same time. His head was pushed farther into the dirt by Donald's foot and he tasted moldy leaves and the taint of piss.

Debbie held his hands behind his back, tying

them with willow branches. He didn't struggle as he submitted to their desires, excitement boiling through him in a sickly fearful way. Adrenaline flooded his synapses and he could almost see between the cracks, between air and time as he lay with his face in the dirt. He was seeing not with his eyes, but somehow with his senses. As he saw the ghosts that were dreams in the waking world.

His pants were loosened and pulled down, his shirt torn away and a multitude of willow switches hailed across him like a storm. They stung, they cut, the pain was deliciously thrilling. A thousand bee stings, a hundred spankings. They started on his back and worked down to his ass. They slipped along his thighs, each little snap whipping by his ear first before it met its mark. Then they would work their way back up again. The right cheek, the left cheek of his round exposed butt. The wide expanse of his back. Long languid strokes, short staccato slaps. His flesh was pummeled and torn, pulled and slashed, until he realized that flesh was only flesh. A sausage casing. A way to hold in the parts that kept him from spilling out. The way to keep form so that others could see and recognize his individualism.

The floggings stopped and he was rolled onto his back. He cried out as the dirt mashed into his wounds, but the pain was soon replaced by gentle touches on his chest, his neck, his face, his belly, his rock-hard cock.

He couldn't see them now as they whirled and swirled around him, through him, dancing in his veins, crawling in through his pores, tickling his nerve endings with the most exquisite pleasure he had ever known. They drew on his tension, teasing him to height after height, until he was rolling along the ground, his hands still bound behind his back, his pants still down to his knees. They were between his skin, riding his blood, boiling in his scrotum, pushing against him, pounding against his inner walls until he could stand it no more and released.

His howls of ecstasy echoed across the graveyard, for once he started coming, he couldn't seem to stop. The seed spilled from him in gush after gush, until he thought he was human no more, but a wave endlessly slapping the beach. And in that moment, he saw it, understood it, how he was everything and nothing at the same time.

Then suddenly, it was over.

The joy was gone.

They disappeared in a wink, as if he had dreamed it all. All that remained was the pain of the lashings and their strange words echoing through his head.

"We are everyone. We are strength. Everything is connected, you to us, we to you . . . the trees, the stones . . . everything is nothing. Emptiness fills us."

He felt as though he had spoken to God himself as he assessed the vision. Their lure permeated his being, he could feel their words etched into his soul, their promises, tantalizingly dangling in front of him. He was curious to know of the pleasures they spoke. Could there possibly be something more intense than what he had just experienced? What waited for him on the other side?

He didn't have a death wish and would wait to taste what more they had for him, both here and there.

He would play out the scene here as long as he could. He pulled himself together as best he could. His T-shirt was more or less a write-off but he got his pants back on.

He was no idiot. He knew that he was playing with fire, he had read enough books, seen enough movies, to know that situations as odd as this one often turned out bad. But bad was in the eye of the beholder. It seemed to him that even if he screwed up here on earth, there was more to go, that they would be waiting for him to cross over, and would show him the next phase of this journey.

The headache started to dissipate and he lit another cigarette. The smoke felt good in his lungs, burning him as if reminding him he was alive and had a whole life to live.

A life that promised riches and power, even if he did have to face some sort of unknown something and provide it with a sacrifice at some point. Something tricky and evil but that somehow already had a clutch on him. He was driven down this path, almost pushed down this path, since the day he saw the cloud above the house. It was as though he had stared at a medusa and his life had been stone ever since, waiting to crack.

He only had a few years to get the money together, to find a partner, to create the sacrifice. He only had a few years to read as much as he could so when the time of double-talk came, he would communicate accordingly and not be lost in the snap moment of a careless answer or unmeditated move.

He wondered what it was he would ultimately be facing.

In the time he had been sitting there, the moon had shifted along the sky and stars had popped out. He picked out the Big Dipper and the Little Dipper. He squinted his eyes, trying to create new constellations, or at least remember some of the more obscure ones. But he couldn't.

The stars were so far away. Balls of fire or gas or energy suspended in space, like the earth. How was it that things were constant, that they never fell, that there never was a hiccup and all the planets rolled into each other? Which one had been the first one? And how far did the universe really go?

Where had Debbie and Donald come from and where was this place they went back to when they finished talking to him? Were heaven and hell somehow in between the stars, a wrinkle slid into the fabric of the universe?

If they were all connected, he, they, the stars, the goddess, what held them together? What connected such different matter and how did they know which form to take? Why didn't their forms just bleed and blend into each other?

His head started to throb again, but not the migraine temple spike, just a plain old headache from burning the ol' brainpower a bit too hard. He was down to the bottom of his bottle and had still found no answers.

One more cigarette and then he would have to get back. He lit it up, wondering what life out of this town was going to be like.

There was a rustling in the bushes, and he stiffened. Had someone been watching him the whole time? If they had, would they have seen the ghosts, or just some insane person rolling along the graves?

"Hey . . ." The word was a whisper and Tony breathed a sigh of relief. It was only Buddy.

"Hey, man," Tony greeted. "What are you doing?"

"Just out walking around." Buddy's tall form appeared in sight now, the moon and stars not giving off much light. Buddy dug around in his pocket and pulled out his smokes. He popped one into his mouth and lit it up.

"Gorgeous night," Buddy said.

"Yep." Tony nodded. The crickets had begun to chirp again, and there was the distant sound of frogs croaking.

"You just taking it all in before you leave?" Buddy asked. Tony nodded, holding back laughter.

"What? Did I say something funny?" Buddy asked.

"Naw . . . jest thinking, is all."

"Huh . . . ?"

"What do you think you're going to do, Buddy?"

"Smoke this here cigarette."

"No, I mean, with your life and all. What do you think you're going to do? What is your dream?"

"My biggest dream, I guess, is to never be hungry and to have a roof over my head. Goddamn old lady's house is a pigsty."

"It's always money, isn't it, Buddy?"

"Not my fault."

"No . . . I'm not talking about you. I'm talking, in general . . . in life . . . as we know it. Just to be human, just to live on this earth and have the simplest things that an animal has, a place to sleep and something to eat, we need money. We have a child, we need to pay to have it. We pay to feed it, to dress it . . ."

"Well, since I've never really had money, I guess I don't really worry about it too much."

"But don't you see, Buddy? We are all animals. We should have these things automatically. Basic things. Then anything extra, like cars and big-screen TVs, are extras. But look around, if you didn't live with your ma, where would you be? You can't go to school. That takes money."

"Can't even hold a fucking job, it seems." Buddy sighed.

"That's because you aren't made for manual labor. You are a thinking man. A man who also can commune with nature. You can talk to beasts."

" 'Tis true. I would go work at the zoo if I didn't think I needed a frickin' education for that. Plus, where would I live? Sure as hell no zoos around here."

"There are lots of animals around here. Hell, look up there. There's an owl, watching us."

Buddy looked up to where Tony was pointing. A white owl glowed on the tree branch. It stared sullenly at them, eyes glowing brighter than the moon. Buddy made a noise. The owl cooed back.

"You could be master of the animals around here," Tony said.

"And who's going to pay me to do that?"

"Maybe you need to guard things. Guard the cave until I return."

"The cave . . ." Buddy shuddered.

"Come on, you know what I'm talking about. You know what we are part of and we might as well embrace it, since we can't shake it. I'll try to take care of you, Buddy, as time passes, if you can guard the cave, the house, make sure that everything is ready when I return."

"I wonder about what we are doing. . . . What if . . . well . . . it all turns to shit?" Buddy said, flicking his cigarette to the ground and stomping it out.

"Then it all turns to shit, I guess."

They stared up at the stars.

"It's already begun and there's not much we can do to stop it. Somehow, we are part of it, I reckon," Buddy mused.

"We are part of it. We were part of it the day we watched them bulldoze that house."

"I somehow wonder if we weren't always part of it . . . " Buddy said. "If this isn't some eternal dance we've played out before."

Tony shook his head. As deep as his thoughts sometimes got, he was amazed by some of the shit

Buddy would come up with. As if reading his mind and then pushing that envelope one notch further.

"Well, if this is a dance, I hope I know all the right steps," Tony tried to joke.

"We better not fuck up this time." Buddy turned to Tony, his eyes glittering in the darkness. "It's about more than money, you know. We are tied to the devil and there is no escape. Mark my words."

"Hey, it's not the devil," Tony said.

"Then what the hell do you see it as?"

"Well, shit, we haven't really seen anything. Except our dreams."

"The word *nightmare* comes to mind. Don't you think that if we were dealing with God and goodness, the dreams would be all sugar and sunshine, not blood and decadence?"

"Are you backing out, Buddy?"

"You know I can't back out now any more than you can. Whatever karmic ties we have to this, we have to finish the deal, no matter how many years it takes. No matter how many pools of shit we have to wade through. This is our destiny."

"You don't sound too happy."

"I reckon I ain't happy at all, Tony. I feel tired sometimes. Tired that I've been dancing and dancing, yet I never get to take a bow. Tired that all around me, people are going off to see the world, finding mates, having sex, building lives as teams, and all I got is me, myself and I. And a mother that is completely and totally fucked up."

"Your time will come, Buddy." Tony patted him on the back.

"Not in this lifetime. But that's okay. I already know how it's gonna go. You and Jeff are gonna do great and I'll still be here, sitting in this graveyard, smoking a butt and wondering when it'll be my turn to shine."

"We'll all shine, Buddy. I won't leave you behind." Tony looped his arm around him.

"We all gotta do what we gotta do. Work from the gut. Instinct. We're all animal that way."

Chapter Sixteen

When Lydia woke again, she was lying on the floor. Her arms and legs were still shackled, she couldn't move far, she couldn't speak. The others lay sleeping, blood and puss seeping from their wounds, the stench of rotting flesh making her want to puke, but she couldn't puke with a ball gag in her mouth. As she looked around, she was aware of being watched. She sat up, her head swimming, her body cramped and stiff, her belly sore. She couldn't even pat her tummy, the chains restrained her. She was too weak to cry or even be afraid anymore.

Both videocameras were trained on her, the red eyes blinking. How she wanted to tell them to fuck off.

She heard movement behind her and, quick as a

flash, she was being released from one set of chains and being led around in another.

She was roughly strapped to a cross, facedown, and she realized that she was naked. Her belly protruded from the side, they at least gave her that much.

A whip slashed her back. She winced. Then she heard Tony's voice.

"With pain, comes enlightenment. You will see."

Lydia shook her head as the whip came across her back again.

"If you choose to join us, Lydia, you can be part of the plan. If not, then you will become like the others. Waiting."

Again the whip.

"But the wait isn't much longer. Not at all. The time is so near we can taste it. Can you taste the change in the wind, Lydia?" Tony was right beside Lydia, whispering in her ear, his hand rubbing her back.

"Be one of us, we can be four. Four strong with all that we dare dream and desire . . . what do you say?"

Tony released the ball gag. Great gobs of drool hung from it.

Lydia moved her mouth painfully, her tongue didn't even feel like her own anymore. "Go to hell."

"Looks to me like you're already there. Why

don't you see what we have to offer you?"

"If it involves torturing innocent people, I'm not interested."

"Lydia, you see, you have to understand . . . we are not torturing. We are bringing enlightenment. We all must be enlightened so that we will be ready. We cannot offer ourselves as those who have not tasted ecstasy. We must offer ourselves as instinct and smell, as raw nerves quivering with experience."

"Be one of us, Lydia."

Lydia stared at the men with their fever-bright eyes.

She spoke again, slowly, as her tongue slipped and slid along her teeth. "If I say yes, then what happens?"

Tony touched her hand. "Then we work together as a team instead of apart."

"For what? To break the law? To be arrested and executed?"

"We are protected. No law can touch us."

"I'm sure Debbie and Donald thought that too. And look what happened to them."

"They didn't follow the rules. *All* the rules."

"And what rules might those be?"

"Promise me you'll think about it. Promise me you won't say no before you consider all the possibilities. For where there is one, there are many.

Where life was created once, it can be created again."

Lydia closed her eyes, turning the words over in her mind. Was he really saying what she thought he was saying? It couldn't be. Had he really gone so mad?

"The baby?"

"Yes, the baby."

"What about the baby?"

"We can always make another that we can keep. People have abortions all the time and don't think twice."

"Abortion?"

"That came out wrong. No, the baby is a gift. We must give the baby to the goddess. That is where Donald and Debbie lost. When the goddess came for the baby, there was none. They were barren."

"Came for the baby . . . Where will the baby live?" Lydia felt as though she were swimming in molasses, her tongue made of molasses, her brain seeping out of her ears like molasses. She had to at least play along with their absurd ideas while she thought of a plan. A way to escape.

"The baby goes with the goddess on that day she appears."

"And?"

"Then anything we desire is within our reach. *Anything.* Look at all we've gotten so far. And that was just a taste. Just enough to fuel our desire."

"But I'm happy with my life. I have my husband, my home, my job, my baby. There is nothing more I need."

"We all always need more. More money, more power. How can we pay for our home, our cars, our children without money?"

"We have jobs."

"The goddess gave us our jobs. If we don't appease her, we will lose our jobs and where will we be?" Tony said.

"I got my own job, long before this goddess shit," Lydia said.

"You are in this, Lydia. One way or another, you are in this and don't forget it. You can do it our way or you too can be . . ."

"Be what?"

"Think about it. Think about it all. And when you realize we are right, we will talk."

Tears streamed down Lydia's face. Give up the baby. But for what? She felt like shit, she needed to lie comfortably, she needed arms that bent on their own. Poor baby inside of her. She had taken such care of him and now she would have to give him up.

Her heart ached at the thought.

She would never give up the child.

Maybe some women had abortions even later

term than she was, but she could already feel his life-form inside of her. She could see him in her mind's eye, spinning in his water sac, little legs kicking, little fingers opening and shutting as they grew longer every day. This was her baby whether Tony wanted him or not, and she would protect him till she died.

Pilar came over and sniffed at her legs.

"Can you at least free my hands so that I can pet my dog?" she asked.

"What do you think, Jeff?" Tony asked. For a moment, he felt sorry for his wife, slung across the cross, her swollen belly hanging on the other side.

"Sure. She's too exhausted to try anything."

Tony loosened the bindings and released her hands. She slid down to the floor, sobbing with aching legs, aching back, aching mind. She cried, and Pilar nuzzled her, remembering the smell of this sad lady from sometime, somewhere once long ago. Lydia reached out to run her hands through her hair and found she wasn't quite real. She was like one of the spirits in the basement, but a tiny bit more solid. She had form but it separated when Lydia put her hands along her.

"What did you do to Pilar?" she asked. "I can't even pet her."

"She is us and we are she. All energy connected.

All full in our emptiness," Buddy said, wandering over, leaning heavily on his staff.

"Will she ever be the way she was before?" Lydia asked.

"Maybe. We'll see what the goddess wants with her."

"The goddess." Lydia sighed heavily, wiping her filthy hands along her eyes. "What is the deal with this goddess? When is this spectacular entrance supposed to take place?"

"Once every twenty years. The cycle, just as you saw in the paper," Tony said. "You know that. You were figuring it out."

"So how does this happen? When does this happen?"

"We have one more day to prepare and then you will see it all. The world will never be the same."

"Yeah, I caught that much already. What happens? Does she just materialize somewhere? Here? Then what? She hangs around till I have this baby?"

"Maybe you should just try to get some sleep. Too many questions. You can't build a religion on so many questions. You have to have faith that things will unfold as they are meant to. Things are happening as our destiny dictated. That is all we need to know."

"Christ . . ." Lydia stared up at the ceiling, at the horrible beast, at the ubuoris.

"Is that creature . . . is that the so-called goddess?"

"That is one of her forms. The one that mortals can see and understand."

"Doesn't it bother you that she looks more like a monster than a god?"

"We are she, and she is us. Maybe we look like monsters to her."

Lydia rubbed her temples. She had pretty much had it with the doublespeak.

"I need to sleep. I'm hungry. I can't go on like this."

Tony led her over to one of the blankets in the prisoners' quarters.

"Can't you just take me home, Tony? In my own clean bed? I'm cooperating. I'm playing the game. Please . . . ?"

"We need you to be here, now that you've arrived. There is no time to be wandering around, keeping track of everyone everywhere."

Lydia fought a sob, a scream, a howl that wanted to slip from her throat, but instead she feigned sweetness and lay her head down. With any luck, she would stay unshackled and if she was at least somewhat free, her chance of escape would be greater. She closed her eyes, hoping to spy on them, but exhaustion overwhelmed her and she slipped into sleep.

"It is time."

"So hard to believe!"

Lydia groggily opened her eyes. She thought for a moment that she was eavesdropping on children at Christmastime, but she wasn't. There were three grown men, dressed in black robes, standing beneath the circular ceiling.

They held candles. Thick smoke billowed from various incense holders positioned around the room. The other prisoners watched wide-eyed, too tired to be any more frightened, to exhausted to wonder if they were going to live or die. They smelled even worse than they had the day before, a fresh new batch of urine and feces staining the floor. It was very dark today, tonight, whatever it was. She could still see their faces, their shapes, but there were only three torches burning. She wondered how many beetles were clicking around.

The videocameras were positioned around the men as they held hands, chanting. A gust of wind whistled through the room, sending the smoke curling and swirling.

The first chant finished, the men dropped hands. Jeff went over to the round mahogany table and sat at his huge velvet-and-wood throne. Tony sat beside him, his glance gazing expectantly from Jeff to Buddy and back again.

Buddy stood alone. Lydia sat up more and could see a giant pentagram drawn on the floor in accordance with the ceiling. That same ubuoris and the red-eyed demon adorned it.

Buddy started to sing. His voice trembled at first, a low trilling sound, but slowly it grew louder and steadier as he intoned words that Lydia could not comprehend. The air became harder to inhale as the incense burned thicker. The walls seemed to breathe, pulsing, rippling and growing tighter, sucking what air was left in the room out.

Buddy took his staff, raising it high over his head. He turned around with the staff still over his head and then laid it down in the circle. It shuddered and then Lydia watched in amazement as, one by one, little grayish white clouds puffed out of the stick. They spun and circled, growing large and longer until each one took the form of a wolf. As the wolf pack materialized around him in a circle, he took off his robe. Lydia was quite amazed to see his strong firm chest, the rippling back muscles, under the shaggy long hair. She couldn't help checking out his ass and penis as he spun around in a circle.

She looked over at Jeff and Tony, saw them kiss,

their lips pressing and parting with hungry familiarity. A pain shot through her so deep it might as well have been a knife. She watched Tony cupping Jeff's face, Tony stroking Jeff's hair. How long had that been going on?

Buddy danced and sang, the wolves materializing and morphing around his feet, howling and panting as they sang along with him. Lydia felt like the biggest fool in the world. How could she have been such an idiot? How could she have fallen so hard for so long for . . . a charade?

This was really, really bad and she couldn't stop going over little things in her head. Little things that, looking back, she should have seen, or noticed. Well, she had seen and noticed a few things, but not the right things. And regarding what she had seen, what did she do? Whine. Stay. Ignore. Sweep under the rug.

For a modern women she sure had been a dink.

Wouldn't most women wonder if their husbands were staying out of town for biz meetings? She honestly didn't know. She had felt such complete love and trust for him it hadn't really entered her head that he might be up to something else.

That was why he chose her, she guessed. A naive woman with not much experience in love. Someone who would be bowled over by his handsome good looks, his attention, his extravagance.

She watched TV, she had a couple of friends, once . . . she knew that wasn't normal for men. Everyday men that weren't up to anything, that is.

It was quite amazing how hindsight is always 20/20. Would haves, could haves, should haves come flying out of nowhere, as if they had been choices all along.

She had no reason, no reason at all to suspect anything at all, at first. Even after they moved into the house, it was hard to tell, since they had to adjust to a new town, the commute, unpacking, her wonder at her own tenacious grip at sanity when it came to the creepy stuff in the basement . . . Who wouldn't be snappy and distant?

She gasped.

Buddy's flesh was flying off of him, landing in meaty strips around the room. The wolves howled and moaned, wistfully staring at the chunks of meat. Pilar had slunk in among them, laying her head across the back of a large male.

The floor inside the pentagram was slick with blood and falling flesh. At last, Buddy stopped spinning and turned his head directly toward her. He was but a skeleton, yet his eyes, glowing green eyes, were still intact.

He picked up his staff and pointed it to the ground. In that instant, a silent command was indicated. The wolves jumped on their meal, teeth gnashing, slobbering snarls filling the air as they fought and feasted, snatching bites from each other, claws slipping and sliding on the dripping gore.

Lydia shoved her fingers into her mouth to keep from screaming. Surely this too was just part of the long unending nightmare that she couldn't seem to wake from. She looked over at the others. The boy, Timothy, was unconscious, safe from his pain for now. The others watched with eyes as large as saucers, fear paralyzing them as they dreaded what the next spectacle would bring.

"Walking Bones . . . you grace us with your presence once more. Your hard work with the guardians is not unnoticed." Jeff nodded to Walking Bones. Walking Bones nodded back and stood at the edge of the pentagram, on the head of the ubuoris eating his own tail.

Jeff and Tony walked into the pentagram. They slowly removed their robes. Lydia admired them for a moment. These handsome, fit men. What a waste. What was it with gorgeous men being the purest of evil?

One of the women, Bev the cashier, was shivering and crying. Lydia edged closer to her, holding her breath from the rancid stench emanating from the woman's mouth, seeping from her pores. The rank stench repelled her, but this was, in the end, just a human, cloaked in misery. Confused and tortured and terrified.

Lydia could stroke her hair, could feel the tangles and chunks of debris in it. She could have unbuckled the ball gag, but that might cost her what little freedom she had. Right now, she had her hands, her mouth, her feet, even if they were shackled, but she could walk a short distance. At least she wasn't still hanging from the ceiling. None of them were now. But she could see they all still had the hooks in their backs, as if ready to be hoisted up at any time.

Lydia held Bev, watching the men dance their weird naked dance. The way they touched each other, looked at each other, even Walking Bones, reinforced her notion that this had been going on for years. Maybe even a lifetime or more.

Again, the pang of stupidity made her want to cry and scream, to pull her hair out. How could she have been so blind, so stupid.

She clung to Bev, watching the strange chanting dance. The way they ran their hands along each other's body, the way they held the goblet for each other to drink, to dip their fingers in the cup and paint their foreheads with whatever was inside.

"Now, we must bring forth one of the sacrifices," Jeff said. He grinned at Tony.

"Which shall it be?"

The three men turned to look at the prisoners. Walking Bones walked over to them, his body clicking loudly with every step. Lydia shuddered as his eyes locked with hers for a moment, and then looked at the others. The wolves followed him, a cloud of cotton with bloodied fangs. Pilar trailed behind, her golden coat still more solid than the rest of the beasts. Her transformation was not yet complete. She trotted over to Lydia and sat in front of her, whining.

"Pilar . . ." Lydia held her hand out slowly. Pilar stared at it, confused, recognizing the scent, not certain why. She stood up, pacing in front of Lydia, as Walking Bones studied the prisoners.

"Perhaps this one will do." Walking Bones pointed to a man. Tony was checking the videocameras.

Jeff grinned, tenting his fingers. "Very good. Everything working okay, Tony?"

"So far, so good."

Tony walked over to where Walking Bones stood. Tony smiled.

"Yes, a very good choice indeed." Tony unlocked the chain that held the shackles to the floor. The man was weak and delirious, his eyes glazed over, dried drool crusted on his chin beneath the ball gag.

He led the man to the pentagram, and fixed the chain to a ring in the floor, just in case.

Pilar shivered and flopped down beside Lydia, putting her head in her lap. Lydia petted the dog, or at least tried to pet the animal that was part illusion.

The man could barely stand, he was dizzy and disoriented.

Jeff stood before him. "Kneel."

The man dropped to his knees, his hands cuffed behind his back.

"Lick my feet." Jeff pushed one of his feet into the man's face. The man obediently licked the soles and then set to work on the toes. When one foot was done, Jeff held up the other foot. When that one was licked inch by inch, Jeff stood staring down at him. He was getting an erection. The man kept his eyes to the ground.

Jeff motioned to Tony. "Prepare the flesh."

Tony held a long whip and snapped it once in the air, to test its weight, before starting to flog the prisoner. Lydia flinched every time the whip ripped into the man's back. Blood poured onto the floor. At last, the man could stand it no more and fell forward.

"Well, that's that," Tony said, coiling the whip around his arm.

"I hope he's not dead. We can't offer him if he's dead."

"I doubt he's dead," Tony said, kneeling beside

the man. He felt his pulse. It was weak.

"Nope, not dead, don't worry."

"We can't afford any more screwups, you know," Jeff snapped.

"There won't be any screwups. We're ready. We're prepared. We've been working toward this our whole lives."

"I don't know. . . ." Jeff looked over at Walking Bones and waved his hand at him. "Like really, what is *that* all about?"

"Keeper of the guard. You know that. If he chooses to feed his wolves his flesh now and again, so what is it to us? We are all each other, he will be whole again, like he always is."

"It's weird, that's all. He's always been weird."

"Jeff . . . I think most people would think *any* of this is weird, so just leave Buddy alone."

"And you . . . keeper of the souls . . . do we have enough? Do we have spares in case there's a fuckup?"

"There will be no fuckups. Don't worry, there is a whole town of souls. If something happens, we will just bring another. The most important is the unborn child. You know that."

"Yes, I know that." Jeff sighed, pacing. He nervously looked up at the ceiling. "Damn it."

"What?"

"I just . . . feel . . . there's something . . ."

"Lydia?"

"I don't know. Something is not going to work. Something is going to fuck up and I can't see what it is."

"I double-checked everything. So did Buddy. So did you. We have the people, we know what to do . . . we saw it in our dreams a hundred times."

"Yes . . . we did." Jeff walked over to the giant crystal ball and peered inside it. He ran his hands along it, just above it, and Lydia could see blue streaks of energy sparking between his fingers and the ball. From where she sat, she saw the ball fill with a cloudy mist and then suddenly clear. But she couldn't see what Jeff saw. He scowled.

"Goddammit all! There is something wrong."

"There is *nothing wrong*. You're just nervous. It's all right to be nervous." Tony patted Jeff's arm.

Jeff pushed him away. "You don't know. You don't see like I do. I am the mouthpiece of the goddess. I am to do her bidding exactly or there will be trouble. And something is *wrong*."

"Nothing is wrong," Tony said again. Jeff pushed him again and again, until Tony fell back against a pillar. He raised his hands to fight back and then lowered them.

"What the fuck do you know?" Jeff said. "You're just a yes man. You're not the boss. You've never had to be in charge, so how the hell do you know what it feels like to be responsible? Solely responsible for how something is supposed to work out?"

Tony glared sullenly at him.

Jeff turned on his heel and returned to the circle. "You are as pathetic as this man here. Both of you are. I could have chosen anyone I desired, and somehow I chose you."

"You had to choose us. We were all there together. We all saw the house fall. We all danced in the graveyard that night. . . ."

Chapter Seventeen

Three boys in their teens sat at the grave of Debbie and Donald. The bruhaha from years ago had gone. Only the victims' parents and friends would occasionally bring something, a picture of their stolen child, a rosary, something to show a symbolic forgiveness even if darkness still raged deep in their hearts.

Tony, Jeff and Buddy sat right on the graves as they had many times before. The first few times, it had been a dare that made them giggle nervously and secretly fear a hand jutting from the earth or a freak with a sickle coming to slice off their heads.

Nothing like that ever happened.

But other things happened.

They saw the spirits, talked to them sometimes.

The spirits didn't talk back, at first, and even the first few times, their speech was garbled. Jeff was the first one to understand how to hear their rapid vibrations and he taught the other two how to listen.

The spirits spoke longingly of what they lost. Their money, their power, the wondrous ecstasy that swallowed them up while they were torturing their victims.

Then came little clues. Tantalizing clues that maybe these three could take up their torch, could continue the work that they had started.

But the boys did not understand. The way they spoke was too fast, too strange. The ways they spoke about were even stranger to these teenagers.

So they had come here tonight, the three of them together, to understand, truly, what it was they were supposed to know.

The circle had been cast, the herbs scattered, the prayers said. Now they sat in rapt contemplation, waiting . . . waiting. . . .

Now and again, they would steal glances at each other, not daring to speak, as they silently willed the spirits to show themselves. To reveal their true purpose.

Buddy hummed as he doodled in the dirt with a knife. Jeff kept his eyes shut and Tony watched first one and then the other and then studied the backs of his hands for a while.

There was only a half-moon tonight and Tony wondered if maybe they should have waited for a full or new moon. However, they had seen things before when there wasn't a particular phase, and he was as impatient as the rest of them. Or rather, they had all finally just gotten their courage up enough to maybe confront whatever it was they needed to, to discover how they too could be rich and powerful and pleasured.

The ground rumbled and suddenly the air grew cold. The boys looked at each other expectantly, watching the breath curl from each other's mouth and nose. The dirt beneath them shifted, as if something was pushing up from beneath them. Buddy jumped up, drawing his knife.

"Calm . . . Buddy . . . " Jeff whispered. "Wait for it."

Buddy held his fighting pose, but he nodded at Jeff, not taking his eyes from the shifting dirt.

Tony grabbed Jeff's hand, his eyes wide. The ground pushed up and up, the boys rising higher and higher, until they were flung like rag dolls away from the graves. They screamed and started to run.

"No. Wait!" Jeff cried. "Wait . . . maybe they are testing us. To see what we are made of."

A geyser of earth shot into the air, spitting splinters of wood and bones and roots. The boys covered their heads.

"We're going to get killed!" Tony cried.

"No, we aren't. I swear, they are testing us. If they were going to kill us, they would have long ago."

After the earth finished belching, the hole undulated and two familiar forms shifted into shape. Their voices were high and slurred, as if a speedy tape were running backward through a machine.

"Take it down." Jeff sighed, raising his hand and lowering it. The other two boys did the same.

"Take it down, we can't hear you," Buddy said.

"Take it down, we want to know you," Tony said.

They walked together toward Debbie and Donald. At last, they were able to tune in to the right frequency and the words became clear to hear.

"You will go there," Debbie was saying matter-of-factly.

"Go where?" Jeff asked.

"To the house. From there you will find the tunnels. And in the tunnels, you will find the chamber."

"Chamber?"

"Yes. You think that it all happened in the basement? No. That part was just for fun, for us. That was before we knew."

"What didn't you know?"

"All of it. All that we have told you before, and more."

"Can you tell us now?" Jeff asked, his face flushed and eager. "Spill your secrets for us, to-night. We need to hear them. We need to see them."

A tree root hurtled from the earth and wrapped itself around Jeff's wrists.

"Hey!" Tony shouted. He reached over to pull at the root and it shot around his wrist as well. As it went for Buddy, he waved the knife. The knife hacked through part of the root, but in less than a second it healed itself and wrapped tightly around Buddy's hands as well.

"Jesus!" Buddy cried, the knife falling to the ground.

"What the—!" Tony screamed.

The boys were all tied in a row, and like a group of prisoners doing community work, they were prodded to walk, the root leading them like a strange serpent.

They walked and walked, until they were out of the graveyard. They walked and walked, down the gravel highway, across a field until they came to a cave. Their cave. Their fort.

"I'm not going in there," Tony said.

"Man, we've been in there a thousand times, what difference does it make?" Jeff said.

"This is just too weird. Too creepy and weird," said Buddy.

"We called the spirits, they will show us," Jeff said. As if in response to his words, the root slipped from around their hands and slithered away along the floor.

"But what is here? It's just a cave."

The root slid into the cave, almost looking back to see if they were following. Behind them stood Debbie and Donald.

"Go in," commanded Debbie.

"Why?" Tony asked. "It's creepy in there."

"The answer will be clear. You will see," Donald replied.

"What about you?" Tony asked them.

"We're coming too," Donald said.

Donald was suddenly in front of them, lighting the cave with his glowing luminescence. Shadows danced across the walls, graffiti written in jest over the years now taking on chilling new connotations.

They walked to what they had always assumed to be the end of the cavern. But it wasn't. On this night, they learned, there was in fact a twist, and then another twist, that led to a narrow tunnel.

Tony shuddered as things brushed his face. Cobwebs, bugs, he didn't know. It was all too much and he wanted to run screaming as fast and as far as he could from this cold damp place, but he could not. He was here for whatever it was they had to face.

Buddy watched the root inch along the ground like the weirdest of inchworms. He thought of the tiny glowing green worms, dangling on a thread, ready to fall or fly with each passing creature. He wondered how far they had fallen tonight.

Jeff grinned, the noise in his temples growing louder. What had been fuzzy static, like white noise, was buzzing into a frequency he could almost hear. This was different than speaking to Debbie and Donald. This was someone else. Someone else that urgently tried to get his attention.

The frightened boys stumbled along the twisting path, past glowing bits of moss, the flutter of startled bat wings brushing their ears. There was no way to hesitate, flanked before and behind by their ghastly masters.

At last, they stood at an opening.

As they peered into the opening, many torches suddenly burst into flame, lighting a giant room with orange brilliance. They stared in wonderment, stepping through cautiously one at a time. The floor was mostly dirt, but there were beautiful stone columns throughout with intricately carved designs on them. There were tables and chairs, very simple ones. There was an altar area, polished wood and jeweled, candles long burned out.

Over in the other section were chains and shackles and, still, instruments of torture such as whips and knives.

The boys wandered around, looking at everything, their jaws practically dropping to the floor.

"All this time . . . we were right above it," Tony finally said.

"Amazing," Buddy marveled.

Jeff stood by the altar, his hand on his ear as if he were listening to someone. He nodded, saying yes several times.

"Jeff?" Tony asked. Jeff waved him away.

Jeff listened again and then looked up at the ceiling.

"Holy shit," he said.

The others looked up, and also saw the amazing stained glass ceiling with the pentagram demon.

"The gateway . . ." Jeff said softly.

Tony and Buddy looked at each other.

"Gateway?"

"Gateway to what?"

"To all we ever desired, and more."

"What do we do?"

The spirits glowed brightly. The root was now on the altar.

Jeff stared at the altar. "We decide if this is what we want."

"But we don't know what *this* is," Tony pointed out.

"We keep telling you, all you desire and more. You only have to serve her," Debbie said, stroking his arm.

"And then we'll end up in jail or dead or both, like you," Tony said.

"And we told you that we screwed up. We didn't fulfill our obligations exactly as she desired."

"So why are you so eager to help us?"

"Don't you see? If we find new guardians, then we will be free to move to the next level," Donald said.

"How do we know you aren't just tricking us?" asked Buddy.

"You don't, do you? That is where your instinct has to come in," Debbie cooed.

"We just have to believe," Jeff stated.

"Did anyone ever stop to think this is wrong?" Tony asked.

"What have we done that is wrong?" Jeff replied.

"What will we do that is wrong?" Buddy asked.

"We don't know what we have to do," Tony said.

"I'm sure the end will justify the means," Jeff said smugly. "I'm positive it will."

"You seem to know so much about this," Tony said.

"I've been reading about a lot of occult stuff, I told you before."

"Are we giving up our souls to go to hell?" asked Tony.

"Tony, we're in the 2000s. The idea of heaven and hell is so yesterday. We do what we do and we evolve or don't evolve while we do it. It's pretty straightforward."

"Sounds like there's no risk. It's not . . . practical," Tony said.

"Maybe. Maybe not. I don't pretend to know all the answers, I just know what I believe for me. I think we are being offered a gift that no one else has been offered, and we should go with it," Jeff said.

"Maybe it's a nightmare," Tony said.

"Maybe you have no sense of adventure," Jeff replied.

"I just don't want to get into something I can't get out of later." Tony paced, scratching his head. There was a whining in his ears, growing louder. His temples throbbed.

Buddy shook his head. "Tony, my man, we are already in, so go with it."

Buddy walked over to the altar. He stared at the root. It no longer looked like the curling snakelike creature that led them here. Now it looked like a walking stick. Buddy picked it up.

"Man, you look like a shepherd or Moses or something." Tony laughed.

Buddy shook his long hair. "I do, don't I. Isn't this cool? How it is just a stick once more?" He held it out to Tony. Tony didn't want to touch it.

Jeff was staring up at the ceiling again. "So it begins . . . ," he whispered.

Tony and Buddy followed his gaze. They saw the beast in the pentagram shifting, eyes glowing red like burning coals. They wanted to run, yet at the same time, they became aware of a sound. The *shssh*ing of white noise.

The beast was trying to communicate.

Jeff nodded. "I understand."

He bowed his head and stared at the floor, breathing heavily.

"Hey, Jeff . . . you okay?"

Jeff looked over at Tony, his eyes glowing red.

Tony screamed and backed away.

A fog billowed into the room and rolled through it, a low groaning sound like an iron gate opening.

The boys were unable to see each other, unable to hear anything but the whirring of white noise and the groaning. The fog tumbled them off their feet, their screams swallowed up. They were tossed and flung about the room. At first it was terrifying, but bit by bit, they grew more aware of their nerve endings and the exquisite sensation dancing along them. The boys laughed, as they saw visions they could never attempt to describe.

That night, the lure had been complete, their young fate sealed.

When it was over, each knew of his role, and his desire.

Each boy knew exactly what must be done when the time arrived.

And that time was now.

"Let's just get on with it," Tony said impatiently. He was tired of Jeff's mood swings, and even more tired of the guilt he felt about his wife. He just wanted the whole mess done with so they could move on.

Walking Bones called the wolves back over to the pentagram. They sauntered over, stealing furtive glances around the room. Sighing, one by one, they flopped down in their spots on the ubuoris.

Walking Bones gave the cry for the last one to come, but she stubbornly sat beside Lydia.

Walking Bones marched over to Pilar and held out his hand. Pilar sniffed it, trembling, yet her tail wagged.

"Don't go, Pilar," Lydia pleaded to the dog. But Pilar was hypnotized by the low murmuring coming from Walking Bones. She took her place in the pack with the others.

"Pilar knows her role," Tony said. "And so should you."

"Fuck off." Lydia scowled, edging closer to the smelly half-conscious cashier.

She looked at the man they had earlier beaten. A pool of blood stained the floor; she was certain he must be dead. She stared at the others, trying to remember their names from the broadcasts. The man on the floor was Jason, the deformed boy was Timothy, the grocery clerk was Bev, the wild-eyed girl on her other side was Karey and the last one . . . Ed. People with names, and lives and histories. People now reduced to quivering, crying chunks of flesh.

The men gathered up goblets and knives and herbs and God knows what, she couldn't really tell. Then, Jeff and Tony went over to another pocket of the room. Lydia gasped as they pushed out two wheelchairs. Sybil and Walter, also bound and gagged. Tony was torturing his own parents. Bile swished around her stomach and she felt it crawl up to her mouth. Before she could stop herself, she vomited.

The rancid sour smell was barely perceptible in the reeking room.

Tears fell down her face as she realized, really and truly, that she was screwed.

* * *

The smoke billowed into a thick fog, swallowing up the chanting songs of the three men. Lydia and the others watched speechlessly at the sight unfolding before them.

The whipped man, Jason, was laid on the altar, so weak he didn't even protest. His body more of a mishmash of flesh than a human. Tony took one of the large gleaming knives and carved him open from his throat to his belly. If they had thought he was dead, they were wrong. The poor man screamed and gurgled, thrashing around as if he were being given electroshock therapy. Blood splattered the men, staining their faces and bodies, smearing the altar. They wore the blood, licking it from each other's faces, drinking dripping streams from Walking Bones's bones. Yet they still sang, and the smell of herbs and death grew stronger, the smoke thicker until Lydia could only see flashes of movement in the gaps of the swirling clouds. Movements she couldn't be sure were real or something her starving brain was conjuring up. She saw her husband engaging in lewd lascivious acts with another man and a skeleton.

Surely she had lost her mind.

Would this nightmare ever end?

The wolves howled, all staring up at the ceiling. Lydia and the others looked up too.

"Holy shit," said Lydia, as she saw the beast in the pentagram breathing. Red eyes glowed, its chest heaved as it drew in gulps of air and smoke.

The beast solidified, magnifying as it sucked in strength. It was enormous, and the most hideous thing Lydia had ever thought could exist. She wasn't even sure what it was.

Maybe it was part bird, with its long sharp beak, and talons on "hands" and "feet." Its covering was a furry feather. Its eyes were huge and red, like a snake's or a crocodile's. Something reptilian and unblinking, its long, scaly tail twitched snakelike.

It—she—dropped to the floor like a cat, then pulled itself to its full enormous height. Eight feet, nine? Ten? Lydia couldn't tell.

The beast stared at the three men lost in carnal pleasure, oblivious of the arrival of their goddess.

"You called?" she asked, her mighty voice rumbling into the floor. The three men froze guiltily. Then panic filled their faces as they considered the abomination before them.

Jeff was the first to move. He approached her tentatively.

"Your Goddessness. . . ." Jeff bowed before her. "We have called you because it is time."

"Suppertime?" she asked in a husky voice. As she cocked her head, her chest feathers lifted slightly to reveal two large rounded breasts with long fingerlike nipples.

"Yes. We have kept our part of the bargain, and brought you all you need."

The beast strutted much like a giant chicken, over to Jason's body flayed out on the altar.

The man was still somehow alive. Guts poured from him and he shivered spasmodically. He saw the beast approach him and tried to scream, but only blood gurgled from his mouth and opened throat.

The beast stood at his head, and caressed his hair, then suddenly plunged her long sharp beak into his skull with a popping, cracking noise. She sucked noisily. Jason's face caved in, body shriveling like a spent balloon, the pull so powerful that the exposed organs all were pulled forcefully up her beak.

She stepped away from the husk, smacking loudly. "Next?"

"Shall we bring her to you?" Tony asked, kneeling in front of her.

"Yeah, sure. Whatever," the beast said disinterestedly, looking around the place. The wolves might well have been stone, they were so still.

Tony grabbed Bev as Lydia tried to beat him off.

"No . . . no . . . are you mad? You can't feed her to the beast. Tony . . ."

Tony pushed her aside and dragged the cashier over to the drooling beast. Lydia ran over, or at least as far as the leg clamp would allow.

"Stop it. Stop it now!"

"Shut up," Jeff said.

They watched the same fate fall to Bev. With excited glee, Jeff started to babble.

"We have been waiting for you, O beautiful goddess. We are your humble servants."

"Yeah, yeah. Where's my baby?" the beast said, looking around.

Tony gulped. This was the time. "It's my baby, I want you to know. I am giving to you the supreme sacrifice of my firstborn because I love you so much."

"So, where is it?"

"It is in my wife . . . you won't take her, though, will you?"

The beast walked over to Lydia and stared unblinkingly at her swollen belly.

"That is the best kind. Still in the shell!" The beast laughed.

"I hate you, Tony," Lydia said. "May you burn in hell, you bastard."

She struggled against the chains, trying to escape. The beast picked her up, as easily as one might pluck a grape from a bunch. The chain broke as the beast dangled her above her head, inspecting her from all sides.

"Mmm . . . the fresh smell of hormones. Don't you just love it, boys?"

"If you are pleased, then we are pleased, Your Goddessness." Jeff bowed again.

The beast looked over at him. "You are so eager to give away your friend's wife and child. What is it you have brought of yours?"

Jeff trembled. "I have no family. I have no one to bring except these people here chained for you. *We* collected them all."

"And the two in the wheelchairs . . ." the beast clucked, glancing at Sybil and Walter, who were watching with wide eyes flooded with tears, their faces red from the stress. "Also Tony's family."

"You must want what I have pretty bad to deliver your parents, your wife and your child. . . ." the bird fixed its beady gaze on Tony.

"It seemed the only way. Jeff and Buddy have no real family. Well, Buddy's is the wolves, and here they are, still guarding your chambers," Tony stammered.

The beast snatched Tony with its other hand. He screamed, struggling to undo her clench.

"What are you doing?" Tony cried. He flailed in the air as the beast brought him close enough to inspect. She turned him side to side. She loosened her grip on Lydia, who fell a few feet to the floor. The beast chuckled and then pierced Tony's skull with her beak. His agony resounded around the room as she sucked him dry with hideous squelching noises, his face, his body all crumbling into an empty shell.

Lydia scrambled and rolled until she was behind a pillar. She didn't want to see what happened to Tony. She could only focus on one thing. This was her chance. The chance for escape that she had been waiting for.

She edged her way back toward where she thought she had stumbled in that day that seemed like a lifetime ago.

Jeff and the beast were arguing. And there was crying, muffled screaming as the hysterical prisoners all strained at their bonds.

The poor deformed boy, Timothy, had woken in time to see the worst nightmare of his life.

The beast returned to where the other prisoners were hanging, and started feasting on them.

Lydia inched over to the table, where Tony had put the keys earlier.

She quietly grabbed them and crawled over to the boy. Jeff and Buddy were still staring in disbelief at Tony's body, Jeff swearing and cursing. The wolves howled and barked.

Lydia managed to unlock Timothy's cuffs with

shaking hands. There was so much noise, she hoped that no one noticed as she helped the frightened man-child to his feet. He was big. Bigger than she, and it was hard work to drag him along, with his slobbering, shaking body, to hide behind the pillars. As they stood behind, watching the beast still feasting on the others, Lydia stared into the boy's frightened eyes.

"If I take the gag off, you will be very, very quiet, won't you?" she asked. "You have to be. Or they'll catch us and kill us. You know that, right?"

The boy nodded.

She unbuckled the ball gag and he groaned softly from the lockjaw.

She massaged his jaw for a moment, before tugging him along.

"Come on, we have to go, before they notice we're gone."

His legs were painfully stiff but adrenaline kept him moving.

"Fuck, where did she go?" she heard Jeff scream at Walking Bones. "And the freak. Where is he?"

Jeff headed toward the prisoner corner but the beast stopped him.

"Where are you going?" the beast asked.

"Your baby, she's getting away," Jeff cried.

"And whose fault is that?" the beast asked. "Aren't you keeper of the souls?"

"That was Tony's job . . . and . . . well . . . you ate him."

"And him over there . . . what was his job?"

"Guardian of the chamber."

The beast nodded. "And you? What was your job?"

"The mouthpiece to the goddess, the one that communicates and executes all your wishes."

"Mouthpiece, huh?"

"Well, that's just the catchall name I gave it as a kid. Maybe . . . communications specialist?"

"Maybe . . ." The beast mimicked his facial expression, his pleading tone. "Maybe you are just lunch."

Jeff screamed as the beast picked him up, punctured his head and sucked on his brains, blood dripping down his handsome face and splattering the floor.

Walking Bones didn't need any more hints. He flung open the nearest secret door and ran, his wolf pack in hot pursuit. Pilar hesitated at the door, staring forlornly where Lydia hid. Lydia willed her to go away, to move on, but she didn't dare speak.

The beast tossed Jeff's empty body aside and then ripped Sybil from her wheelchair. She bore her beak into Sybil's skull. Sybil's eyes rolled up in her head, moaning and twitching. Then Lydia beheld a strange sight. As the beast tried to suck her up, an energy emitted from the woman, streams curling and uncurling, trying to escape the breath and beak.

The energy must be her soul, Lydia thought. A soul trying to flee. Sybil's soul was as stubborn as the old bitch had been alive.

Lydia watched the tug-of-war with fascination, while trying to discover how she could possibly get by the beast with the boy, without detection.

The battle for the soul raged, this one was stubborn. Lydia watched the door where Walking Bones had fled. She knew there were other doors, many other doors, but she didn't have the luxury of looking for them.

She grabbed the child and turned his head from the sloppy scene.

She pointed at the far door, praying he would understand.

"Now," she whispered, and pulled him as they fled from one pillar to the next.

The soul had escaped the body and the beast and now hung suspended above it, taunting it. The beast swung its hands at it, trying to catch it as it hovered annoyingly just out of reach.

Lydia and the boy tore over to the next pillar. It was not an easy task, the boy was badly hurt and she wasn't much better. But fear and adrenaline spurred them on.

They made it to the pillar and then the next while the beast finally snatched the soul and slurped it down. Just as Lydia pushed the boy through the door, she felt the nasty clutch of the beast's grip around her waist.

"Nooo!" she screamed, kicking her legs uselessly as once more she was lifted from the ground.

"You thought I didn't see you trying to escape. As if I'd lose sight of the most precious one of all," the beast sneered.

"You are a strong one. Stubborn too. You're going to give me quite a fight as well, aren't you?"

"I'll never let you have me. Never," Lydia cried.

The beast lumbered over to the altar and laid her down on it. It held her arms with one hand, her legs with the other. The beast stared at the swollen stomach, trying to figure where to position the beak.

"Fuck you!" Lydia screamed, writhing under the grip.

The beast lowered its beak as if measuring. Suddenly it was jarred by a mound of flying fur and teeth. The beast was startled enough to release its grip, and Lydia didn't have to think twice about leaping off the table and running to the door. Pilar wrestled with the beast, tearing at its throat with sharp teeth. The beast plucked her from its body and flung her aside. Pilar whimpered as she hit the floor.

Lydia heard the thump of Pilar but didn't stop as she pushed the boy down the pitch-black tunnel. She wondered how many bugs and bats and God knows what were down here. The boy cried as she pushed him ahead, waving his stiff sore arms in front of him, terrified of what might be just before him. How she hoped the tunnel was too small for the beast.

Chapter Eighteen

The beast watched Lydia and the boy run out the door.

That girl was feisty, and if it was games she wanted to play, then let her. She had been part of the plan for many lifetimes and the beast knew the cycle would be complete in this round.

The tunnel was too small. She knew that. She had planned it that way, this entire labyrinth was of her design, back in her human days, back when there was only one race of humans running from her power.

She wanted her humans to come and go unnoticed by others, to feed her as she needed to be fed, to appease her and keep her mammoth form safe with promises and gifts. Some were illusions, some she could deliver, it depended on what the humans craved, on what they truly desired in their hearts, how hard they truly wanted to sweat.

Funny how it was almost always men who found her. Almost always men who smelled the scent of riches and power, of omnipotence over their fellow man. And the women who followed them, almost always weak and brainwashed . . . a far cry from the rebellious Eve who bit the apple, the independent Lilith who had walked away from servitude in disgust.

Yet now and again, there were some who amused her with their strength, and this Lydia was one of them. How exquisite her soul would taste, what wondrous fuel she would add to the fire burning in her belly, and maybe, just maybe the baby soul would be as strong, the one she had been searching for all these eons, to create the child she herself so desired.

She would play cat and mouse with Lydia a while longer, the night was dark, the moon was full. But in the end, there was no escape. Not now. Not ever.

The hunt was eternal as the ubuoris.

The beast, the goddess, the muse of lust and power, clambered up one of the pillars, which crumbled under her immense weight. She reached her arms out to the ceiling and, bending her long legs, leaped into the air like a giant lizard.

She reached up to the window and pulled herself up. With long, earsplitting crashes, she pecked at the glass. Her beak was numb with the constant slamming. At last, the tiniest crack formed and she worked on it, hitting and hitting, chipping away at the tiny gap until the pane splintered and shattered. The glass broke away and fell to the floor with a crash.

There was no sky above but the surface was not far. She clawed with her long talons, raking away the dirt, dreaming of the tasty meal to come.

She dug and dug through clay that had settled for hundreds of years. She dug through layers of rock and stone, her talons and beak chipping as she frantically tore her way through the ceiling.

At last, a shower of dirt and rock fell to the floor and she slipped to the edge just in time. With the full moon shining down through the hole, she hooked her claws around and pulled herself through.

It was tedious work, pulling herself through, the hole was tight around her, and she was wedged for a moment or two. She shook and flailed and another section caved in. As it crashed down, she flung herself up and over onto the land.

She sniffed the air and, finding the scent she was looking for, headed toward it.

* * *

Lydia stumbled through the tunnel with the boy. Tears ran down her face as the wretchedness of what she had seen started to break through. She pushed away the thoughts, of Tony, of the beast, of all that had gone on. Fear would make her weak and she didn't have time for that. In the darkness, she could see swirling forms and realized the spirits were here with her. They pushed with their cold dampness, urging her on, seemingly picking her up and guiding her.

At last, she was in the mouth of the cave. She peered out. The last time she had been outside, there had been tons of snow. Now it had all but melted. More of the bizarre nature weirdness, the greenhouse effect or whatever it was, that was plaguing the earth. It was wet and slippery out there, but no mountains of snow.

There was no sign of the beast as she panted, getting her bearings. She didn't know where to go, she just knew they had to keep moving.

As they emerged from the cave, they saw a dark form in the moonlight ambling toward them. Her veins turned to ice. It was the beast. Somehow it had gotten through before them and was heading their way.

They ran, slipping and sliding across the muddy

field. She didn't think the beast had seen them yet, as she looked back and saw her examining the mouth of the cave.

She pushed the boy toward the woods, toward the water.

When they were in the woods, she found a fallen tree and had the boy lie down. He was so tired, so afraid.

"Stay here and don't make a sound. It's me she wants," she told him, covering him with mud and debris. The boy shivered, he was going into shock, could not speak but only made grunting noises.

She ran farther, the beast gaining on her with every step.

The beast was catching up, her claws snatching at Lydia's back as she tried to outrun her. At last, Lydia realized she had no choice and dove into the icy cold water. Her body felt as if it were being pierced by shards of glass as she dragged herself along the water. She swam frantically, hoping that her strong arms would take her farther. The beast waded in after her, its mammoth body splashing, creating giant waves. Lydia pushed farther, heading down toward her swimming hole.

The beast screeched unearthly noises, frustration mounting as it fought to balance in the water. Lydia looked back, and saw, to her amazement, that the beast could not, seemed not to be able to, swim.

This gave her another surge of hope and she kicked as hard as she could, going deeper and deeper, ignoring the way her hands and feet seemed to no longer belong to her. The beast's cries were louder, echoing across the water.

The beast had reached the mysterious deep part, and lost her footing. She sank down, the water closing over her head, her tail thrashing above her. Lydia heard her anguished cries as she struggled to keep her head above water.

Before Lydia was the float. Not much farther. She was so tired and cold. If she could just make it to the float, she could rest for a moment.

There was bubbling and she could no longer see the beast.

She pulled herself up on the raft, panting and heaving, drawing in great gulps of air.

She stared at the water, but there was nothing. No more bubbles. No more splashing.

She panted, laying her head upon her arms, listening to the stillness of the night.

She closed her eyes, drowsiness sweeping over her as she shivered.

The raft vibrated, then lurched sideways. With a scream, Lydia toppled over and the giant claws snatched at her. She kicked and struggled as the beast held her, trying to pull her under. The beast was jumping, trying to suck in the air. Lydia tore at the hands, saw her own blood staining the water, black in the moonlight as she tried to loosen the iron grip.

She fought to keep her own head above water, felt the beast weakening as it couldn't find the surface.

The beast rose up again, one last mighty jump, and its head broke the surface. As it strained for a gasp of air, something flew from the sky and landed in its throat. A gush of blood sprayed out and, with it, a blinding shower of sparks.

A long stick hung from her neck. The beast grabbed at the stick, loosening her grip on Lydia. Lydia paddled from her reach as fast as she could, kicking and gasping, her freezing fingers finding the side of the raft to hang on to.

Clinging to the raft, she saw who had thrown the giant stick. It was Buddy. Buddy once more in the flesh, standing waist deep in the water. She gasped for air, trying to understand it. She recognized the stick as Buddy's walking stick.

The beast still fought for life. She had nearly pulled the stick from her throat as she tried to jump up again, jaws inches away from Lydia. Lydia took a deep breath, then leaped up, jamming the stick deeper, feeling it pierce through the throat. A fresh burst of blood and more sizzling sparks shot up. Wisps of smoky fog escaped. They soared and roared, circling the beast. Lydia saw the faces of those who had just died. Tony, Sybil, Jeff, Bev, Jason. They swirled together, making a ring around the creature that grew tighter and tighter until the beast was gasping. The hole in the neck ripped open farther as more souls struggled to escape. More blood and meat poured out as the anguished ones absconded and joined the formation. The beast stiffened, eyes bulging, then with an earsplitting shriek, sank down into a foam of bloody bubbles.

Buddy swam the remaining way out to Lydia. He clambered onto the raft, then reached over and took hold of her.

Lydia was crying and shaking as Buddy pulled her up.

"Don't touch me!" she screamed.

"I want to help."

"You tried to kill me."

"But now I tried to save you."

"Why?" Her teeth chattered as he rubbed at her arms. He was shivering too.

"There is nothing for me now," Buddy said. "It is over. It is all over."

Lydia stared at the water, waiting for the creature to rise again, but there was nothing.

She laid her head down and cried.

Chapter Nineteen

Lydia sat in a rocking chair by the tiny window of her new apartment.

She rubbed her humongous belly and felt a strong kick. The baby would be coming soon. Pilar sat on the floor beside her, watching her, as she had always watched her. Pilar's fur was missing in places, she was still raggy and torn. She was far from the beauty she once was, but she was here and alive.

Lydia looked at all the boxes around her. Not so many to unpack this time. She was starting over. She was starting fresh with much less baggage.

The skyline twinkled, its familiar glow bringing comfort to her as she stroked her stomach.

"We will be safe here now," she whispered to the

baby. "Far away from that nightmare place."

Pilar whined and Lydia petted her.

"We should never have left New York," Lydia said.

Pilar barked in agreement.